Once More with You

A FABLE NOTCH NOVEL

BOOK ONE

ELENA MARKEM

Dedication

♥

For my mother, Hilda,
who gave me my love of reading
and encouraged my every dream.
Your support has always lifted me up. I love you.

Chapter One

♥

Theo Hanson wasn't surprised the joy from his promotion was short-lived. If there was anything he knew for certain, it was that happiness didn't last.

That Friday morning, after a few weeks of salary negotiations, piles of contracts to sign, and a firm handshake, he was the newest investigator at Prometheus Consulting, one of the most respected fire and arson investigation companies in the country. In a few years, he hoped to become a partner. Sometimes he didn't recognize his own life. When he joined the army at twenty, he didn't care if he came back. Now at thirty-one, he had a successful career with a promising future.

After a celebratory lunch with his co-workers, there was a note on his desk: *Call Martin Sinclair.*

His heart raced. A note meant Martin told the receptionist not to transfer him to voice mail. Something was very wrong. *Not again*, said a voice in his head. Theo looked at his cell phone to see he'd missed two calls while he was out. It had to be about Millie, Martin's wife. Something terrible had happened. Why else would he call?

On the first ring, Theo ran his hands through his hair, gripping the back in his fist. After almost seven years stateside, he still marveled at how long it felt. When the phone rang a second time, he stood. By the third, he was pacing. Finally, a familiar voice answered, "Hello, Theo. Don't panic. Everything's fine."

"Everything can't be fine, or you would have left a message."

"Stop pacing, sit down, and don't pull your hair."

Sometimes he hated how well Martin knew him, but since Martin and Millie practically raised him and his brothers, it wasn't a surprise. Theo took a deep breath and sat. "So, Millie's okay? You haven't had another heart attack? Because, seriously, you nearly gave me one."

"Sorry, son. We're both fine, well mostly."

"What do you mean, 'well mostly'?"

The brief pause was enough to make Theo worry again. "We had a fire in an office building Tuesday night. Two of us went in looking for hot spots, and the stairs gave out from under me. I've broken my arm and wrist and bruised a bunch of other things." A sheen of sweat broke out over Theo's body. He knew what it was like inside a burning building, even though as an arson investigator he didn't have to go into the blaze. Not that this kept him safe. His hand went to the scar on his leg, which was a constant reminder of what had happened less than a year ago. "Theo," Martin said, bringing him back to the present. "This was the third property destroyed by fire in a little over a month."

Now he understood the reason for the call. Martin getting injured was terrible, but three fires in such a short time were unheard of in their small New Hampshire town. They could go a year and not have as many. "You suspect arson."

"I do. I haven't told anyone else, except Millie and my team, but rumors are flying." Rumors flew easily where Theo grew up. "I won't beat around the bush. I need you to come home, take over my job while I'm laid up, and investigate. If it is arson, and I'm convinced it is, our volunteer department is not equipped to handle it."

Theo didn't hear much beyond "come home." It had been years since he'd been in New Hampshire, let alone Fable Notch. His reason to even consider returning to where he'd grown up was long gone. He loved Martin and Millie and all they did for him and his brothers, but they understood why he didn't visit.

Ever.

Theo didn't want to make the trip if there was another way. He hadn't even gone back after Martin's heart attack. It was the only time he'd offered. Truthfully, he didn't care if the town burned to the ground, but Martin felt differently. Shaking off his thoughts, Theo switched into professional mode. "Why don't you send me what you have on the fires so far, and I'll help where I can from here. I can show you how to use Skype or Zoom, and we can talk face to face."

"And when the next fire happens, and no one knows how to look for or collect evidence?" Theo gave a small smile. Martin had been listening over the years when Theo shared information about the process he used to solve cases. It wasn't something most firefighters or police understood.

Theo scrambled for options. "Why not call the state investigator?"

"I did, but there've been some issues down in Manchester, so they don't have anyone available. You know I wouldn't ask if I thought there was another way."

Which was likely why it took three days for Martin to call and ask for help. The thought grabbed Theo's attention. "How long has it been between the fires?"

There was a pause before Martin answered. "Over two weeks between the first and second, and then a little less than that before the third."

Theo looked at the calendar on his desk. "You have less than a week before the next."

"How do you know?"

"He's speeding up. He's enjoying what he's doing and is getting a rush from the chaos and concern it's causing.

He won't want to wait to experience that power again. I'd guess he'll wait no more than ten days from the last to the next, which means a week from today, a week from tomorrow at the latest."

"So you'll come?"

Back to where he was pitied because his father abandoned them, and his mother was a drunk? Back to where everyone remembered every piece of trouble he and his brothers had gotten into? Back to a place where he'd experienced his greatest heartbreak? Theo couldn't believe what he was about to say. "Yes. I'm not in the middle of an active investigation. I could be there by Sunday night."

"Thank you, Theo. This means a lot to me."

They talked for a little longer before Millie grabbed the phone from her husband and gushed over how much she was looking forward to seeing him. As they spoke, Theo heard children's voices in the background. None of the boys raised by the Sinclairs — Theo and his two brothers, along with their own son, Ryan — had children, and none lived in Fable Notch. "Who's there?" he asked.

"Grace Duncan and her twins. Didn't Martin tell you?"

"Tell me what?" Of course there was more.

"The second fire destroyed a building with four apartments. Grace and her twins are living here. Which reminds me, you're more than welcome, but if you stay with us, you'll be surrounded by two energetic eight-year-olds."

"No problem. I'll find somewhere else." He knew a place that might be available even with Harlow, his arson dog, accompanying him. May as well jump completely into the deep end.

A few minutes later, he hung up and stared at the phone. Like it or not, he was going back to Fable Notch.

Theo spent the next day and a half preparing for the trip. He got approval from the senior partner to work remotely and to list this work as a pro bono case, so Prometheus would pick up the tab for any samples Theo sent to the lab. He'd check in regularly and join meetings via video conference. As he packed, he called his younger brother, Nick, to find out if he could stay in their old house, which Nick had renovated and rented to tourists. Fortunately — or maybe not — Nick was having the basement finished, which meant there were no bookings for the next three weeks. Theo hoped it wouldn't take him that long. The less time he spent in Fable Notch, the better.

On Sunday, after two restless but mostly dreamless nights, he and Harlow set off for New Hampshire. Eight hours later, they crossed the state border, and it wasn't long before he saw mountains in the distance. As he drove north, the highway dropped from three lanes to two and then one as the White Mountains loomed before him. Less than two hours after entering the state, he got off at the exit and was soon passing the sign welcoming him to Fable Notch. His stomach clenched as if he needed a reminder he didn't want to be here.

Driving into town, he saw familiar stores and businesses, as well as a few new ones. The Triangle Market, at the intersection of the main street and the diagonal one that met it, was the first place most tourists stopped. A Thai restaurant was an unexpected addition. There were several souvenir shops, and when he saw a sign telling him there were tastings and tours at the Seven Brothers Brewery, he wondered which members of the large Stewart family opened it. Plenty of places to trigger memories and remind him of one person in particular.

There was hardly anywhere in town where he hadn't spent time with Eden, his high school girlfriend and first love. Only love, if he were being honest. She'd gotten out of Fable Notch years ago to pursue her dream of being a professional dancer. At one time, he thought he'd be by her side, but they'd split because he didn't want to hold her back.

There was enough light in the summer sky to check the sites hit by the arsonist before heading to the old house. At least he could be productive while delaying the inevitable. Pulling out the addresses Martin gave him, Theo drove by each site to get a quick impression of the destruction. After taking in what was left of the properties, he headed back into town and made a stop at DeMarco's picking up a sub for dinner.

It wasn't long before he turned onto the street where he grew up. Despite money being scarce, they'd never been in danger of being homeless because his mother's parents owned the place. He never imagined willingly staying here again.

As he pulled into the driveway, he thought he might be at the wrong address. Several years ago, Nick convinced Theo and Cole he could turn the house into a profitable rental property for leaf peepers, hikers, and skiers. Truthfully, it was the only building Theo would have gladly set fire to himself, but since Cole agreed, Theo did too. He never looked at the plans or pictures Nick sent and donated the quarterly checks he received to the school that trained Harlow.

He shut off the engine and stared at the updates. Nothing but the basic structure remained, and Nick had built an addition on the side where his mother's bedroom used to be. When he was a kid, the outside had been faded blue with the paint peeling, the porch sagging, and shutters missing. Today it was cream color with forest green shutters. The porch looked deeper and now wrapped around one side. There were even oversized chairs and a swing. If the inside was as different as the outside, maybe it wouldn't be too horrible staying here.

He got out of the truck and Harlow followed as he went to the back to get his bags. There was a tiny Mini Cooper parked next to him in the two-car driveway, which he assumed belonged to the person Nick had called to open the house and bring in supplies. It seemed like a ridiculous car to have in an area which got so much snow, but when he saw the AWD on the trunk, it made a little more sense.

He found the key where Nick said it would be, gave himself a mental "you can do this", before going inside.

He was right — nothing looked the same, and he let out an involuntary sigh of relief. Harlow sniffed around the room as Theo marveled at the changes. He put his dinner on the kitchen island, then realized he'd forgotten to bring in Harlow's food and dishes from the car. "I'll be right back, girl," he said. As she bounded up the stairs, he headed to the door. He was halfway out when a scream brought him racing back.

Chapter Two

♥

E den Barrett had a lap full of dog.

One moment she was lost in the sexy, romantic world of Alisha Rai's *Hate to Want You* and the next she was staring into the snout of a big and quite beautiful dog. Her scream hadn't bothered the animal, since he — or she — remained on the bed, but when Eden heard heavy footsteps running up the stairs, she leapt up and looked for something to use as a weapon. The room, designed to please renters, had nothing useful and the bedside lamp was too large to pick up.

"Harlow, where are you?" called a voice. A familiar voice.

She was imagining things. The book was about two people who met once a year because even though they couldn't be together, they couldn't stay apart. Eden understood the heroine's yearning but didn't have the once-a-year benefits. She'd never see her first love again, so thinking she heard Theo's voice was ridiculous. Not that she wanted to see him. How could she when her life had turned into such a mess? Fortunately, it couldn't be him.

"What the hell?"

She could be wrong.

She stared at the man who appeared in the doorway and thought of the expression about having no luck if it weren't for bad luck. Hadn't she had enough in the last few weeks? There was a moment of stunned silence before he said, "Eden? Is it you?

After years of missing him, needing him, and making several poor decisions, she'd finally landed on her feet. Sure, since the fire destroyed the apartment she was renting, Eden was back to questioning nearly everything to the point where there were days she couldn't choose what to have for lunch, but she was managing.

Of all the times for him to come back, why did it have to be now?

And why was he even more gorgeous than she re-membered? Her body reacted as quickly as her heart. As they stared at each other, she found herself lost in his familiar blue eyes and noticing the changes of time. His light brown hair, which he had worn rebelliously long as a teen, was short. His lips were still full. Would he kiss the same?

Stupid, runaway thoughts.

She finally found her voice and said, "Yes, it's me. What are you doing here?"

"I could ask you the same thing." He'd gone from sounding curious to curt. "Harlow, come, girl." That answered the dog's gender question. Harlow, who had been walking around Eden's legs, left her side to stand by Theo. Eden didn't need protecting, but somehow, she felt vulnerable without the dog's nearness. "And I have two versions of that question. What are you doing in this house, and what are you doing in this town?"

She understood the first question, but he had no right to ask the second. He wasn't around when her life fell apart and had no idea what she'd gone through in the years after he left. So she answered the first one. "My apartment burned down three weeks ago. Millie checked the online calendar and said the place was available for the next several weeks. She told me I could stay until my renter's insurance check came in, and I found something else."

"Your place was one of the sites hit by the arsonist?"

"You know about the fires? It's definitely arson?" Too many questions. And too many others she didn't want to answer.

"Martin suspects arson, so he called me. I need to investigate before I can say for sure. Which answers your question." Theo scraped a hand over his face and pulled at his hair. Such a familiar move. The silence continued until he said, "Look, it's been a long day. I had a ten-hour drive, and I'm starving. I have to get some things from my truck for Harlow and then eat. Can you meet me in the kitchen in a few minutes? We need to talk."

Eden nodded once, and he returned the gesture before turning and leaving the room, the dog at his heels. Eden sank onto the bed and dropped her head in her hands. Where was she going to go? On the night of the fire, she'd stayed with her closest friend, Janelle Novak, in the apartment above the thrift shop she ran, but all Janelle had was an extra sofa and Eden had been stuck three times in the night by pins trapped in the fabric. Eden's father offered her a place, but that wasn't an option. It had taken long enough for her to get away from him. She was *not* taking a step back.

When Millie Sinclair came to the gym where Eden worked and suggested she stay at the Hanson house, Eden jumped at the chance. Not having to worry about rent for a few weeks was wonderful. She admitted to herself that being in Theo's old room made her feel closer to the person she'd been when they'd dated in high school, a woman she wanted to be again. But if Theo was here, she'd have to look for a new place as soon as possible.

Great, one more thing for the to-do list.

Maybe he would go somewhere else. It's not as if he liked this house. He spent as little time here as possible when they were younger and left as soon as he could.

You were a part of that. No, her father was. Patrick Barrett never approved of her relationship with Theo, but he couldn't keep them apart until he dropped a bombshell the day after her high school graduation. If she stayed with Theo, she'd get no financial support for attending the Boston Conservatory where she'd been accepted to study dance. Eden wanted to have both, but Theo had gone along with Patrick's ultimatum, refusing to consider other options. Not only had she been hurt and forced to give in to what her father wanted, it started a pattern of not standing up for herself that took years to change.

She listened for noise coming from downstairs to know when to join him. She considered staying in her room, but what was the point? May as well get this conversation over with.

Taking a deep breath, she went to the kitchen to face her past. A dog's water and food bowls were now on the end of the island. Theo was searching for something, even though he'd taken several bites from a large sub. A pile of fries was next to the sandwich. He moved around the kitchen, opening cabinets and closing them with a bang.

"Can't find what you need?" she said.

"I don't even know where to look." His expression was somewhere between frustrated and amused. When he found and pulled out a plate, he gave an exasperated, "Finally. When Nick renovates a place, he doesn't hold back."

"I thought I was at the wrong house when I met Millie here."

"Same. If it weren't for the basic structure and the neighbors' houses, I would have turned on my GPS to make sure." He opened the refrigerator and gave a mocking laugh. "Would you look at that? There's something other than ketchup and milk in here. Although ketchup is what I need. Another change. I suppose all this food is your doing."

"Only some of it. There's more in there than when I left this morning. I thought Millie had come by and stocked things for me. I wondered when I saw the beer."

Taking out the ketchup, Theo closed the refrigerator, then proceeded to nearly drown the fries. Something that hadn't changed. He ate one and said, "Nick called some service he uses to have the place stocked. He told me the place was available."

"Guess we got our wires crossed."

Theo waited a beat before saying, "In more ways than one."

Before he could say anything else, she said, "So why are you staying here? You hate this house almost as much as this town. Maybe more."

"I do, but because of Harlow, the places I can stay are limited. She's a service animal — an arson dog — so hotels can't keep her out, but since she doesn't have to be with me 24/7, sometimes it's easier for both of us if I leave her where I'm staying. I usually book efficiency apartments in extended stay hotels, but there aren't any around here. I can't stay with the Sinclairs because they took in a family who were also left homeless from the fire."

"Yes, Grace and her kids." Eden was glad they were staying with Martin and Millie who would provide the extra care the family needed.

"It never occurred to me to let them know where I'd be." From his tone, she guessed he regretted that decision.

She decided this time it was her turn to leave. "I'll start looking for a new place in the morning."

"You haven't looked?"

He sounded shocked. Did he think she was lazy? It had only been three weeks. No one else had suggested she was dawdling. "Too many other things going on, things to replace. I haven't been able to focus enough to get that done. I was just happy to have underwear."

Underwear? That's what you choose to mention?

As her face warmed, she waited for him to comment on her choice of joy, but instead he said, "It's not uncommon after losing a home to fire to be unbalanced for a while. No one realizes how much they have or what it means until it's gone, especially things that can't be replaced. Unlike underwear."

They needed to talk about something other than her underwear. "It's not something you can be prepared for."

"There are lots of things you can't prepare for." There was a world of meaning in the one sentence, none of them she felt prepared to discuss. Fortunately, Theo didn't seem ready either, and he asked, "So, you've been here since the fire?"

"Yes."

He sighed, ran his hand through his hair, then ate a fry. She let him think. This was always his way — give all the pieces careful consideration before deciding. Except for his last decision. That one he made quickly and never gave her a chance to change his mind. Finally, he said, "You've been uprooted enough. Probably feeling settled for the first time since this happened."

"Yes, it's been helpful."

"Millie would never let me hear the end of it if I kicked you out."

She lifted her shoulder in a half shrug. "You're not kicking me out. I offered."

"That's not how she'll see it." More of his fries disappeared.

"We can explain. You need a place for Harlow. I'll manage."

"I don't doubt it." His simple statement surprised her. She'd been without acceptance for so long she couldn't help but notice how easily he believed in her. "Look, my priority needs to be solving this case, not finding a place to stay. This is on my time and mostly my dime, not the company's. If you're okay with it, we can both stay here. Then if it doesn't work, we'll figure something out."

The tightness in her throat relaxed. She may have sounded casual to Theo, but the thought of having to find a place quickly filled her with dread. She wasn't ready for more upheaval. Of course, Theo being back — and being in the same house — was an upheaval of a different kind, but if she could keep her emotions in check, she'd keep her balance. As he said, he didn't plan to stay long. "There's plenty of room. Nick made the place bigger."

"So I see," he said, gesturing to where the back wall had been knocked out to make the living room huge.

"I'm staying in —"

"In my old room," he interrupted.

She nodded but didn't comment. The silence was worse than the mention of underwear, so she suggested, "You could stay downstairs in the master suite. Do you get up early?"

"Usually," he said.

"Great, because I don't start until later."

"You never liked mornings." He smiled for the first time, and she hated how it made her heart hitch. "You always complained about morning dance practice."

It wasn't fair for him to still know her so well. "I'm sure we can stay out of each other's way."

He looked up from his food and met her eyes. Not since her audition days, did she feel so scrutinized. He continued to stare at her as he said, "We're good at staying out of each other's way, which brings me back to my earlier question — what are you doing in Fable Notch?"

Clearly, he hadn't heard anything about her since leaving. "A lot can happen in twelve years."

"I'm aware, but you were all set, acceptance to the Conservatory in hand." He picked up the ketchup bottle to put more on his fries. She could hardly see them. "Why aren't you performing or touring with a major dance company?"

No, no, no. She was not having this conversation. She was not going back to those painful memories and certainly not with him. "Things change. It was a long time ago, and you chose not to be a part of my life."

"Chose? Do you think I had a choice?" The bottle slammed on the counter, and she jumped. He didn't usually yell, especially because he knew she hated it. And why was he angry? He was the one who agreed to her father's demands. He was the one who left, who joined the army, putting thousands of miles between them and never reaching out to her again. "I went along with your father splitting us up was so you could dance. You deserved it. Needed it. I couldn't take that from you. So why didn't you go?"

"I did. I was at the Boston Conservatory for two years."

"And then?"

This was not good. Only a few minutes in the same room and she was already shaking from the feelings of vulnerability. Maybe she would look for a new place to stay after all. "And then my mom was diagnosed with stage four ovarian cancer. I found out when I came home the summer after my sophomore year. I deferred in the fall. She died a few weeks after the New Year of what would have been my junior year."

His face softened as his hands moved to his jean's pockets. "I'm sorry. I liked Donna. She was a kind person."

"She liked you, too. She was always on our side." Which helped, but in the end not enough.

"Didn't you go back?"

"No." She couldn't bring herself to say more.

"You gave up dancing?"

"I had to." She held up a hand before he could say anything. "Don't ask me to explain." Numb from her mother's death, she'd all but hidden away in her room, counting the hours until she could leave again. She planned to stay in Boston permanently once school started, but that summer changed things for her more than the summer when he left.

"So you've been here since then?"

"Pretty much. At least one of us got their wish of leaving this town and never coming back."

"Never imagined I'd have a reason to return," he said.

Would she have been a reason? If she'd tried to find him, tell him what happened, would he have come back? No, he didn't even visit Martin and Millie. Her dream may have been dance, but his was never coming back here. "You're here to help Martin." She said it to remind herself that his being here had nothing to do with her.

Theo gave a non-committal shrug. "He's out of commission because of his injury. Said he needed me."

I needed you, too, her heart cried out. Stupid heart. Eden kept her features schooled. She was good at it.

Harlow gave a yip, pulling her out of her traitorous thoughts. "Yes, you can have some chicken," Theo said.

He took his plate and put food in her dish. He came close enough for Eden to smell the soap he used and sense the heat of his body, if only for a moment. As he walked to sit at the dining room table with his sandwich, she noticed something else. "You're limping."

"No, I'm not," he said, but his rapid answer and tone said he knew otherwise.

"Is it from an army injury?"

"No, I got out of there without breaking or seriously burning anything. About ten months ago, a beam came down on my leg when I was going through a warehouse hit by a firebug in Pittsburgh. Open femur break. It sometimes acts up at the end of a long day, and this has been a very long day."

She winced and ignored the comment about his day. "That would be a hell of an injury. The fact that your limp is barely noticeable is impressive."

"You sound as though you're speaking from knowledge."

More than he knew. "I'm a physical therapist. I've got a practice over at Maximum Results, the shiny new gym off of 3. I also teach a few classes there." It was the only dancing she could do.

"Why? I mean, how did that happen? I mean... hell, I'm not sure what I mean." He ran his hand through his hair, then took a bite of his sandwich. Harlow came over to where Eden was standing, and she was glad petting the dog gave her something to do. "So, about this living arrangement — you're okay with it?"

"I think we can manage," she said, looking at the man she once couldn't imagine being without. There was so much to say and nothing to say. "I'm getting back to my book, then going to sleep. Unless you need help finding anything else."

"No, nothing. Good night, Eden."

"Good night, Theo."

As she headed upstairs, she tried not to think about what his being in town was going to mean. Telling him she quit dancing was hard enough. How was she going to tell him she'd gotten married?

Chapter Three

♥

Theo's first waking thought was of Eden, asleep upstairs. After years of being apart, this morning she was only a few rooms away. It seemed impossible. Then again, a week ago, he would have said willingly coming back to this town was impossible.

To himself, he could admit he'd never stopped thinking of her and comparing other women to her. She was so beautiful. His memory didn't do her justice. She may not be dancing professionally, but even wearing leggings and a t-shirt, he could see how strong and graceful she was. Sexy. Her arms were muscled, and he assumed her legs were too. He shouldn't think about her legs.

Her blonde hair was shorter now, a few inches past her shoulders rather than to the middle of her back. What had changed the most were her eyes. They were the warm brown he remembered, but missing the sparkle that was part of what drew him to her. And he knew why — because she wasn't dancing anymore.

Her dream was the reason he left. Did that mean none of it had been worth it?

He'd agreed to her father's ultimatum so she could dance. Since he didn't have dreams of his own, hers had been precious to him. Her father, Patrick, never thought Theo was good enough for his daughter, and on some level, Theo agreed. When the old man told Eden to either give up Theo or he wouldn't pay her tuition for college, to Theo it was a no-brainer.

It had been the hardest thing he'd ever done. She told him they'd figure it out when she got back from her graduation trip. But by then he'd gone on the road with his brother, Cole, and his band. He made certain Eden had no way to contact him.

And still, the pull was too great. To keep himself from going to Boston to be with her, he joined the army. Several thousand miles of distance did the trick. He'd told Millie and Martin to never bring her up, which he assumed was why they didn't tell him she'd come back.

He'd known before agreeing to Martin's request, this trip wasn't going to be easy. Eden being here was going to make it harder. He'd ached to reach out and touch her last night. Was her hair as soft as he remembered?

No, that didn't matter. He needed to stifle that urge.

Theo got out of bed, stretched, and did a quick physical inventory. His leg was a little sore, but not bad. As he got dressed, he realized with a shock that he hadn't had any nightmares. Stress made him prone to violent dreams either about his time in Afghanistan or being trapped under the beam that broke his leg —— or both. It had to be the total exhaustion from the drive. Quiet, dreamless nights like last night were something to be grateful for. Especially considering he spent the night in mother's old room.

He stared at his surroundings, amazed. Not much of the original room remained. The master bedroom had been enlarged, so besides a four-poster king sized bed, there was a sitting area with an enormous television over a newly created fireplace, and a luxurious bathroom. He would never get over the changes Nick made. His brother may be brilliant at whatever financial thing he did on Wall Street, but he also had an eye for design.

A glance at the clock told him he had time for coffee and taking Harlow for a quick walk before meeting Martin at the Kinsman Diner. Throwing on a hoodie with the

Prometheus logo to remind himself this was a job, along with jeans and work boots, he went into the kitchen, put food in Harlow's dish and a mug under the Keurig machine. A few minutes later, he took his first sip and looked around the room in the morning light.

More changes. Everything in the kitchen was new. The last time he was here, only one burner on the stove worked and the oven was sketchy — things either burned or were completely undercooked, which was one of the many reasons why back then he ate most of his dinners at the Sinclairs. Instead of a wall dividing the kitchen from the rest of the house, there was an island in the center, which opened into a dining area, then into an immense living room created by Nick having knocked out the back wall. Theo never imagined the place could look this good. All he ever imagined was getting out.

Now he was back, and Eden had never left. It was a lot to take in.

Taking his coffee with him as he and Harlow walked through the neighborhood, he noticed how much cooler the morning air was in New Hampshire compared to Maryland. May was barely the beginning of spring. When they got back, he put his mug in the sink and pretended he wasn't listening to hear if Eden was awake before they jumped in his truck and headed out. The streets were quiet, and he was at the diner in less than ten minutes.

The Kinsman Diner, a classic train car diner with the name painted in big letters on the front, looked the same. Knowing how little room was in the place, he cracked the windows and left Harlow in the car. Inside, everything looked the way it did when he left. For once, he was glad things hadn't changed.

At a glance, he took in the black, white, and aqua tiles on the floor, the long counter running the length of the train car, and the round stools with no backs. A short-order cook on the grill out front, a third of the griddle taken up by hash browns cooking along the side, the rest by orders in process. The specials were written on a blackboard over the cook's head. Fresh baked muffins the size of his fist and iced pastries beckoned from under a plastic dome. About fifteen years ago, they'd built an extension to the side to accommodate more tables, larger groups, and a handicapped entrance turning the building into an 'L'. It hadn't been enough to stop a line from forming out the door on the weekends.

"Oh my goodness, as sure as there is still snow on top of Mt. Washington, it's Theo Hanson," said a familiar voice.

"Rosie Kinsman," he said, as she came over. Holding the hot coffee carafe at arm's length, she gave him a hug which pressed the entire length of her compact and ample body against him. She fit under his chin. Her grandfather had owned and operated the diner and people said Rosie was waiting tables as soon as she was big enough to see over them. She was Millie's best friend and held a special place in his heart. He couldn't imagine the place without her. "You are one hot momma."

"You're damn right I am," she agreed. "Didn't you grow up fine? If you've been back more than a day without comin' in here, you are getting none of my cinnamon French toast."

"I got in last night, and I want a double order."

She laughed. "You may have gotten older and stronger, but it's good to see your appetite's the same. Bet you drink coffee, not Coke, now."

"I do. Black, one sugar."

"Sugar's on the table. Pick yourself a booth, and I'll be over with a mug." He slid onto the black vinyl of a middle booth and chose the side facing the door. "Something must be up if you're here. Gotta be at least a decade since we've seen you," Rosie said, putting down and filling his mug in one practiced move.

"Been nearly twelve years. Martin called me because of the fires."

"I shoulda known. With all that's been going on, it's no surprise he's called you in. He took a nasty fall. You gonna help him at the station?"

He nodded as he added sugar, then took a careful sip of his coffee. Piping hot, the way he liked it. "I am. What have you heard?"

"Same as everyone. Those fires are big news. Hottest topic in town, no pun intended. No one hurt except Martin, thank goodness, but a lot of damage. People out of their homes and work. You know we don't usually get that kind of activity. Hell, we've gone years without anything burning, 'specially when there's a wet spring or fall." She sat on the opposite bench and leaned forward. "Helen and I were saying the other night, it seems suspicious." Helen was Rosie's wife. The two women had been together as long as Martin and Millie, maybe longer.

"Martin thinks so, too," he said in a lowered tone. He never could keep his mouth shut with Rosie or Millie. The two of them always got him to spill everything running through his head. He continued without thinking. "He's hoping I can help uncover who's behind these. But don't mention it around."

"Of course not, silly child." He smiled at the ludicrous endearment. "If there is someone doing this, I know you'll catch them. We don't want any more of our folks getting hurt."

For Rosie, calling the locals "our folks" wasn't an exaggeration. She had grown up in Fable Notch, practically raised by the customers in the diner. "I'll do whatever I can."

"I know you will," she said, patting his hand. She stood and took a step away, then turned back. "Should I get you some bacon for the pretty puppy sittin' in your front seat?"

"She'd love it. Thanks."

"Good morning, Rosie," Martin said, coming up to the table and putting down the stack of files tucked under his arm.

"Morning, Chief. Let me get you coffee and put in an order for a breakfast sandwich. I know Sal's got crispy home fries on the side of the griddle you'll love. And a double order of the French toast is on the way," she assured Theo before walking away.

Theo stood up to hug Martin, still somewhat surprised to be taller than the man who came into his life when he was thirteen and saved him and his brothers in every way possible. As he pulled back, his investigator's eye made note of the changes in the man. It had been over three years since he last saw Martin at a professional conference in Boston. The recent accident, along with a heart attack, had aged him. Theo took in the heavy cast that started at the wrist and went past Martin's elbow and the cane gripped in his good hand. His hair was almost completely gray, and he'd lost weight. While the weight was a good thing, seeing Martin look older made Theo do some quick mental math. Martin was almost sixty-five. He couldn't quite wrap his head around that.

"Bet she chose your breakfast for you, too," Martin said with a smile as he sat down. Theo nodded as he sipped his coffee. "What time did you get into town last night?"

"Around seven. Drove by the sites for a quick reference, grabbed dinner, and then went to the old house."

"Why did you stop there?"

"Didn't stop by. I'm staying there for this trip.

"Guess that's the first time since you've been there since — oh damn." Martin's voice trailed off.

"Yeah, I was surprised, too."

Martin waited until after Rosie poured his coffee and left to continue. "Son, I'm sorry. It never occurred to me to tell you about Eden because I never thought you'd go there."

"You couldn't have mentioned in our conversation on Friday that she was here? And one of the victims?"

"Truthfully, I didn't quite know how to bring it up. I knew you'd find out, but I guess I thought you'd see her name in the file, and I'd tell you then. I certainly didn't expect for you to run into her first."

"Actually. Harlow ran into her, and I ran in after."

"You lost me." Theo explained how he and Eden came face to face and their current decision on living arrangements. "You're both going to stay in the house?"

Theo nodded. "She's not ready to look for another place, and my having Harlow limits my choices. We're adults. We can make it work. It's not like I'll be here long."

Martin didn't say anything, and Theo was glad when their food arrived, giving them something else to focus on. He wasn't as certain about the living arrangement as he pretended. Fortunately, breakfast gave him a distraction. When he forked a huge mouthful of the cinnamon-y, eggy toast into his mouth, he couldn't stop the moan.

"I heard that," called Rosie. He didn't even see her. "Glad you like it."

"This is why I don't even whisper around her," Martin said. "She hears everything."

"Yes, I do."

After taking several more bites, Theo asked, "Are those the files on the fires?"

"It's what I have so far. All my notes and pictures. A few interviews."

"I want to review the first and the third fire sites today, see how he started and what he did most recently."

"I'll join you, at least for the first one. You're going to have to schedule times to talk to the owner and residents of the professional building. I haven't gotten to those for obvious reasons."

"No problem."

"You won't say that when you hear who owns it."

Theo let his fork drop to the plate. "Patrick Barrett."

"Got it on the first shot." The French toast turned into a lump in Theo's stomach. Seeing Eden was one thing. Seeing her father? That was something completely different. As if reading Theo's thoughts, Martin said, "A lot of time has passed."

"And you think he's changed?" Theo couldn't keep the sarcasm from his voice.

"No, I think you have."

Theo said nothing, just sipped more coffee. It wasn't that he couldn't see the changes in himself, but he also knew not all of those were good. And the things Patrick didn't approve of back when Theo and Eden were dating — coming from a broken home with an alcoholic mother and absent father, barely graduating from high school — those remained true. His financial situation had improved, but he had personal challenges that would not be welcomed by any woman or accepted by her father. Who would want to be with a man who traveled regularly, suffered from nightmares, and came with the baggage he did?

As they ate, people came over to talk to Martin. From the conversations, Theo could tell most hadn't seen him since the accident. Martin introduced or reintroduced him to at least a half-dozen people as Theo tried to finish his breakfast. He watched their faces register surprise at seeing him and looked for disapproval, waited for the first cruel remark.

"No one thinks badly of you," Martin said after another person left.

"Why do you say that?"

"I can see the tension in your body. I know you have a lot of mixed memories about this town. But, son, those are the memories of a boy who was barely an adult when he left. A boy who had been through too much loss and hardship. Just because people didn't approve of what your parents did, doesn't mean they didn't approve of you."

Theo raised an eyebrow. He remembered the looks from teachers, parents, and other adults that went from pitying to mistrustful, as though he'd grab a purse and run at the first available opportunity. They were either 'those poor Hanson boys,' or 'those wild Hanson boys,' depending on who was talking. And Theo lived up to his reputation, pulling pranks and skirting the edge of breaking the law. "I'm never going to have this town's approval. It's enough to know that you and Millie love me."

"That we do," said a warm voice.

Theo almost jumped from his seat to give Millie a hug. As she wrapped her arms around him, the smell of violets brought back a thousand memories of her care. After years of his mother's indifference, it had taken Theo a while to accept Millie's love, but she'd proven it repeatedly with her support, understanding, and rock-solid confidence in him, his brothers, and Ryan, her son. She changed his life.

"I'm so glad you're here," she said when they sat again.

"Good to see you, too." And he meant it. Not seeing Martin and Millie for so long had been hard, but as much as he loved them, he hated this town more.

Like her husband, Millie looked older too, and he still thought she looked like Ellen Burstyn. Most importantly, the warmth of her smile was the same. Seeing the two of them was more emotional than Theo expected. He might not believe in happiness for himself, but he believed others could have it because of what Martin and Millie showed him.

"Theo is staying at his old house while he's here," Martin said.

"But he can't because...." Millie stopped. "Oh, Theo, I'm sorry. I had no idea. It never occurred to me you might go there."

"It's okay."

"Where is Eden going to stay? I suppose one of you could come to the house after all. There's another bedroom, or I could rearrange things in my music studio. You could stay there. Please, don't make her move. She's had so much upheaval recently." Millie's hands flitted about as though she were moving people around.

"Relax, Ma." As soon as he called her "Ma," she calmed. He'd never forget the first time he called her that. It had slipped out one day when he'd thanked her for something, and they both teared up. It was as true now as it was then. "I didn't kick her out. We're both staying there and being as adult as possible."

"Ooh, that sounds—"

"Stop. Don't get any ideas. We've worked it out, but my focus is on these fires. Nothing more. Once the case is solved, I'm heading back to Baltimore." Theo didn't want to have this conversation a second time. "I'm going to inspect the first site."

Martin reached into his pocket and said, "Here's my work phone for you, and grab the extra squawk box in my car. You should have it with you in case there are any calls."

Theo's shoulders tensed. He'd forgotten he was also here to step in as chief while Martin healed. Although chances were there would be little to do in that regard, it was one more responsibility, and Theo felt the weight of it. He preferred coming in after the fire was out. "Is there anyone who will be annoyed at being passed over for the chief job, even if it's temporary? What about Lloyd Wilson?" Theo named the part-time deputy chief, the only other paid firefighter. He didn't want to make enemies no matter how short his stay.

"I don't think so. I met with most of the volunteers after they discharged me, and I told them I was calling you. They agreed it was a good idea. There's no doubt we need someone with your experience."

"You don't think my being in town will raise eyebrows?" Theo asked.

Martin shrugged, and Millie said, "Maybe one or two, but if anyone is curious, it's because you never come around. People know the amazing things you've done since moving away, how you served our country." Theo knew exactly who'd told them, too. "And everyone knows you'd always help my Martin. There's no reason for you to feel unwelcome."

As if he'd felt welcome back then. He knew how the people in Fable Notch saw his family. His mother was the town drunk, and her sons were a trio of trouble-makers. It didn't matter how they'd turned out. Cole was literally a rock star. Nick worked on Wall Street and made more money than God. But if you asked anyone, they'd be quick to mention Cole's pool shark days, Nick trying to make time with the rich ski bunnies, and how Theo was run out of town for dating the wrong girl.

Who he was now living with.

He ran his hands through his hair. This was not good. Too many memories.

"Thinking about the cases or something else?" Martin asked.

"The cases," Theo said, but when he looked at Martin, he knew the man saw through him. He hadn't been able to lie to Martin since the day they met. Why would years away make any difference? Theo emptied his mug, grabbed the top file, and said to Martin, "Meet me at the Northcott Estate when you're done."

"I'll finish my coffee and be right over." Theo knew 'finishing coffee' could take Martin an hour or more, depending on how many people there were to talk to, and with Millie there, it would take longer. He didn't mind. He needed the time alone.

As he walked to the door, Rosie handed him a bag and a to-go cup with coffee. "I have a feeling you're going to need both of these," she said.

"What's in the bag?" he said, giving it a shake.

"Something for you and something for the pup."

He kissed her cheek. "See you soon."

"You better."

He got into his truck and gave a little laugh at the smell of bacon. "Rosie's going to spoil us both while we're here." Harlow gave a quick bark that Theo assumed was approval. At least someone was happy.

The fires were already the big topic around town, and Theo knew his arrival would soon be at the top of the list of what people were talking about. And if they heard he and Eden were staying in the same house? It would be the *only* thing people were talking about.

Chapter Four

♥

As soon as Eden woke the next day, she looked out the window to see if Theo's car was next to hers. When she saw her Mini Cooper sitting on its own, she sighed in relief. It was a temporary reprieve, but she'd take it. Hopefully, the next time she saw Theo, she'd be more prepared. To say his appearance last night shook her was an understatement.

The last year had been filled with important and empowering changes, including leaving her marriage. Her apartment being destroyed by the fire had shaken her up, but she was determined to keep moving forward. Having her past walk back into her life at this moment was not what she wanted, but she would get through it. She would not let Theo's temporary return to Fable Notch throw her off.

Like you could ever control your emotions for Theo.

Great, the voice in her head decided sarcasm was the best way to start the day. Unfortunately, it was also true. From the first time she saw Theo when she was a sophomore in high school, she'd been drawn to him. And by the end of their first date, had lost her heart. She'd never gotten it back and learned to live without it instead.

Staying in bed wasn't going to change or help the situation, so she got up, dressed in her usual leggings and t-shirt, and headed down to the kitchen, hoping that coffee would help. Then she saw his mug in the sink. Did he still take it with sugar, or did he prefer it black now? And what did it matter?

She shook her head to clear her thoughts as she took a sip of her coffee. Maybe while Theo was in town she could get closure, say the things that had gone unsaid when he left her. That way, when he left again, she'd be able to move on.

The sarcastic voice said, *We'll see*. Totally not helping.

The sound of a car pulling into the driveway made her stomach flutter. Great, she wasn't even halfway through her first cup of coffee, and she'd have to manage a conversation with Theo after all. He was right — the sooner he could find the arsonist the better. Then she could put him and the fire behind her and get on with her life.

Eden took a deep breath and braced herself, but instead of Theo, two fast knocks brought her friends, Janelle and Dani Vaughn, into the house along with Dani's huge dog, Otis, who came bounding over for the first hugs.

"This is a pleasant surprise," she said, embracing each of them. "What are you doing here? It's nearly nine. Shouldn't you both be at work?"

"It's not like I can't open Tailor Thrift late," Janelle said. "I've yet to have a line waiting for me when I unlock the doors." Janelle owned a clothing thrift store, which also featured pieces where she took previously hideous clothing and redesigned them.

"And Beth is opening the clinic. I don't have a patient until eleven." Dani was the new veterinarian. She'd recently moved permanently to Fable Notch after spending summers with her aunt, Rosie Kinsman, when she was a kid. "I have some news," Dani said.

"And when she called to tell me, I thought it would be better to let you know in person," Janelle said.

This couldn't be good. "Now that I'm nervous, spill it."

An unsure glance passed between the two women before Janelle finally blurted, "Theo Hanson is back in town. He's here to help Martin investigate the fires."

On the bright side, it wasn't more bad news. "I know."

"How?" Dani asked as she went over to the coffeepot and poured herself and Janelle a mug. "Aunt Rosie called me while he was in the diner having breakfast."

Eden wasn't surprised the diner was one of his first stops. It had always been a favorite. "Guess where he's staying while he's here?"

Two coffee cups hit the island almost simultaneously. "You're shitting me," Janelle said. Eden couldn't stop the smile. She loved the way Janelle expressed herself. She sometimes wished she could talk the same way.

"Do you think I'd joke about this?"

"Of course not, but.... Holy hell, Eden."

Eden tilted her head in agreement. "Yeah, that sums it up."

"Tell us what happened. Don't leave anything out," Dani said.

Eden went into the refrigerator to get scrambled egg cups for herself and her friends and tossed one to Otis after a nod from Dani. As she popped them in the microwave, she told them about Theo's unexpected arrival the night before.

After a stunned silence, Janelle said, "I feel the need to state the obvious — that had to have been uncomfortable."

Eden plated the food, scrambled eggs mixed with cheese and chopped veggies cooked in muffin cups, and handed them to her friends. She was stalling. "It wasn't the best night I've had recently, but it wasn't the worst."

Janelle gave a quick laugh. "If your apartment building hadn't burned down three weeks ago with practically all of your belongings in it, this would rank higher on the suck-scale."

"If that hadn't happened, Theo wouldn't be here at all." *It's not like there was anything else to bring him back to Fable Notch*, she thought bitterly.

"How long has it been since you saw him?" Janelle asked.

"The weekend we graduated from high school."

"I don't know what I'd do if I ran into Nick unexpectedly," Dani said. Nick Hanson, Theo's younger brother, was the big heartbreak from Dani's past. "I mean, I know it's going to happen since, unlike Theo, Nick comes to visit, but I'm hoping I'm a little more prepared than you were."

"That wouldn't take much."

"So, which one of you is moving out?" Janelle asked. "You were here first, but this is Theo's place, I suppose."

"For the moment, we're both staying." The twin stares she received were almost comical. She explained their decision. "I know, it's crazy, but we're grownups. We can make it work."

"Are you sure?" Janelle didn't look convinced.

Eden shrugged. "I've been so comfortable here after the stress of the fire that I haven't looked for a new place. Not to mention any building owned or managed by my father is out of the question." It was bad enough Patrick was one of the biggest real estate developers in the area, but as the biggest controlling influence in her life, she was doing all she could to separate herself from him.

"You're welcome to move in with me again," Janelle offered. "I mean, I know it was crazy the night after the fire, but I can find space for you. We'll make it work." Janelle lived in the one-bedroom apartment above her shop, which meant her work — and a lot of thrifted clothes — filled her space. Because Eden had nowhere to go, she'd stayed with Janelle and slept on the couch in the living room. She'd found three pins in the cushions when they stuck her. The next day, Millie Sinclair suggested this house, and Eden jumped at the chance.

"You could stay with me and Otis. I can move things out of the second bedroom. It wouldn't take more than a day. We'd love the company as long as you don't mind the fur."

Eden put down her coffee mug and took her friends' hands into hers. She loved these women. Dani, with her warm smile and gentle voice, effortlessly put her animal patients and their owners at ease because her kindness came from the heart. Janelle would be intimidating with her natural beauty and style if it weren't for the fact she looked for and found the beauty in others.

Eden could hardly believe that less than a year ago she was married to Keith Peters and rarely saw anyone without it being part of a social life Keith dictated. She'd never had an easy time making friends because dance took so much time and attention. But she and Janelle had easily reconnected when Janelle moved back to Fable Notch after pursuing a fashion career in New York City. Eden wouldn't have made it through her divorce without Janelle.

Her friendship with Dani was newer, but no less important. Eden hadn't known Dani well when they were younger, but because Dani was often with Nick, Eden saw Dani's friendship with Nick turn into love. Time and life had separated them, as it had Eden and Theo. Dani came back to Fable Notch two months ago. She and Janelle had run into her at the Seven Brothers Brewery, which was run by Dani's closest friend, Laurel Stewart, and soon Dani was joining them during their weekly visits. The past three weeks were more bearable because of her friends.

"So?" Janelle's question brought her out of her reverie.

Eden gave their hands a squeeze. "Thank you, but I'm going to stay put for now. There's plenty of room, and I'm not ready for more changes. Maybe I'm crazy, but it's not as though I can avoid him while he's here. He'll need to talk to me about the fire, if nothing else."

"That's a far cry from living with him," Dani said.

"Are you hoping something might re-spark between you?"

Leave it to Janelle to ask the question she didn't want to think about. She responded with the painful truth. "It doesn't matter if it does or doesn't. I'm sure Theo's dislike for this town hasn't changed. As soon as he finds out who's been setting these fires, he'll leave again."

Janelle gave her an "are you sure look" which made Eden wonder if she was kidding herself or if she had ulterior motives for wanting to stay with him, but she didn't have the energy to analyze her decision. Maybe they were both being stubborn by staying. Wouldn't be the first time in their relationship.

Not that they had a relationship anymore.

"He must have been as surprised to see you as you were to see him," Dani said.

Eden nodded. "Especially considering he left me so I could study dance, and I don't do that anymore. I think he was shocked and disappointed. I suppose I am, too."

Janelle put a hand on her shoulder. "Of course, you were shocked."

"I meant disappointed. I never wanted Theo to know I stopped dancing. If he didn't come back, he'd always think his leaving gave me my dream. Now he knows we broke up for nothing."

"Stop," Janelle said. "You were kids and your father asked you to make an impossible decision. And yes, I know you didn't see yourself ending up back here — hell, I didn't either when I left to conquer the fashion world — but things happen. You make choices, and you live with the consequences. Theo doesn't get to be disappointed in you. He has no say in your life. And you don't have to be disappointed either."

Don't I? But she didn't say it out loud.

Dani covered their clasp hands in reassurance before letting go. "Okay, you've decided to stay and make this situation work. How can we help?"

"You already have. Running over here and making sure I'm okay. It means a lot."

"Not a problem. But remember, if it gets too weird or uncomfortable, my second bedroom is always available."

"And my couch. This time I'll run the pin magnet over the cushions before you go to sleep." She was grateful for her friends. Millie came through with a place to stay, but it was Janelle, Dani, and Laurel who brought her clothes and toiletries, took her shopping for necessities, and made sure she didn't curl into a ball and hide. Eden smiled at her friends and felt the beginning of tears.

"Hey, what are the tears for?" The kindness in Dani's voice made Eden's eyes well up more.

"I'm lucky to have you in my life." For years she hadn't cried and always presented a brave face. Any time she cried with Keith — whether or not it was because of him — he told her to stop being so emotional. Being comfortable with her own feelings was another new part of her life. Her therapist told her it would make her stronger. Eden hoped it was true, because as long as Theo was in town, she was going to need that strength.

Chapter Five

♥

It took Theo less than fifteen minutes to get to North-cott Estate from the diner. Of course, nothing was far from anything in Fable Notch. As a teen, he'd been able to get almost anywhere he wanted with a bike, including this place. The Northcott house, a large Victorian painted slate blue with darker blue shutters, had seen better days, but was still beautiful. It was three stories high with a rounded turret on the left, wood details along the trim, and a large wrap-around porch. It had always been one of his favorites. He, Nick, and Cole occasionally rode over on their bikes. They'd stare at it and imagine what it would be like to live in a place that grand. Even then, it wasn't in the best shape. Taking care of an immense house was expensive, and the family had fallen on hard times, but to a boy whose home was more prison than castle, it looked magical.

Shaking off the useless memories, he got out of the truck, grabbed a camera out of the bag in his back seat, and instructed Harlow to stay. He'd call her over after his initial review. He took in a deep breath of the fresh, May air before he moved his focus to the building. Years in the army taught Theo the value of taking in the details of his surroundings carefully and completely, a skill which translated well to reading fire sites.

According to the file, no one had lived here for several years. The owners let it go for so long it had become impossible to sell at the price they wanted. The For-Sale sign looked as ragged as he felt. Looking around, it was clear the arsonist had only been interested in the carriage house, which was several hundred yards away. If the owners were responsible, they'd be more likely to burn the house hoping to collect the insurance money. To him, burning the carriage house felt like a "test run" for the arsonist. A safe location where neither he nor the fire would be seen.

Almost nothing remained of the building except a few of the thicker beams. The second-floor loft had collapsed and only one partial wall remained upright. He walked the perimeter at a distance, taking pictures and looking for anything that stood out. When he was ready to move closer, he took his kit from the car and released Harlow with a call of "Seek".

While he waited for the dog to give her signal, he took more pictures and tried not to think about how bothered he was about being here in the first place. He wanted to help Martin, but he couldn't give a shit about most of the people in this town. They may need him now, but where were they when he and his brothers had needed help? If the Sinclairs hadn't started caring for them, they would have probably ended up in foster care.

It wasn't long before Harlow stopped and barked, pulling him from his thoughts and making him notice his knuckles had gone white on the camera. Her bark, indicating she'd found the remnants of an accelerant, was in the same location noted in Martin's file as the probable starting point. The man may not fight a lot of fires in a year, but he understood the ones he did.

He met Harlow where she sat, gave her a treat, then released her. She continued her search while he took out a pair of rubber gloves and an evidence bag from his kit. Once he was gloved, he ran his hands over the fragments, picking things up, then checking for residue. Most arsonists who didn't create explosives like bombs or electrical short-circuits used readily findable accelerants — gasoline, kerosene, even spray paint in a microwave. When he noticed a shiny residue on his gloves, he packaged samples to send to the testing facility Prometheus used.

A car horn interrupted him. He looked up to see Martin arriving. A glance at his watch told him he'd been combing the site for nearly an hour. At least he got his timing right on how long it would take Martin to finish his coffee. He waved and went back to work.

As Theo finished. Martin walked up to him, pushing some debris aside with his cane. "It's impressive to watch you. You're methodical."

"A learned skill, as you know," Theo said. Patience had not been one of his virtues as a boy, assuming he had any. As an army firefighter, he'd been trained how to work with a team, something he'd never done before, but also on how to prioritize and execute a plan to save as many people and as much property as possible. Difficult to do when the world around you was on fire. He preferred the procedure and process required in arson investigation. It was better coming in after the fact than during. "A hard, but worthwhile lesson."

"Aren't they all? And who is this?" Martin asked as Harlow came over to check out the new arrival.

"This is Harlow, my arson dog and partner. She and I have been working together for nearly two years. Harlow, this is Martin." Harlow walked once around Martin, sniffed his hand, then sat between the men. "You've been approved."

"Interesting name choice."

"Well, she is a beautiful blond."

"No argument. So, what is your professional assessment? Did you two find anything?"

Theo rubbed the back of his neck with his hand. "There was residue at the point of origin, which Harlow found, and you got right. It started at the back left corner, which gave the fire time to build before becoming visible, even if someone was driving by. I won't know what they used until I get the results back from the lab. Reviewing the other sites will confirm it, but the fact that this wasn't accidental, combined with the increasing severity and frequency of the other fires, makes me agree. It's arson."

"Can't say I'm surprised, but I was hoping to be wrong."

Theo put the camera back in his truck and took out a tablet so he could write some notes. "What was it like on the night of the fire?" Theo could imagine from what remained, but it was a help to hear Martin's account.

"When we got here, the place was ablaze. Couldn't get near it. It had been burning for a while before neighbors saw anything." Martin gave Theo more details, which he noted on his tablet. "We assumed at the time it was unintentional. Kids hang out here sometimes, smoking and drinking."

"I'm shocked," Theo said sarcastically.

Martin gave a small laugh. "They can't get into the house, but the carriage house wasn't as securely locked. I'm pretty sure I know the answer, but what are the chances this is over?"

"That there won't be any more fires?" Martin nodded. Theo straightened as he gave the man the bad news. "Slim to none. Arsonists don't usually stop until they're caught — either for the fires or another crime. The only time I saw a series of fires stop was because the arsonist ended up in jail for eighteen months on a breaking and entering charge. As soon as he was out, the fires started again."

"So there are more coming."

Theo knew Martin was thinking about who could be hurt and what might be lost. "There are. And as I said when you called, we'll see the next one before the week is out."

"I should put the other area towns' departments on alert so they can be ready to help us and see if they've had any suspicious fires."

"That's a good idea. I can give you more information after I review the other sites and when I learn what accelerant he used. I'm going to head over to the third site, go through this process again, then find somewhere to print these pictures." He worked best with a visual in front of him. It helped to discover patterns.

"We've got a one-hour photo place in town. It's part of the new pharmacy."

Theo gave a nod of recognition. "I noticed it as I drove in. Never thought I'd see a chain store in this town."

"There are a few now. Some people hate them, but they create jobs and are helpful to the tourists. I like the convenience for getting some of my new prescriptions and knowing they'll have what I need."

New prescriptions. An unpleasant reminder that Martin was getting older. Theo made a mental note to visit with the Sinclairs after this was done. "I can see that, but kids can't hang around outside a CVS the way we could Nash's Pharmacy." Theo and Adam Stewart used to sit for hours on the front sidewalk in front of Nash's drinking sodas and killing time. It was one of the few places Theo felt welcome. Stella Nash was kind and that meant a lot. She'd add candy when he bought a drink, bottles of aspirin when he picked up his mother's medications after she injured her back. He'd felt protective of the place and Mrs. Nash. He'd once got his childhood tormentor, Dylan Cioni, caught when Dylan tried to sneak out with a bunch of contraband under his jacket. Theo had tripped him. When Dylan fell, merchandise went flying. Theo had gotten slammed into a locker the next day, but the bruises had been worth it.

He pinched the bridge of his nose. Could you get frequent flyer miles for trips down memory lane? If so, he was going to be racking them up. "Are you up for joining me at the next site?"

"You mean am I strong enough to stand around while you work?"

"No, that's not it at all," Theo said, hoping he hadn't offended Martin. Theo hated when other people underestimated what they thought he could do, and he didn't want Martin to think that's what he meant. "It can be boring watching Harlow and me go over everything piece by piece — almost literally. If there's something you need to do back at the station, I understand."

"The third site was the worst, and I haven't been back since it happened. I'd like to look at it with you, give you insight into what we saw."

"I'd appreciate it. The aftermath can tell me a lot, but knowing what happened that night helps, too."

"Then I'll give you and Harlow time to do your walk through before I come by. In the meantime, I'll head to the station to see what I've missed in the last few days. I'm also going to give our volunteers a call, see if they can come by tomorrow afternoon and tell you what they saw."

"You sure it's a smart idea?" He didn't know who was on the team, but it was likely that someone who knew his history and reputation would be there.

"I do. They need to meet you, and they may have information that can help. They're good people."

"If you say so." It was going to take more than Martin's word to convince him.

"Ready to go?"

"Let me wash Harlow's paws, and we're off." Theo called for Harlow, and she followed him and Martin to his truck. He grabbed a jug of water and filled the paw cleaner.

"That looks like an oversized travel mug."

"It's called a Paw Plunger." Theo took one of Harlow's paws and pushed it through a hole at the top of the cup. "We do this after going through a site. Keeps her from licking it later and from getting soot all over my car."

"Clever. She doesn't seem to mind it."

"It was part of her training. I also think she's happier when her paws don't have crap stuck on them." Theo finished with Harlow and put things back in his car. Everything was in its place, so he could find it easily whenever he needed it. "Okay, I'm heading out. See you over there."

He took the most direct route to the professional building where Martin had been injured and as he drove, he noticed more of the changes—businesses like the Nash's were gone, new ones had appeared. They had converted the old paper mill to a ritzy shopping center anchored by the Seven Brother Brewery. There was a day spa he couldn't imagine the locals using and a coffee place called Jitters. Maybe it looked different on the outside, but it was going to take more than chain stores and lattes to make Theo think anything had changed.

Arriving at the site, Theo got his first close look at the damage. Instead of a pile of charred wood, this time the outside of the structure remained, but every window was broken, the outer bricks stained by flames. Built in the 70s, the building was a big stone square, and it would have been like a kiln when the fire got going. The volunteer crew was lucky Martin was the only injury.

He started with a thorough exam of the exterior. When he released Harlow, she walked the perimeter, sniffling and snorting, separating the smells left by the fire from those left by the humans who fought it. At the back exit, Harlow barked and gave her indication. Theo rewarded her with a treat, then squatted down to go through his evidence collection process again. The more he could give the lab, the better the chances of a clear result.

He had Harlow wait as he went back to the truck for a hard hat, which he put on before they stepped inside to inspect what remained. The interior was piles of plaster and bricks mixed with plumbing and office furniture, including filing cabinets and metal desks, which survived the blaze. Harlow indicated two more locations, one beneath a section of the building that burned so hot it had broken through to the floor above and brought down the ceiling tiles. Places where the arsonist literally added fuel to the fire. Theo made a mental note to get a blueprint of the building and information on what businesses were located where. He needed to know if the arsonist had a specific target in mind when he set the fire.

Moving through the space while listening for sounds of weakened beams breaking, Theo let out a curse when he rolled his ankle, stepping over debris onto an uneven surface. Pain shot up his injured leg. Damn, he hated the reminder he wasn't done healing yet.

When Martin arrived, they walked the perimeter, and he told Theo what he experienced the night of the blaze. People driving by honked in greeting and a few stopped to talk with Martin and see how he was doing. By the time they were done, Theo's head was spinning with information and images. He'd had more small talk in the past few hours than he did in a week, maybe a month back home.

They were walking to their cars, Theo thinking about his next steps, when Martin asked, "Are you okay, Theo? You're limping a bit there."

"Walking over uneven ground for several hours does it to me sometimes, and I rolled my ankle earlier. Eden told me she's a physical therapist. I'll probably call her and see if she has an appointment open." Was he looking for another reason to see her?

"You still need that?" Theo appreciated the worry in Martin's voice.

"It helps. You'll need to see her after your cast comes off."

Martin scowled, and Theo laughed. Neither of them enjoyed being fussed over or told what to do. Much to Millie's consternation, none of her "boys" liked when she mothered them.

Martin changed the subject. "Let's head to the station. Millie said she'd drop lunch over."

"Sounds good," Theo said. "I'll drop the pictures off for developing and meet you there."

It wasn't long before Theo and Harlow were sitting in the station's kitchen. During lunch, he and Martin talked about likely suspects, starting with the people affected by the fire. It was possible one tenant of the professional building had a beef with Patrick Barrett. The man didn't make or want friends, but other than that, there wasn't anyone who stood out.

"After we're done, I'll send the samples I took from the sites to the lab, and then I need to set up an incident board. Do you have something I can use?"

"Probably. Don't tell Millie, but I've got as much stuff stored here as I do in the shed." Theo laughed. It was a tradition for Millie to ask Martin every year to clean out the shed and get rid of the things they didn't need. Every year, Martin agreed and did nothing. "Listen, about Eden. I'm sorry we didn't tell you she'd moved back. I tried to let you know when it first happened, but you made it clear you didn't want to hear about her."

"I'm stubborn like that."

"Which is why I didn't push it, but now you know. Are you sure you're going to be okay living in the same house? It's a lot to ask of both of you, especially given how things ended."

"You mean Patrick forcing me out of her life?"

"And you agreeing."

He'd been stubborn then, too. When it came to a choice between him and her dream, he couldn't let her make the wrong choice. His mother had once been an artist and wanted to sell her work, be a professional. His father, Russell, had drilled that dream out of her. Depression and alcohol did the rest. Theo remembered his brothers pooling their money to buy her paints and canvas the first Christmas after their father, Russell, left. She'd looked at the gift, cried, and ran to her room. She'd never used it. No, you couldn't get back broken dreams, and he'd seen the damage firsthand.

"It was the right thing to do," he said. He was sure of his decision then, but had it been a mistake? "I think enough time has passed. We can manage this. I won't be here long, and I don't want her to be pushed into moving if she's not ready. I've interviewed people after house fires. It's tough under any condition. You did the right thing offering her a place to stay."

"One of us should have called and told Nick, then this wouldn't have happened. If it doesn't work, we can find room for you and Harlow at the house."

"Thanks. I know you will."

"Thanks for being willing to help. I'm glad you're home."

Theo gave a small smile and put food in his mouth as quickly as he could. This wasn't home, and he wasn't truly willing. But he wasn't going to say that to Martin.

After lunch, Martin helped Theo get comfortable at his desk and set up an incident board on an old bulletin board they found at the back of a supply closet. After Martin left, Theo ran out to pick up the photos as soon as they were ready, then came back to the station to make a list of people to call and interview. Patrick Barrett was at the top. Theo was dreading it. He stared at the pictures hoping some answers would magically come to him.

"You look like you could use some ice cream." The voice was familiar but unexpected, so when Adam Stewart stepped into the work area and put a bag down on his desk, Theo almost jumped out of his skin. Harlow barked in response and went on alert.

"Jesus, man, if you're delivering the ice cream, shouldn't you have a bell to warn people?" He stood up and gave his old friend a hug. Adam had been his closest friend in high school, but they hadn't stayed in touch after Theo left. He couldn't see a reason. "It's good to see you."

"You, too. Never expected to. And you have a dog. If I'd known, I would have brought her one of our special dog treats." Adam kneeled and reached out a hand, which Harlow sniffed. Theo introduced them and immediately the two were playing on the floor.

As Theo watched them, he said, "Millie told me you opened an ice cream business. What's the place called?"

"The Bright Spot," Adam said, separating himself from Harlow and brushing fur from his jeans as he stood. Theo raised an eyebrow. "Yeah, go ahead and laugh. I used my mom's endearment after complaining about it for years."

"So, why did you pick it?"

"Because everything clever sounded stupid after a while. Brain Freeze, Thrills and Chills, Cone-ection, Udderly Delightful. One of my brothers suggested Pemigewasset, as if anyone can pronounce that river's name."

Theo groaned. "Hell, how long did it take before we could spell it in school?"

"Exactly, and those were the better options. One afternoon I was hanging with my mom and complaining and when she said, 'Don't worry. You'll come up with the right one. You'll know it when you hear it, my bright spot.' I looked at her and we both laughed. It was so obvious. Besides, isn't ice cream the bright spot in people's day?"

"Usually," Theo said.

"And it made for a great logo." Adam took a container out of the bag and Theo saw a simple drawing of the sun coming out from behind the peak of a mountain before Adam dropped the pint back in. "Got it on shirts and bags, too."

"I can't believe you turned your sweet tooth into a career."

"Hey, you were practically raised by the fire chief and look what you do." True. Theo had unintentionally gone into the family business. Although since the other options were alcoholism or deadbeat dad, it was the right choice. "Besides, can you tell me a better way to spend your time than making ice cream and putting a smile on people's faces?"

It was an ideal job for Adam, who had a knack for making people happy, hence the nickname from his mother. "Good point. Sounds like you like it."

"I love it. And in addition to making something everyone wants, I get to be my own boss. I like following other people's rules almost as much as you do."

It was true. Adam and Theo got into their fair share of trouble. They never did anything harmful or which could land them in front of a judge—they didn't want to test Martin or Robert, Adam's father—but there were plenty of cut classes and other pushed boundaries. Joy rides in their brothers' cars, tricks played on younger siblings, and one memorable night encasing their principal's car in plastic wrap. "I got better with rules when I was in the army."

"I can imagine. I thought Martin was kidding when I heard you'd joined, but guess it was good for you."

"Yeah, turns out a little discipline isn't all bad. Okay, maybe a lot of discipline, in my case."

"True. I'm a great boss, but when I first started working for myself, I was a terrible employee. I'd put things off, ignore my own deadlines. It wasn't good for business. When I got serious about the fun, the fun got serious."

"Things are going well?"

"Very. I've got contracts with several of the local restaurants and hotels, and I'm thinking of opening a second shop in the next year. Maybe something in the Lake Winnipesaukee area. That will help with my next goal, which is to buy my building from Patrick Barrett."

"You rent from him?"

"Yeah, sorry. I know how you feel about the guy. It wasn't my first choice, but the location is ideal. I put the option to buy after five years in our contract."

"He could turn you down." Barrett could be an asshole just for the joy of it. Theo had seen it several times.

"I know, but I'm hoping to make him too good of an offer. And you're doing well professionally, or so I hear."

Theo gave Adam the basics of his work and recent promotion. "Guess we turned out okay for two troublemakers."

"Yes, we did. And no one, as far as I know, has ever trumped our trick of breaking into the high school and switching the teacher's desks."

Theo laughed. "That was backbreaking, but worth every minute of the confusion it caused. Hard to believe those boys turned into us."

"Speaking of being a boss, I saw signs for the Seven Brothers Brewery. I assume it's run by someone in your family."

"It is." Adam was one of eight kids — seven boys, one girl. Three of the boys were cousins who became part of their family when Adam was six and his aunt and uncle died. Robert and Valerie Stewart opened their home and hearts, and the family became the biggest one Theo had ever known. He'd always thought it was lucky they ran a hotel with cottages. They were used to crowd management.

"Which one of your brothers owns it?"

Adam laughed. "Laurel."

Not the answer Theo was expecting. "It's your sister's place?"

"Yup. You'll have to stop by and get her to tell you the story of how she decided making craft beer was her dream career."

"Gotta be a hell of a story."

"It is. There's a restaurant too. She serves my ice cream. So, what else is happening?"

"You know Eden is still in town."

"Of course. She and Laurel sometimes hang out, and I went to her for a shoulder injury last summer. Poor posture while scooping ice cream. Who knew there was a wrong and right way to do it? Or that physical therapy could hurt so much?" From his own experience, Theo knew how painful the process could be. He also knew how much contact was required between a physical therapist and her client. He didn't care for the way his pulse jumped at the thought of Eden having her hands on his friend. "Have you seen her?"

Theo didn't need to hide anything from Adam. "We're living together."

"You don't waste any time, do you?"

"It's not like that." Theo told Adam about finding her in the house.

"Must have given new meaning to uncomfortable. I wonder if her divorce is final."

Theo's mouth went dry. "Divorce?"

"Shit, man. Guess she didn't mention it. Until recently, she was married to Keith Peters."

"When did she...never mind. It doesn't matter." But it did. Theo couldn't help it. If he'd experienced a twinge of jealousy at the thought of Eden touching Adam when he saw her as a PT, a husband was another matter entirely.

"From what I heard, it was her decision to leave him. Don't know if that makes a difference."

From what I heard. Yeah, people in this town loved to talk.

"I'm sure she'll tell me eventually," Theo said more casually than he felt. "It's not like I gave her a reason to wait for me."

The silence became awkward until Adam said, "I need to get going and you better get that ice cream in the freezer. You don't want it rock hard, but soup isn't right either."

Theo peeked in the bag and saw the flavor name. "Chocolate peanut butter?"

"Has your love of Reese's changed?"

"Not one bit. You remembered."

"Some things you don't forget." Theo didn't respond knowing there were several meanings to his friend's words. "Let's get lunch or something this week."

"Definitely. We'll have to have a beer at your sister's place." He shook his head. "God, that sounds weird."

"Which part? Us being legal to drink or Laurel running a brewery?"

"Both," Theo said.

They walked out of the firehouse together. Theo gave Adam his number so they could make plans and then went into town to pick up the pictures from the pharmacy. On his drive back to the station, he took a few unnecessary turns to see more of the town.

Back at the station, Theo put the new pictures in their spot on the incident board. After an hour of making notes and writing questions for which he had no answers, he went to the kitchen, grabbed a spoon, and got the ice cream out of the freezer. He took a healthy bite, and the tastes of chocolate and peanut butter filled his mouth with delightful sweetness. His friend made amazing ice cream. It made him wonder how many more surprises were waiting for him before this case was closed.

As Theo continued to stare at the pictures of the fire sites as though they would magically give him an answer as to who set the fires, his phone buzzed breaking him out of his revery. He looked at the caller ID then smiled as he answered. "Hey, Nick, how's it going? How's the world of high finance?"

"Plenty exciting to me, but if I told you what was on my agenda for today, you'd nod off."

"Probably. I enjoy having money, but I've never quite had your fascination and determination to make it. Are you on track to be a billionaire before you're forty?"

"You know I am."

Theo wasn't surprised. Nick joined an after-school investor's club his sophomore year of high school and was instantly hooked. Before the first semester was over, he had mapped out two decades of goals, complete with monetary achievements. Theo had been a senior. His only goal was to leave town with Eden. He'd gotten half of that. He hoped Nick's plans worked out better. "Good to hear New York continues to live up to your expectations."

"It does, but more importantly, how are you managing in Fable Notch? Haven't run away screaming yet?"

"Not yet, but it's barely been a day." Even in that short time, his emotions had been tossed all over the place. He still couldn't quite wrap his head around the knowledge the Eden was minutes not hundreds of miles away.

"I'm amazed you went back even if it is to help Martin."

Cole came up when his band was playing in Boston. Nick visited the area to ski a few times a year when he could. Theo stayed away completely. On the occasions when he was in New England, Millie and Martin came to meet him. "That makes two of us."

"What do you think of the house?"

"It's amazing. I hardly recognize the place, which is its biggest draw."

"When I had the renovation done, we tried to restore mom's drawings in our old bedrooms, but the cheap paint she used to cover it up was like brown glue."

Theo's heart tightened as Nick's words brought back a forgotten memory. Nick didn't let a lot of people see it, but he had a big heart. "I'm glad you tried."

"Are you staying in your old room?"

This was going to be fun. "No, I'm in the master bedroom. I like the king size bed. Besides, Eden is staying in my room."

There was silence. Theo smiled and waited. He would not be the first one to talk. "Eden. Your Eden?"

"She's not mine, but yes."

"Okay. I knew she'd come back, but why is she at the house? And before you ask why I never mentioned her, it's because you made it clear no one should bring her up."

"Martin and Millie said the same thing. And she's there because her apartment was hit by the arsonist."

Theo explained how Millie offered the house to Eden, and how they decided they could handle living together.

"Damn, that sucks. It's too bad my new place isn't ready. I'd tell you to go there, but I'm sure you'd prefer a few necessities like electricity and running water."

"You're renovating another house?"

"Building one. But it won't be livable until July."

"Another thing off your Master List?" Nick's plans had plans. Theo never understood how his brother's mind worked, but it made him happy, and that's what mattered.

"Absolutely, and I'm getting this one earlier than expected, thanks to a few great years. It'll be another rental property except when I want to stay there."

"You and your goals amaze me," Theo said.

"Seems fair, your ability to not think too far ahead amazes me."

If Nick had experienced things falling apart the way Theo did, he'd understand Theo's preference for living one day at a time. Whenever he made a plan, it was ruined by something or someone. Have a life with Eden — ruined by her father. Come back with his entire army unit — ruined by an explosion.

Stay away from Fable Notch — ruined by an arsonist.

Yeah, no making plans for him.

They talked for a few more minutes, and Theo promised to give his brother a call on the drive back to Baltimore to see if they could get together.

After he hung up, Theo focused again on the incident board. He'd divided the board into squares, putting pictures and notes related to the fires in the corresponding areas. He stared at the pictures in the boxes for sites one and three, adding post-its with the names of the people impacted and who owned the buildings. He noticed Eden's building wasn't owned by her father. Interesting. He'd get those pictures tomorrow.

The empty fourth square bothered him the most. Nothing he'd seen gave him what he needed to create a targeted suspect list, which meant every day was one day closer to the next fire. He let out a harsh breath and ran a hand through his hair. Hopefully, the arsonist would continue to keep his focus on property, not people. Theo didn't want anyone hurt. He had enough to worry about.

He called the tenants of the third building, talking to some, leaving messages for others, including Patrick Barrett. Theo was dreading meeting with Eden's father and wanted to get it over with as soon as possible.

He wondered what Barrett thought of his daughter getting divorced. There was no way he approved. Theo shouldn't be surprised — or hurt — that her life went on, but it was still a gut punch. He stood and paced, stopping when there was a twinge in his leg. Maybe he should visit the gym. See if the muscles needed help.

Liar.

Fine, he wanted to ask her about her ex-husband, but he also knew better than to ignore pains in his injured leg.

He got ready to leave the station when Phyllis, the secretary and dispatcher for the police and fire departments, came in to tell him Ida Northcott Matthews was on hold for him. He'd called her after learning she was the current owner of the Northcott property. He didn't think she was responsible — especially as she lived in Florida — but it was best to be certain. Assumptions could be deadly.

Ida was more than happy to talk at length about the house of her childhood and her many memories of the place. He could hear the sadness in her voice that no one in the family wanted it. "And I thought we'd priced it fairly, but the only offer we received was so far under our asking price it was insulting. I mean, can you imagine offering almost $100,000 less than an owner wanted to sell for? He had a lot of nerve. I wish I'd been able to talk to him directly to tell him what I thought of his bid, but our real estate agent said it wasn't a good idea. What a horrid man."

"If you don't mind, could you tell me who made the bid? I'd like to find out if he had something to do with what happened to the property."

"Do you think he could have done it? Set fire to my grandfather's beautiful carriage house so we'd come down on the price?"

"It's possible, ma'am, and something I'd like to check out."

"If it's him, I hope you catch him and put him away. His name is Keith Peters."

Chapter Six

♥

Seeing her friends in the morning helped Eden, but as the day went on, images of Theo made it hard to focus. He was every other thought during her yoga class.

Deep breath in. *I wonder what he's doing.*

Child's pose. *Did he leave a girlfriend behind in Baltimore who will be upset if she finds out about our living arrangements?*

Downward facing dog. *How am I going to manage living with him?*

Warrior One. *The army certainly made his body stronger. Was his chest always so broad?*

It was a long class and Eden had trouble focusing during her first two clients of the afternoon. She hoped they didn't notice. She reminded herself if she had the strength to end her marriage, she could get through a few days with Theo.

Eden tried to focus on paperwork that afternoon, but her mind continued to wander. She was ready to give up and grab dinner when there was a call from the receptionist.

"There's a Theo Hanson here to see you if you're available."

It was as if she'd conjured him. "Send him to the treatment area."

She didn't know if he was stopping by to talk about the fire or if he needed her help with his leg, but she had less than two minutes to compose herself. She gave up after one. Nothing was going to make her feel calm. When he walked into the space where she worked with clients the look on his face suggested this wasn't related to the fires or his muscles.

"I hear you married Keith Peters," he said by way of a greeting.

"Where did you... Never mind." This was going to be fun. She knew he'd learn about it sooner or later, but hoped she could break it to him gently. But there wasn't a good way to say, 'Hey, remember the football player you used to make fun of? I was married to him for almost five years.' She wondered who had done that for her. "Did you hear I divorced him?"

He threw his duffle bag on the floor and said loudly, "Yes, but how did you manage to end up with that asshole?"

Nope, not fun at all. She cringed at his raised voice. Nothing put her in a defensive position faster than someone yelling. All her life, she'd done what it took to keep first Patrick and then Keith from getting angry. Her father's outbursts were legendary, not only in their home, but with his employees and tenants too. Eden's mother had been good at calming him, and Eden watched and learned. It had helped on the nights Keith came home in a lousy mood, looking to start a fight to release whatever was bothering him at work.

She nearly snapped at him that it wasn't his business, and he had no right to question her decisions. She was better at accepting and expressing anger and frustration. Unfortunately, that wasn't going to help. Sure, it would keep Theo at a distance, but why bother? She wasn't angry at him and, most of the time, she wasn't angry at herself anymore. Her therapist would be proud. "A lot changed after my mother died. Keith was working for my father, and he was there for me through a lot of tough times."

"And he was your best choice?" His voice rose further, and before she could answer, he held up a hand. "Sorry, that was uncalled for, and I shouldn't have yelled."

He remembered. Maybe it was foolish, but it warmed her heart. Very few people knew how much yelling upset her. With Theo, there had been no yelling. He didn't like it any more than she did. He'd told her how often his parents yelled before his father left, and the more his mom drank, the shorter her temper. They both worked to talk, not yell when they were together. Then again, they weren't together anymore. "Maybe we should focus on the reason you're here with me."

With me. Her words hung in the air, and they stood staring at each other. Flashes of moments spent together ran through her head like a poorly edited movie. Holding hands in the hall at school, eating breakfast for dinner at the Kinsman Diner on a Friday night, talking out by Silver Lake until they stopped talking and started....

She could not do this. Focusing on the past was not going to help her deal with him being here. Yes, it would be nice to heal the old hurts, but he'd be gone once this case was solved. She had to remember there could be nothing more.

"I rolled my ankle walking through the remains of the third site. I avoid walking on uneven ground when possible, but without a team, I'm on my own." There was more to that than the reference to the job. "I called, and the receptionist said you didn't have any appointments, so I took a chance and came by."

"Any pain?"

"On the 1 to 10 scale, I may be nearing a two, but I've learned not to ignore that."

"Learned the hard way, I assume," she said.

"Isn't that the only way?"

He had no idea. "So I've heard. Do you know which exercises help?"

"I mostly work on a mat, but I need props and help with resistance."

Which meant leaning against him, touching him. "No problem," she said. Her brain screamed, *Big problem!* "Let's get started." He moved into a prone position on the mat that took up most of the space in the center of the room, and she positioned herself at his feet. It would be the perfect set up for flirting if there weren't more than a decade of emotional distance separating them.

She evaluated his condition as they moved through several strengthening exercises, too many of which required her to lean against him or for him to press against her. She needed to turn up the air conditioning. After a half hour, she stopped and sat next to him on the mat. "I think you're fine. Anything you're feeling is from walking on the rolled ankle. Nothing new has been strained. Injuries like yours usually cause more lasting damage. I hope you know how lucky you are to have so much mobility."

"So I've been told. I was used to strict discipline from the military, so I didn't hold back on my rehab, and I was in good shape before the accident."

Your shape looks good now. Her internal monologue needed to shut up. "Let me know if there's anything else I can do to help." The sentence was supposed to sound professional, but it brought up a wave of emotion. There wasn't anything she could do to help fix the years between them.

In the silence, he reached out and brushed a hair from her face that had escaped her ponytail. The gentle touch loosened something in her chest. "Eden, why did you stay here?"

She knew he was going to ask again, and she wanted to tell him about the accident and her injury, but it was too much on top of talking about her marriage. "After my mother died, it was hard to think clearly. My dad put pressure on me to stay and I gave in, hoping for some kind of closeness. And then I met Keith. Marrying him seemed like a good idea. It wasn't."

"You knew your dad liked to — needed to — control you."

"I did, and yes, I admit I let him. And Keith wasn't any better. Over time, I stopped trusting myself, stopped remembering what I wanted for myself. It was hard back then, harder than I can express." She got up and walked to where she'd left a bottle of water, needing a little space. She took a sip and when she turned to look at Theo, his expression was miserable. Could he be hurting as much as she was?

"I was certain I was doing the right thing for you when I left."

"I tried to tell you there was no part of us being separated that was right, but you wouldn't listen."

Theo stood and ran his hands through his hair. She watched as he struggled with a response. There was nothing to be said. Nothing could change what happened. "No, I didn't listen."

"In less than three years I lost the two people I was closest too. I was alone. My mom was gone. You were gone. You forgot me." Her voice cracked as the belief she didn't know she held broke from her lips.

"I never forgot you. Not then, not now. How could I forget this?" he said, and in two steps he was directly in front of her, reaching for her face and leaning in for a kiss.

At the first touch, his mouth was hard, insistent, and she felt his frustration with their situation, but in a heartbeat, his lips softened against hers and his hands caressed the back of her neck.

As she melted into the kiss, Eden learned there was something that could unnerve her more than someone yelling.

Chapter Seven

♥

For a moment, logic surfaced, and Theo considered stopping. Neither of them needed this complication. He would leave as soon as the arsonist was caught, and she'd continue with her life here. But then her body melted against his, and he was lost.

When he left Harlow with Phyllis and headed to the gym, he told himself it was to get what he needed for his leg. He wasn't going to say anything about Keith. But when he saw her, he imagined them together, and he couldn't stop the angry words. When Eden accused him of forgetting her, he needed to show her how wrong she was.

She gasped as he deepened the embrace, and he let his tongue slip into her mouth. Her taste was familiar and new, a heady combination. She put her hands on his shoulders, and he wrapped an arm around her waist, pulling her closer.

How many nights had he dreamed of having her in his arms again? How many times had he ached to be with her? For years she was his first and last thought of the day and while time eased that, it hadn't stopped. He stroked the back of her neck, caressing an area he knew she liked, and she shivered at the touch. This was the woman he remembered — responsive, sensitive.

Time fell away and memories came rushing back. They'd been apart more than three times as many years as they'd been together, but it was as if they'd last kissed yesterday. He thought he recalled the feel of her against him with perfect clarity, but now he noticed all the things he'd forgotten. The softness of her skin. The floral scent of her shampoo. The perfect way her body fit against his. The way his heart raced as she sighed.

No kiss could ever compare to hers. No woman had been able to either. Part of his brain screamed, *You're holding Eden again,* even as his emotions warred with knowing that no matter how wonderful this was, it couldn't last.

When he broke the kiss, they stared at each other, breathless. His thoughts were a jumble, his emotions tangled. The only thing clear was that he wanted to kiss her again. If he was being honest with himself, he wanted more, but he couldn't let himself think about this. He took a step back before she could notice how hard he was.

"I never forgot," he said. "Don't ever doubt it. Leaving you was the hardest thing I've ever done. And that includes being on the front lines of a war."

He left without saying anything else, got Harlow from the station and went home. By the time he pulled into the driveway, he was regretting his actions.

He shouldn't have kissed her. He didn't need this complication. Shouldn't have let himself remember how good she felt in his arms. He couldn't get involved because there was no way he was staying after this investigation was done. Some things said about him were accurate. Theo was a bad bet and always would be. He might have a good job, but he had no idea how to create a home or what it took to stay with someone. Eden deserved better than Keith *and* him.

And what if she didn't want him to kiss her? Yes, she'd responded, but he'd all but grabbed her. No matter how badly he ached, he'd never forced himself on a woman. God, he owed her an apology. His inability to resist her was no excuse for his actions.

He knew coming to Fable Notch was going to be a challenge. With Eden here, with all these emotions still alive, it was torture.

Theo scrubbed his hand over his face and tried to get her out of his head. Yeah, like that was going to happen. He hadn't been able to manage it in the time they'd been apart. It certainly wasn't going to happen now.

He went into the house, dropped his keys and wallet on the island, and looked in the refrigerator to see if there was anything for dinner. He found a foil wrapped rectangle with a post-it that read *Meatloaf - 30 minutes in the oven at 350. Make a vegetable. Love, Millie.* The woman knew how to take care of people. Completely different from his own mother.

He set the oven, put the meatloaf in, and decided to take a walk with Harlow. They both needed the exercise. Anything to clear his head.

The spring sunset was beginning, and the night was beautiful, something he couldn't appreciate as a kid. Coworkers talked of visiting New England to go skiing, see the foliage. To Theo, it was all something to be avoided, like memories of Eden and his parents. As he walked, he found his thoughts going not to the painful times, but to the fun ones. Minor league baseball games in Manchester with Martin, Ryan, and his brothers. Listening to Millie teach Cole how to play piano and encouraging him to write music. Sunday dinners with everyone over at the Sinclair's house, his own worries far away.

And Eden, who made the painful moments bearable. He needed to be careful. She was just getting her life back. He would not ruin that for her.

When he got back to the house, the smell of Millie's cooking filled the air, and he was again thankful for her care. If he was honest with himself, even though Eden's being here complicated things, part of him was glad to help Martin. The Sinclairs never asked for anything in return for taking him and his brothers into their lives.

Their generosity and love came without strings, but he'd always hoped for a way to pay them back. When he started to make a decent salary, he'd sent them a check every month. After a year of the money not being deposited, he stopped. With the fires, finally, he could help.

He heated a bag of frozen vegetables — somehow if he didn't, Millie would know — and brought his plate over to the living room to watch television while he ate. Harlow made short work of the piece he gave her and was soon sitting next to him, hoping for more. As he channel surfed, he smiled at the size of the television. When they were kids, Nick complained how small their set was. They could barely afford basic cable, and it frustrated all three of them. It was another reason to spend time at the Sinclairs' house, even though there were frequent fights between Nick and Ryan over what to watch.

When Theo finished dinner, he decided to see what other changes Nick had made to the house. As he walked upstairs, he realized even they were new. Nothing creaked or sagged. He couldn't imagine what it cost to make this many updates, but whatever Nick invested had been worth it.

At the top of the stairs, he stood for a minute, looking at the doors of the three bedrooms. That had been the one good thing — they'd each had their own room. How many times had these doors slammed in anger and frustration? How many times had they listened to their parents screaming at each other while hiding in their own spaces — or ending up in Cole's room for comfort? When his father left, the yelling stopped, and his mother's heavy drinking began. It wasn't a good trade off.

Theo went into Cole's room first. No band posters, no sheet music all over the place. Just a queen size bed, a dresser, desk, and nightstands all done in greens and browns, like an indoor forest. It was cozy. Nick's room, which would be the one over the expanded living room, was decorated in shades of blue, cool and inviting. It was larger than it had been when they were kids and held bunk beds and a double bed. He smiled at the bunk beds. Another thing Nick always wanted. It was nice to see the old dreams Nick brought to life with this place.

He hesitated before the door to his room for several reasons. First, this was where Eden was staying and second, because of the memories. Good, bad, horrible. A few times of hope, more times of anger and despair. Finally, he took a deep breath and walked in.

The night before, he had been too focused on Eden to notice the changes. Done in shades burgundy and black, it had the identical furnishings as Cole's room with different prints of autumnal New England scenes on the wall. Unlike Cole's room, there was evidence of someone living here, someone female. Shoes under the dresser, jewelry on the top along with lotions, a romance novel on the bedside table, make-up and a mirror on the desk. He could imagine her getting ready in the morning, brushing her hair. Always beautiful and shiny. God, would the memories never stop?

He sat on the messily made bed, and he swore he could smell her shampoo. Last month marked twelve years since he was here last. One of those last memories had been wonderful. He and Eden made love for their first and only time in this room, the night of their graduation.

Everything had gone to hell the next day.

Theo sat there as older memories came back. He saw the room as it had been when he was and a maple tree mural covered the wall, stretching out and arching over his bed, a swing hanging from a branch. His mother, Susan, had painted something special in each of their rooms. The tree in Theo's, a motorcycle for Cole, and a cartoon moose for Nick. Every time he looked at the tree, he'd felt loved. She'd been so happy while creating their rooms, her talent shining through. A week after they'd learned their father had died in a car crash, almost two years after leaving, Theo walked upstairs and smelled fresh paint. For a moment he'd thought — hoped — his mother had started painting again. She had — but not in the way he wanted. He found her in his room covering the tree and the entire wall a hideous brown, painting layer after layer over her work.

He'd screamed, "What are you doing," and tried to get the brush away from her, getting his shirt, arms, and face covered in the process. She'd looked at him, not seeing him at first, and he knew she was drunk. Again. At three in the afternoon. "Stop, please."

"No, this hideous tree has to go. It's awful. It's worthless, useless."

Theo recognized the words his father used when he talked about Susan and her work, when he told her she needed to get a better job, and the night he threw her sketchbooks and other work into the fireplace. Theo tried to stop her. "Mom, it's wonderful, and it's mine. Like the pictures you made for Cole and Nick. Please, don't take it away."

"Those had to go, too."

It took Theo a second to understand her words, but when he did, he ran to his brothers' rooms to see the same brown paint covering their walls. Her work, along with the comfort and beauty it brought to their house, was gone. He'd gone back to his room, grabbed the paint bucket, opened a window and tossed it out. She'd screamed at him and went to look for more, but there wasn't any. She went into her room and slammed the door. When Cole and Nick came upstairs and saw what she'd done, Nick cried the tears Theo wouldn't allow himself. He'd fallen asleep staring at the remaining ends of the branch with a few scattered leaves that escaped his mother's mania and accepted there was nothing in life you could count on or hold on to. If you could lose something that was part of a wall, nothing was safe.

It had been a hard lesson. Losing Eden reinforced it several years later.

"What are you doing in my room?"

He jumped. For a second, he thought he'd conjured Eden with his thoughts. He'd been so lost in the memories he hadn't heard her come home. "I'm sorry. After dinner, I decided to explore the house to see the changes Nick made."

"It's unrecognizable."

"Which is the main attraction, if you ask me."

"I saw the lights were on in the living room. Guess you noticed the enormous television."

"Hard to miss."

She laughed and leaned against the door frame. He wondered if he should move aside to let her sit on the bed with him, but Eden sitting so close might be too much of a temptation — he'd want to touch her, run his fingers through her hair, press his lips to hers like he had earlier — so he didn't suggest it. "I didn't know they made them that size. I had a movie party last weekend. It's not quite as big as a theater screen, but the setting is better."

"Nick used to talk about what he'd want in a dream house. A big television was on the list. He's improved everything." Better to focus on the house than her.

"He's in the process of having the basement finished," she said.

"I heard. That's why the house wasn't being rented."

The conversation lulled, and he didn't know what to say. Just when he was about to get up and leave her to her room, Eden said, "You want to talk about whatever had you distracted when I came in?"

There was a time when she would have been the first person he went to when he was upset, confused or angry — all of which he was experiencing to different degrees. But it had been so long, and he was out of the habit of sharing his feelings. The last woman he'd dated for more than a few months accused him of being "more remote than Pluto." He didn't disagree. Counting on people, opening up to them, took time and a good reason — like his team in the army. But there was always a cost, which made him careful about who, if anyone, he talked to. "This first day back has been overwhelming." He sighed. "The things that have changed. The things that haven't. Oh, and earlier? I'm—"

"Please don't say you're sorry," she said, coming to sit next to him. She took his hand in hers. "I'd hate it if you regretted kissing me." The pain in her voice made him long to ask what was underneath her comment, but the years apart took away his right to pry.

"I've never regretted kissing you. I promise," he said, glancing at her lips and wishing he could kiss her again, if only to prove his words true. "But I made the decision and acted on it without thinking it through, and I wasn't sure it was okay with you."

"You didn't notice how I responded?" Her teasing tone eased his worry.

"Of course I did," he said. He noticed every sigh, every movement of her hands on his back, and remembering was enough to get him worked up again. "Although I was a little lost in my own reactions. I shouldn't have assumed it was what you wanted."

"Are you concerned about consent?" She sounded surprised.

"Yes. I'm not suggesting you didn't like it or wouldn't have pushed me away if you didn't want me to continue, but I did move in kind of suddenly."

"You did, and I was surprised," she admitted. "But I wanted that kiss as much as you did. I may not have realized it at first, but it's true."

That was a relief. "Good to hear. You're not dating anyone, are you?"

She gave a harsh laugh. "No, most people still think I'm married, and it will be a long while before anyone goes near Keith Peters' ex-wife. Or Patrick Barrett's daughter." Her tone was self-deprecating, and she let go of his hand to move back on the bed and lean against the headboard. "You were one of the few people who wasn't scared of my dad. I'm not going to have to worry about men beating a path to my door any time soon. Not that I have a door to beat down at the moment."

He saw the worry in her eyes and wanted to make it disappear. "You will. This is a temporary setback."

"You sound like Janelle."

"Glad to know she's still smart."

"Oh, that she is. Smart aleck, smart ass." Eden laughed. "I couldn't have gotten through that night, or several others, without her. I'm lucky to have her in my life."

Because I left you alone. He couldn't help but think of Eden's comment from the gym. Would he have come back if he'd known what happened to her? Maybe she would have been with him and not had her life burn down around her. The thought that she could have been in the building when it caught fire made his heart tighten. He moved to sit next to her again and, with an effort, kept from touching her. "Were you home when the fire happened?"

"Not when it started. I had a late class at the gym and after I was done, I saw the call telling me what was happening. The place was ablaze when I arrived. I've never seen anything like it. The heat, the noise."

He kept himself from shuddering. He wasn't looking forward to facing a live fire. "No, nothing prepares you for it. I'll be walking through the site tomorrow. I'll talk to the Duncans and the other couple from the building, but would you be willing to join me there to tell me what you saw?"

"As long as it doesn't have to be in the morning."

"Yes, I know, no mornings if you can help it." He could be okay with some things not changing if it was about Eden.

"No, it's not that." She paused, and he waited, wondering what was wrong. "I have an appointment."

Since she wasn't specific, he figured she wasn't comfortable enough to tell him. He couldn't blame her. "No problem. I'll go to the station first, make calls and set up interviews. At some point, I'm going to have to speak with your father since he owned the third site."

"Better you than me."

He laughed. "Could you make it by 11:30?"

"Yes," she said. "Anything else?"

Everything else. He wanted to kiss her again and not stop this time. He wanted to create a new memory for this room that didn't include pain and loss. He wanted... which was the problem. And the best reason not to start. "That's it. And now, before this conversation gets any more awkward, I'll go downstairs and let you get on with your night."

"Probably a good idea." They stared at each other and he wondered if she wanted to be kissed. Finally, she saved them both by saying, "Good night, Theo."

"Good night."

Back in his room Theo got ready for bed but listened for movement upstairs. He couldn't stop himself from wondering what she was doing, thinking... wearing. He ached to go to her, but if a simple kiss drove him this crazy, he needed to keep his distance.

As he opened up a book on his Kindle, he ignored the *good luck with that* voice taunting him.

Chapter Eight

♥

Tuesday mornings Eden drove an hour south to Concord to see a psychologist. There were plenty of therapists closer, but she didn't consider it an option. This was something she did for herself and the last thing she wanted was her father or her ex-husband finding out. It had been tough enough to tell Janelle, although her encouragement after she did was wonderful.

Going out of the area gave her the anonymity she wanted, and she enjoyed the drive each way. She listened to podcasts or music and let her mind drift. Some weeks she'd be clearer and energized after her appointments, other weeks left her thoughts and emotions swirling. On those days, she took back roads, so when she got to work, she was able to focus. Either way, the sessions were good for her. Her divorce lawyer suggested it, and she was grateful.

During her appointment, she talked about Theo and the emotions his return stirred up. Stir was an understatement. It was more like a blender on liquefy. It had been only two nights, and he'd been the last thing she thought of before sleep and the first thing she thought of when she woke. Not to mention the number of times images of him entered her head throughout the day. Images now coupled with thoughts of how wonderful his kiss felt, how she wanted more, even knowing he wasn't going to stay. It was like being strapped into a roller coaster that didn't have an end and she couldn't see the tracks. She shifted from terrified to exhilarated to hopeful, then back to terrified at lightning speed.

Keeping things — and people — calm had been one of her biggest coping mechanisms growing up. Her father's temper taught her and her mother ways to diffuse his anger or, better yet, ways to avoid it completely. Emotions had to be kept hidden. They were a sign of weakness. Eden allowed herself to feel when she danced and when she was with Theo. Then she'd lost both. It was only since leaving Keith and embracing her love of teaching and helping her clients that she allowed herself to come alive again.

Now Theo was back, and her emotions were all over the place.

After her appointment, she looked at the clock and did some quick calculations. Taking the highway would get her to Fable Notch too early to meet Theo. If she took the back roads, she'd be a little late, but calmer. She could be late. She selected a classical music mix on Spotify and headed north.

By the time she arrived, she was glad for her decision. The extra time allowed her to think about what she discussed in her appointment. In previous sessions, she'd gone on about how it felt years before when Theo sided with her father and left her. To her it had been a betrayal of everything they'd gone through together, all the times she had to fight or sneak out to see him. It was as though he'd turned his back on her and their love. She found herself seeing how she never released that pain or loss, simply accepted it. And for the first time, it was clear that Theo thought he was doing the only thing he could do to support her. That even though the decision broke her heart — and his as well — he was trying to be her hero. She may not like or agree with what he did, but she could come to understand it. She took a deep breath as she neared the site, realizing what a big change this was.

Maybe it would make it easier to enjoy the time Theo was here and stay strong after he left. There were no guarantees, but for the first time since seeing him, she didn't feel as though she was at risk of falling completely apart.

His truck was in the lot when she arrived, and he and Harlow were walking slowly around the site. She sat there watching how intent he was, how focused, and remembered how she loved when his focus was on her. For the first time in years, she didn't try to push the memories away.

She also noticed how sexy he was. Tall and confident in his pseudo-professional dress of jeans, construction boots and company logo jacket. He had a large messenger style bag across his chest and what looked like an expensive camera in his hands.

As she watched, Harlow gave a sharp bark, stopped, and sat. Theo walked over and pulled something out of his pocket, which Eden realized was a treat as the dog took it from his hand. He put away the camera, took out a plastic bag and slipped on a pair of examination gloves. Then he squatted down to run his hands through the debris. At a signal from Theo, Harlow walked away and started working again. A few minutes later, she gave another bark, and they went through the routine again.

Her professional brain kicked in as Eden noticed the muscles needed for this work. Slow walking, sometimes over uneven terrain, then squatting for periods of time. No wonder physical therapy was important. It was more than personal mobility. His work required it. Eden wouldn't have thought arson investigation was a particularly physical job, but it definitely wasn't a desk job.

That didn't surprise her. Theo didn't like to be bored or sedentary. He'd told her once that he hated having to sit in school all day and was one of the reasons why he'd loved cross-country running. Back then, it was a way for him to compete as well as his favorite way to think.

Caught up in her memories, she didn't notice Theo and Harlow coming toward her until they were only a few steps away. She got out of the car to great them. "Good morning. I hope I didn't distract you."

"As distractions go, you're a good one, but no, we've been working for a while."

She smiled at the compliment. "The two of you were very focused."

"You looked lost in thought, yourself. What were you thinking about?"

She hesitated, then decided there was no reason not to tell him. "The day we met, the track meet."

"Sophomore year. I think we won. You came because Janelle had a crush on someone on the team. I can't remember who, but I remember not hearing a word they were saying to each other once I saw you."

"That's what I remember. Us talking, although I can't recall what about."

"Nope, not a clue. I remember thinking how beautiful you were, and that I wanted to keep talking."

Her cheeks warmed at the memory. "And you suggested the four of us get together on Friday night. It was my first double date."

"Same. And we saw *Stardust*, even though," he stopped and snapped his fingers, "Sam Kimble, that's who it was Janelle liked — he wanted to see *There Will Be Blood*. We figured something romantic would be better, make a better impression. Make it more likely we'd get lucky." Theo wiggled his eyebrows, and she laughed.

"It worked on Janelle. I think they were kissing less than an hour into the movie."

"And I was too shy to make a move."

But he had kissed her softly good night after their date and asked if he could see her again. She said yes. They'd spent hours kissing for the next two years. No one's kisses had ever done to her what his did. "We eventually made up for it."

They stood in silence. Eden assumed Theo was as lost in memories as she was. Was he aching for another kiss because that was all she could think about as she stared into his blue eyes? A bump against her leg from Harlow brought her back to the present. "And how are you today, Harlow?" She knelt to give the dog scratches behind the ear, then stopped. "I'm sorry. Is it okay to do this? I know you're not supposed to disturb service dogs while they're working."

"It's fine. We're on a break. Just don't let her get her dirty paws on you, or you'll have to change."

Eden gave Harlow a little more attention until the dog wandered off. She stood and said, "When she barked, you went over to her. Is that part of what she does?"

"Yes, she's trained to search out specific scents. Her bark told me she found an accelerant. Where she identifies it, I look to see if there's debris with traces I can send to the lab."

"Which explains your gloves and the bags."

He nodded. "She found two spots in the back, at the corners. The arsonist made sure not to be seen when he set the fires. My notes say this building was two stories with four apartments in total. Were they all occupied?"

"No, the one across the hall from me on the second floor was vacant. It was mostly used as an Air BnB. Grace and her kids were under me." She gestured to the right side of the building where her home used to be.

"What do you remember about the fire?"

"That it seemed to be everywhere. The biggest fire I'd ever seen before this were the school bonfires by the lake." She stopped, and the memories came back, the feelings of loss, anger, and shock. Of being aware, once again, of how quickly things that mattered could be taken from her. "I tried to run in to see if I could save anything, but it was impossible."

"It's a natural reaction, to want to save things. The report said Grace called in the fire a little after 5:30."

"Yes, normally Grace is home earlier, but on Mondays the twins take an art class at the Artists' Exchange with Helen Massey."

"Is that the only day of the week she's home later?"

Eden had to think for a second. She didn't know her neighbors well. It was more of an "in passing" kind of relationship. Enough to say hi and talk for a few minutes if neither of them were busy, but not much more. "There may be other days, but I keep odd hours. I know about Monday because Grace sometimes takes a class with me while the kids are busy."

"And the other couple. Are they usually home when you come home?"

"Sometimes, but generally, they both work later. He's a doctor at the hospital and she's in sales at one of the resorts."

"With the empty apartment, six people living here. The fact that no one was expected home when the fire started tells me the arsonist learned people's schedules. He didn't want to injure people, and certainly not risk children."

Eden gave a shudder. "That's a scary thought — someone was watching us, learning our comings and goings."

"True, but I'm grateful the buildings and not the people were the target with all the fires so far."

"So far?"

"I don't know this person's end game. It looks like property damage is his focus, but which ones are significant and why? It's one of the answers I'm looking for. I noticed your father didn't own this building."

"It was one of the reasons I chose it." She knew Theo would understand.

"He must have loved that."

"Almost as much as he loved me leaving Keith. Maybe it was spiteful, but when I left my marriage, I needed to be on my own, away from them both."

"Good for you. He only has the control you give him."

"That was hard to understand when I was younger, but I see it now." It was something she continued to learn as she took charge of her life and decisions.

"I think you should know Keith has the most connection to these fires."

"What do you mean?"

He explained about the bid on the Northcott estate. "You lived here, and the third building is owned by his employer."

"Is he trying to get to me or my dad?"

"Maybe both, maybe neither. It could be a coincidence, but I don't like those. Can you think of any other links?"

"Not off the top of my head, but as you were always fond of noticing, this is a small town. You'll probably uncover other connections as you go forward."

He ran his hands through his hair, and when he was done, she couldn't stop herself from reaching out and smoothing where it was standing up. He stared at her, and she held her breath wondering what he was doing to say or do.

Then Harlow gave a muffled bark, and they both jumped.

Theo looked down at the dog, gave her a scratch between the ears and said, "She and I are going to have to have a talk about manners and interrupting." Harlow bumped into Eden's leg and then dropped whatever she had in her mouth. "What did you find?"

As Theo bent to pick it up, Eden recognized it and grabbed it from him. She squealed with joy. "My charm bracelet? I can't believe it." The bracelet, a thirteenth birthday present from her mother, was one of her most treasured possessions. Its loss had been one of the hardest parts of the fire. "I leave it home a lot because it's too distracting to have it on when I work, and I left it in my office a few times when I would take it off there. I tried looking through the rubble after the fire was out but didn't have any luck. I never thought I'd see it again."

She bent down and threw her arms around the dog's neck, giving her a huge hug. Harlow took it as her due.

"Since that's a piece you wear often, your scent would be strong on it, at least to her."

"Harlow, you are amazing," she said. The dog barked in agreement, and Eden kissed her furry forehead. She got a chuff in response.

"Can I put it on you?" he asked.

"Yes, please," she said. Handing him the bracelet and holding up her wrist.

As he opened the clasp, he looked at the charms. "Where's the one from me?"

The ballet slippers, his graduation gift to her. She blushed then rushed out the words, "I took it off after I heard you'd joined the army."

"I suppose I deserve that."

She could hear the hurt in his voice. She'd cried for hours the day she removed the charm but seeing it every day was worse. "I kept it, but I stopped wearing it." She couldn't bear to part with the beautiful gift and knew exactly where it was. Sitting securely in a safe deposit box. It had been in the back of her jewelry box, but one night she'd come home to find Keith going through her drawers. He'd made up an excuse, but afterward, she'd rented a box and kept her valuables there.

"I hope you'll consider having it reattached."

"I will," she said. He fastened the clasp, which looked small in his large hands. He bent forward, and she wondered if he might kiss the exposed part of her wrist. The thought sent a shiver through her body. Feeling bold, she leaned in, wondering if he'd take the hint, but a car's honk made her move back. Good reminder. This was not the place for anything physical. Eden looked up to see a familiar SUV and driver go past.

Theo watched her wave and said, "Was that Janelle?"

"It was. She came back from New York two years ago. Said the city was draining her creative energy and her bank account too fast. She opened a thrift store a few years ago"

"Tailor Thrift? I couldn't help but notice the name."

"Isn't it great? She runs that along with creating a really popular a YouTube channel. She's amazing. Best thing about my leaving Keith has been seeing my friends more." He looked back at her, and Eden wondered if they were going to pick up the intimate moment again, but his phone buzzed. "Guess interruptions are the order of the day."

"Unfortunately." He pulled the phone out and looked at the message. "I need to get back to the station. I'm glad Harlow found your bracelet." He took hold of her hand and spun the bracelet, looking at the charms. "I haven't seen the Eiffel Tower. From your graduation trip with Donna?"

Eden nodded. "The other new one is the linked hearts. She bought it for me after her diagnosis. To remind me she'd always be with me."

"She was a special woman."

Her voice was barely a whisper when she said, "I miss her every day."

"I don't doubt it. She loved you very much."

As they stood there, Eden wondered if he was being tormented by as many memories as she was — good ones about her mother and times she and Theo were together. Or was he focused on her hand in his, because while part of her brain was remembering their shared past, another part was aware of the warmth of his skin, the nearness of his body, and how she ached to kiss him again.

Which was a bad idea, at least out in the open like this. Coming to her senses, she took her hand back and stepped toward her car. "I need to get to the gym before my 1:00 class. Is there anything else you need from me?" When his eyebrow raised, she heard the other meaning in her words. "Concerning the fire."

"No, but if you remember anything, you know where to find me."

Closer than he'd been in forever. "Sorry I wasn't much help."

"You were. Knowing the timing was deliberate could be important. I think.... That is.... If you don't mind..."

She didn't understand why he suddenly looked uncomfortable. "Yes?"

"I should get your phone number and give you mine, in case you think of something or if I have other questions," he said.

Phone numbers. Now she understood his hesitation. All those years ago, Theo left her his old cell phone, then changed his number went on the road with Cole, making sure she had no way of getting in touch with him. This was a new bridge should she want to build it. Before she could answer, he said, "Never mind. I'll see you at the house. It's not important."

His rapid speech said more than his words. His nervousness helped make her decision. She took out her phone and said, "No, it's a good idea. And this way, if one of us gets delayed somewhere, we can tell the other. If I'd been late today, I couldn't have let you know."

"Speaking of which," he said as he put his number in her contacts, "I'll be late tonight. Martin has arranged for the volunteers to come to the station to meet me, talk about what they know, and what I've learned about these fires. I don't know how long it will last."

"Then I'll see you whenever."

Eden gave Harlow another hug, both to thank the dog for her wonderful find and to keep herself from hugging Theo. They got into their vehicles, and Theo waved as he left. When she put her hands on the wheel, the sun hit her bracelet and tears came to her eyes. She never thought she'd see it again. Like Theo.

It had been a long morning. It was exhausting to move back and forth between feeling strong and feeling unsteady. Just when she thought she had her balance, something knocked her off kilter. First the fire, now Theo. Less than two days and old responses were resurfacing faster than she could manage them. She wanted to kiss him and keep her distance. But it wasn't possible. Being with him and remembering what they shared risked a piece of her heart. How was she going to hold on to her newfound strength against this onslaught of emotions?

Chapter Nine

♥

Theo grabbed lunch for himself after stopping at the pharmacy to upload the next set of pictures and sending the evidence he'd collected at site two to the lab. Back at the station, Harlow napped at his feet after he gave her a piece of his sandwich and he stared at the incident board as he finished eating, mentally adding the images from this morning and trying, unsuccessfully, not to think of Eden and how it felt to take her hand in his.

"I don't think they're going to magically give you the answers." Theo turned to see Lloyd Wilson standing next to the cubicle partition with a cup of coffee. Lloyd, the station's deputy chief, was tall and slender, his hair gone completely gray with a bit of a comb-over since the last time Theo saw him. He was a few years younger than Martin but looked older. Theo remembered him as a smoker, which was probably the cause. "Although if they do, you'll have to teach me that trick."

"Sorry, no magic, but sometimes I notice a pattern after a while. Good to see you, Mr. Wilson."

"Call me that, and I'll have to call your Mr. Hanson."

Theo gave an involuntary shudder. Mr. Hanson made him think of his father, a memory he didn't need. "Definitely not. Too weird."

"Then it will have to be Lloyd. Agreed?"

"Yes, sir. I mean, sure, Lloyd."

The other man laughed. "You'll get used to it. What can you tell me?"

Theo brought Lloyd up to speed on what he and Harlow discovered about the fires. "I'm waiting to hear from my lab on what accelerant was used, but it's likely to be a household product and not helpful." Back in Fable Notch less than two days and already failing.

"Gotta say, I'm glad these fires happened after tax season ended. I needed a full day to recover after the last one, and I didn't have time to spare back in April." Theo had forgotten Lloyd was also a CPA. After years as a volunteer, he'd scaled back the other business to take the part-time job as deputy.

"Interesting. I wonder if the time of year is a factor."

"How so?"

"Arsonists have a trigger. A person, a site, a reason to cause chaos. Let's say you were our arsonist. You might want to start fires at the beginning of April to avoid the coming work. The season, the month, could be significant."

"The when could be as important as the where?"

"Exactly," Theo said. "I need to figure this into the process."

"Let me know if you want to talk anything through or want help. I'll be at my desk until the meeting tonight."

Theo managed not to cringe. The volunteer meeting. More uncomfortable conversations. More people watching him flounder without having answers. He could hardly wait.

After a few hours of phone calls to follow up with people affected by the fire—including making an appointment to meet with Patrick Barrett—and taking a quick break to get the most recent photos, Theo was interrupted by Phyllis speaking on the phone as she came into the room. "Yes, Mrs. Costa, I'm telling Deputy Chief Wilson and the acting chief now. Stay out of the house, pull your car out of the driveway, and keep the kids with you. They'll be there with the pumper in no time." Phyllis ended the call and handed a paper with the address to Theo. "Sounds like an electrical fire in the kitchen. She doesn't have a fire extinguisher. She tried beating it down with a dish towel. It caught fire, too. Then she opened the window to let the smoke out."

"Jesus," Lloyd said, frustration edging his voice. "She did everything wrong. Gas or electric stove?"

"Electric," Phyllis said. Theo was impressed. He wouldn't have thought to ask.

"Something to be thankful for," Lloyd said. "Guess we're up. Coats and helmets are in the truck. I know where she lives."

"Then you drive." Theo made it sound as though this was a decision based on logic. The truth was, his heart was hammering in his chest. The last time Theo had gone to fight a fire, he'd been in Afghanistan. While the fire today would be small with no chance of casualties, his body was reacting as though a bomb had gone off. "Phyllis, will you be here to watch Harlow?"

"Of course."

"Thanks." Before he could think more, he followed Lloyd to the garage and grabbed the coat Lloyd handed him. His stomach flipped, and he started sweating as soon as the weight of the jacket settled on his shoulders. *Get yourself under control, Hanson.* Not since his first fire had he been so on edge.

He got into the truck and worked to get his thoughts focused. As they drove, seeing green lawns and old-growth trees reminded Theo he wasn't in a desert, there was no gun fire, insurgents weren't trying to burn out civilians. Lloyd kept up a steady stream of conversation on the new engine they were riding in, talking about its capabilities the way others might brag about a child's athletic achievements. Theo half listened while he worked to bring his breathing under control. When he agreed to take over for Martin, he knew he'd be part of any fires that happened. Unfortunately, knowledge didn't change the dread.

When they arrived at the Costa's small Colonial, he saw the smoke coming from a front and side window and a woman standing outside with two boys who looked under ten. Lloyd was out of the truck in an instant and moved to release the hoses and valves. They wouldn't need much yardage since the kitchen faced the driveway. Theo joined Lloyd and handed him a helmet. When he pulled down the face guard, his pulse jumped again. He could hear his breathing in the enclosed space. It had been years since he'd worn a face guard, but putting it on brought back the memories of previous fires. Part of him wanted to rip it off and run, but that wasn't an option.

Lloyd took a step toward the house. Theo hesitated for a second that could have been an hour. He knew what to expect, the acrid smell that lingered in his nose, the heat that would wrap around him like a deathly robe. He didn't see flames yet, but in his mind, he saw four years of blazes he'd battled, the friends who were injured, the one who was lost. He'd lost count of the number of fires he'd fought, but not of the bodies they'd pulled out.

And then his training kicked in. Theo shut his brain off, and as he'd done in the army when fear threatened to paralyze and keep him from doing his job, he focused on what needed to be done and nothing else. Get in, find the center, soak the worst of the flames. There was no one to evacuate, no unknowns, minimal danger. One step and then another.

Theo braced himself as they entered the house, but there was no need. Although the kitchen was nearly engulfed, the fire was manageable and out in minutes. He hardly felt a rise in temperature compared to what he'd been imagining. If the family had a fire extinguisher, they wouldn't be here at all. When Lloyd went to get the hose to pump foam to be certain nothing would reignite, Theo checked the room for hot spots. The fire had worked its way through one wall and from what he could see the laundry room had damage. The ceiling would need inspecting. He'd tell Mrs. Costa to move whoever slept in the room above, at least until someone could examine the space properly.

A quick layer of foam, and they were done. They put their helmets in the truck and Theo opened his jacket to let the air cool his sweat dampened skin. His shirt was practically soaked through. He needed to control himself. A bigger blaze was coming, and he couldn't afford to panic when it did.

They walked to the bottom of the driveway to talk to Mrs. Costa. She had tears in her eyes. Theo hoped Lloyd knew what to say. He didn't respond well to emotional women.

"Thank you, thank you so much. Both of you. I know I messed everything up." She gave them each a hug, and Theo did his best not to stiffen. This wasn't usually part of his job. "I'm grateful you got here so... oh my goodness. Aren't you Theo Hanson?"

A new tightness in his chest. Nothing to do with the fire this time, everything to do with who he was in this town. No way around it. "I am." He braced himself for a different kind of reaction.

"I'm Amber Costa, was Roberts a lifetime ago. My son, Felix," she gave the taller boy a squeeze, "takes piano lessons with Millie. She said you'd be coming to town. I was in the same class as Cole, so you probably don't remember me."

"Sorry, no."

"I had such a crush on your brother. Guess we all did, but he only had eyes for Mia. I heard you fought fires in the army. It's great that you came to help Martin. He must be glad you're here. I'm sorry. I'm rambling. This has not been the night I expected." As she chatted, Theo nodded in what he hoped were the right places. How much longer did he need to stand here? "I guess I should let you two go and see what the damage is. Thank you again for your help."

"No problem. Call your insurance company in the morning."

She nodded. "And then go out and get a fire extinguisher. I'm such an idiot." Theo didn't know how to respond. He hoped the smile he tried didn't look as forced as it felt. He was still on edge from the unnecessary adrenaline. "Guess it's takeout for dinner for the next few days."

The boys jumped up at the news and the younger asked. "We can have pizza tonight?"

Before he heard the answer, Theo and Lloyd headed to the truck. As the last of the hoses were stored in the engine, they were interrupted by the kids. They muttered between them, an important debate clearly going on, and finally the older boy asked, "Can... can we see the truck before you go?"

Theo was shot back in time to the day he and his brothers met Martin Sinclair. Theo, Cole, and Nick were bored. Their father had been gone for more than a year, their mother too busy working or drinking to focus on her children. They were playing in the backyard, tossing matches at the shed, watching the old wood and grass spark for a second then go out. They didn't notice something ignited until the flames were consuming the small structure. One of their neighbors called the fire department as Theo and his brothers argued and fought over what to do.

Martin arrived alone in the smaller pumper truck the town had. Like tonight, the fire was out quickly, but that wasn't the scary part. The three of them stood and waited for Martin to tell them he was calling Family Services after he learned their mother wasn't home, and they didn't know when she would be. Instead, he'd piled them into the truck, taken them to the station, then switched cars and brought them to his home for dinner. Before they'd left, Nick had asked to see the truck and Martin agreed.

That fire had saved Theo's life.

"Please," said a quiet voice bringing him back to the present.

"Sure," said Theo as Lloyd gave a nod. They walked around the engine, answering the boys' questions and letting them wear some of the gear. Theo couldn't help but smile at how silly the kids looked with the helmet falling down over their eyes. Their laughter and enthusiasm broke up the tension in Theo's body, and by the time he and Lloyd headed back to the station, Theo was calmer.

"Guess I'm not going to look like the put-together professional," Theo said, looking at his wrinkled and damp clothes as they pulled into the station garage. "It's hotter in those jackets than I remembered."

"We've got extra t-shirts in one of the closets if you want to change before the meeting."

"Thanks. Saves me the trouble of going home to change."

Theo found a shirt and headed for the bathroom. He took off the polo he was wearing, got it wet in the sink, then ran it over his chest and arms to cool his skin. He splashed cold water over his face and dared a look in the mirror. Maybe a little pale, but no one would know.

In two days, he'd made it through seeing — and kissing — Eden and his first fire. Now he had to get through something worse. A meeting.

Chapter Ten

♥

Eden's day turned out surprisingly well given its emotional start. She kept the bracelet on, even though it wasn't practical with her work. Seeing it made her smile, and she needed that. Messages from her friends helped, too. She checked her phone as her early afternoon class broke up to find the beginning of a group text from Janelle, Dani, and Laurel.

How's it going with Theo? Janelle wrote. Eden was surprised they waited more than a day before they asked.

Yeah, how's living together? Dani added.

She was about to respond they weren't really living together, but no matter how she rationalized it, they were. And she didn't hate it. *So far, so good*, she wrote. Vague, but truthful.

She should have known they'd want more.

Not good enough. We need details, read Janelle's reply followed immediately by, *Has there been kissing?*

Her stomach gave a flutter. Oh, yes. Wonderful, deep kisses she wanted more of. Kisses that stirred memories and desires. Kisses that made her want to ask for more.

She's taking too long to respond, Laurel wrote. *That means yes.*

There was no way to avoid telling them. *Yes, there was kissing. Yes, it was hot. And awkward and even though I shouldn't, I want him to do it again.*

Now it was her friends' turn to be silent. Yeah, she didn't know what to say either.

I'd tell you to be careful, but since I never am, that should come from someone else, wrote Janelle. Janelle's pattern was to fall in love with men who didn't want relationships or weren't sticking around. She got her heart broken a little bit on a regular basis. She said it made her strong.

Maybe trust yourself but be a little cautious. Dani was practical. It made her a good veterinarian and a good friend.

Stick to your head, not your heart, if you can, added Laurel. Laurel saved her heart for her business and her family. She claimed relationships took too much time and effort. Eden suspected there was a story behind Laurel's words.

And keep us posted. Either send us details or send for help. Eden laughed at Janelle's candor. It was one of her friend's best qualities, whether she was listening to a problem or telling someone an outfit wasn't right for them.

Everyone come to the brewery Friday night. You can try my newest ale and we can talk.

A chorus of 'Can't wait' and 'See you there' followed.

These women were terrific, and Eden was grateful to have them in her life. After years of being isolated by her marriage, she understood the value of friendship, of the give and take that helped get you through the tough days, and of not being alone during the scary, vulnerable moments. She was looking forward to Friday. Time spent with her friends always made her feel good.

All the joy disappeared, however, when she walked into her office and saw her father sitting behind her desk as if it were his. Nothing like an unexpected visit from Patrick to ruin a good mood. Visits from her father were never welcomed, less so when she had no time to prepare.

"Hi, Dad," she said in a monotone. She hung her jacket and bag on the back of her door and did what she could to calm her racing thoughts before turning to face him.

Patrick was in his early sixties but looked younger with a full head of nearly black hair and unreadable brown eyes. He was not quite six feet tall and narrowly built. He never worked out, but he watched his weight since his appearance was important to him. Looking at Patrick, Eden wondered, not for the first time, why he never remarried after her mother's death. He was good looking, rich, and available.

"Hello, kitten," he said with a smile.

She groaned inwardly and tried not to wince. The endearment told her whatever his reason for being here, he was going to try to influence her with kindness. Sometimes it was harder to resist than his anger, but she heard Theo's voice in her head. *He only has the control you give him.* She squared her shoulders, ran her fingers over her charm bracelet, and allowed herself to experience some of the confidence she had before the fire. She wouldn't let Patrick change her good attitude. "What can I do for you?"

"Can't a father simply come by to visit his daughter?"

"Yes, but that's not your style. You always say the phone is for setting up appointments. Talking face to face is for getting things accomplished."

"I should be pleased to know you listen to me."

"You know I do."

"Then I want you to listen to me now. It's time for you to come to your senses. You've made your point. You want your independence. I respect that, but it doesn't mean you leave your marriage and live in a crappy apartment."

"At the moment, I'm living in a rather lovely house." *With Theo,* she thought, but didn't say.

"It wouldn't be necessary if you'd go back to your husband."

"What bothers you more? That I left Keith or that I was living in an apartment building you didn't own?" She watched her father's cheeks redden. They both knew she'd chosen the place on purpose.

"I'm worried about you. Suppose, God forbid, you get hurt again. You're alone. How would you get help?"

Was this how he'd kept her mother close. By reminding Donna of all the ways she was fragile and alone? It was how Eden felt for years — scared she couldn't manage, certain something would go wrong again no matter what she did or tried. As the familiar anxiety rose, Eden tapped it down with a slow breath. Yes, bad things could happen, but she was fine here and now. Nothing her father said changed what she knew to be true. "Good point, Dad."

"I knew you'd understand." As he watched, Eden woke her phone, opened an app and started typing. She didn't look at her father, knowing his expression would make her laugh which wouldn't help. Finally, he said, "What are you doing?"

"Writing myself a note to look into smart home devices that can call 911. Otherwise, maybe my phone will do it."

"That is *not* what I meant. No one in our family gets a divorce. You and Keith need to work things out."

"Dad, we've had this conversation countless times. It's too late for Keith and me." This would be the perfect time to tell him the divorce was already final, but she wasn't prepared. It could wait. It's not like it would change anything.

"You're being ridiculous and acting like a child."

"I am neither being ridiculous nor childlike. In fact, the reason you don't like the situation is because I'm acting like an adult," she said, surprised she said it out loud. She'd thought it often enough.

"Kitten, come to your senses, please." He was back to coaxing and kindness, and the part of her that wanted to please him wavered.

She needed to remember all the times he'd manipulated her to get his way, and the times she gave in. *I won't support your tuition if you stay with that Hanson boy. He's no good for you.*

It's okay if you don't want to go back to the Conservatory. Dance is such a risky career.

Why don't you live at home and go to college locally? It will be one less thing to worry about.

Keith is the kind of man who can take care of you. I'm glad you're together.

She was done with doing things the Patrick Barrett way. It was time to make the decisions she wanted. She squared her shoulders and said, "My senses are fine, Dad."

"Not from where I'm sitting," he grumbled. His kindness was reaching its limits.

"You shouldn't be sitting there anyway." She hoped he'd take the hint and move. He didn't. As usual, he ignored her words and focused on the results he wanted. It may work for him in business, but it wasn't going to work with her. "This is my office, and it's my life. I am a grown woman and your days of telling me what's right for me are over." If only she'd said that a long time ago, but better late than never. She was shaking inside and hoped it didn't show. If he noticed any hesitation from her, he'd pounce, and her confidence was too new to withstand a direct attack.

He stood up from her desk and walked toward her. Needing to keep her distance, she stepped away, changing places with him as she sat in her chair. She hated that it was warm from his body. Still, it was good to be in the position of power. It added to her self-assurance and reminded her of every step she'd taken, every recent change she'd made to make her life what she wanted, not what someone else thought was right for her.

"I don't understand you anymore," he said. He sounded resigned, even a touch sad, but Eden recognized it as another ploy.

"Dad, you've never understood me, but I don't need you to understand my decisions, only to accept them and hopefully support them."

"How can I do that when I think you're making a horrible mistake?"

"Making a mistake? By not staying married to a man I don't like, let alone love?" She chose not to give him the details of how Keith treated her. Patrick would find a way to make it her fault. "By focusing on my business instead of a family?"

"Yes, all of those things. You shouldn't be on your own. There's no need for it."

"You're wrong, dad. I most definitely should. I will not spend my life standing in the shadow of someone else's goals like mom did."

"Your mother..."

"Is not someone I am going to discuss with you. We both know she was unhappy and wanted more, and we both know you discouraged her whenever you could, but she made her choices and I'm making mine. I will not let you stop me."

"I paid for all those years of dance lessons, missy. Don't you forget it." He leaned forward and slammed both hands down on her desk. She was proud of herself for not startling. The convincing her with kindness portion of the conversation was officially over. She braced herself for the guilt. "I supported your rehabilitation after the accident, your college tuition and your fancy wedding."

"And for those things, the wedding not included, you have my gratitude, but that does not mean I owe you anything. I am your *daughter*, *not* your employee."

Before her father could answer, his cell phone rang. "Hate these damn things. Shouldn't be able to find a man anywhere he is." But since it was likely business, he answered it. No surprise. He never put family over work.

As he spoke brusquely to the person on the line, she closed her eyes and remembered the things that made her feel powerful — her students, her patients, and her mom. It was a technique her therapist gave her. An image of Theo came to mind. Picturing him and knowing he was near was helpful. She was grateful they talked about their breakup. There was more healing to do, but it felt possible. And she remembered how strong she'd been with him, something Keith and her father had eroded over the years.

Then she thought of his kiss and another image came to mind. Theo naked and looking into her eyes. A flush came to her cheeks.

"I have to go," her father said, breaking her out of her thoughts as he'd tucked the phone into his pocket. "Did you know Theo Hanson is back in town?"

So that's what the phone call was about. "Yes, he's helping Martin investigate the fires."

"It seems I'm part of the investigation. My secretary made an appointment for him to see me tomorrow morning."

"You are the owner of the third building destroyed. It's logical he'd need to see you."

"But he's got no reason to see you. Stay away from him."

"I've already seen him. I'm one of the fire victims, too." Okay, there was more to it, but she was not bringing that up.

Her father said nothing. His silence was more intimidating than his words. She knew he was trying to decide how to respond. Finally he said, "We're not done."

He walked out before she could answer, but she responded out loud anyway, "Yes, we are."

Chapter Eleven

♥

By the time Theo came into the kitchen, Martin and Lloyd were talking to the earlier arrivals. A stack of pizza boxes and a collection of sodas were on the table. Theo introduced himself and Harlow to the men, and she walked around, enjoying the attention and taking in their scents. Knowing there were occasions of firefighters becoming arsonists, he watched to see if she gave a signal of any kind and was relieved when she had no reactions.

Then, once again, Theo heard a familiar voice. This time instead of thoughts of friendship and fun, images of getting slammed into lockers, having his lunch taken, and everything from his family to his face ridiculed came into his head. Goosebumps broke out on his arms. He turned, knowing who to expect, only to be surprised at what time had done to his childhood bully.

Theo remembered Dylan Cioni as tall, muscular, and threatening. In his memories, the boy towered over him with hands always balled into fists. The man he was looking at today was barely his height, carrying close to fifty extra pounds on his frame and already had a receding hairline. Apparently, memories weren't always accurate. The teenager in Theo wanted to laugh out loud. "Hello, Dylan. Didn't know you'd be here."

"I was wondering if you'd remember me," Dylan said, his hands in his pockets, his eyes not quite meeting Theo's.

"I remember." Theo added nothing else as he stood there doing what he said. Remembering. He remembered bruises, humiliation, and anxiety that had him avoiding certain hallways at different times of the school day.

"Yeah, guess you would. Hard to forget the people who were lousy to us." Something in the sentence made Theo wonder who Dylan meant, but he wasn't going to ask. He managed not to cross his arms in front of his chest, but couldn't stop himself from clenching his jaw. Dylan looked at the floor. Was he embarrassed? "Is it too late to offer an apology?"

Theo almost swallowed his tongue. "No, it's not too late."

Dylan held out a hand and said, "I'm sorry. I was a first-class asshole."

Theo didn't answer at first, shocked at the surreal moment. He saw Martin over Dylan's shoulder, and he gave Theo a smile and nod. Theo took Dylan's hand and while his feelings were mixed, he accepted the apology. "So you've stayed here?" Great, he was stating the obvious.

"At my mother's insistence, God bless her, I went to college. Nearly got thrown out after the first semester for partying and tanking my classes, but I buckled down and discovered there were things to like in school. Learned I could be something other than a jerk. I got my degree then a Masters. I teach at the high school. History. I'm also the coach of the wrestling team."

More surprises. "Thanks for coming tonight. Couldn't have been easy."

"I almost didn't, knowing you'd be here. Figured one of the other guys could fill me in, but then if you saw me at a fire it would be awkward for us both and bad for the team. That's not the example I want to set for my students or my kids. Got a son and daughter of my own — and if someone does to them what I did to you, I'll pummel them. Decided I couldn't skip the chance to say sorry." Dylan paused in his rambling and Theo saw the sheen of sweat on Dylan's forehead. It wasn't warm in the station. "Funny how time can change your perspective."

Theo understood the sentiment, and he appreciated the courage it took for Dylan to show up. If Dylan could be so honest, he could take a step, too. He put a hand on Dylan's shoulder and said, "Time is good for that. Grab some pizza and a drink. We'll go over everything after."

As they ate, the men asked Theo about his work, and he got to know them. It wasn't a large team, and he was impressed by the job they'd done. They were lucky there'd been only one injury. As Martin pointed out, they could go a year without three significant sized fires. This had been a rough ride for them, and he sensed they were on edge. Whether it was because they knew it was arson or they weren't sure about him, Theo didn't know, but he hoped to put at least one of those concerns to rest by the end of the meeting.

After everyone had time to eat and talk, Theo started the meeting. He brought in the incident board and said he wanted to get their impressions of the fires and ideas on anyone who might be suspects. Theo explained that while he was working from evidence and experience, he didn't know the people and dynamics in this town, and those likely played a large part in these fires.

Using the pictures along with his and Martin's notes, Theo showed them what he learned from the remains of each site, and they told him what they remembered. The Northcott fire had been straightforward. As he suspected, they were more worried about the fire spreading to the woods and the house than the carriage house itself. And no one considered arson.

The fire at the apartments had been bigger but manageable since it wasn't next to any other building. Tim, one of the more experienced volunteers, suggested going for drinks after the fire with some of the other guys, and they'd agreed it was larger than a simple electrical fire, which is what most residential fires in the area are, as Theo experienced earlier. It was the first time someone mentioned the fire being intentional. When Theo showed them the two origin points, it connected to what they'd faced.

"So we weren't crazy to think it was bigger than it should have been," Tim said.

"No, your instincts were right. The accelerant increased the size and intensity of the blaze. By the time you got there, more was burning than should have been."

Dylan asked, "I assume the same is true of the Barrett building?"

"Yes, the arsonist used more accelerant there than on the others and had two points of origin. All the fires were started at the back of the building, giving them time to build before anyone saw and called them in."

Theo pointed out images on the board, pictures of the samples he sent to the lab, and passed around the files for the men to review. "In addition to knowing the schedule of the people who lived in the apartments, there's reason to believe the person has a working knowledge of the professional building because he chose one without a sprinkler system. A more modern or larger structure would have one, and the fire wouldn't have gotten as out of control."

"We have several buildings in that category," Martin said.

"Could you get me a list of those locations?" Martin nodded and made a note in a small spiral notebook.

"That night was brutal. We had to call in another department to get it under control. Never had that before," Dylan said. Looking around the table, Theo noticed Dylan was the only one who looked Theo's age. The rest had at least five to ten years on him, some more, other than one new volunteer, who'd introduced himself as John and appeared to be in his twenties. Theo made a mental note to suggest Martin might want to recruit younger members. Maybe a few women if there was an interest.

"It was one of the roughest I can remember," Lloyd said. "I almost thought we'd call in a third. Glad we didn't have to. It's hard to work with so many guys around. We're not used to it."

"You did a great job," Theo said, and he meant it. Fires like this weren't easy even when there was a paid staff. Having nearly all volunteers added a challenge, but these men had met it.

"We were lucky no one was in the buildings," Lloyd said.

Martin agreed. "That's one of the things that made us suspicious. Three fires, no people in the buildings? Didn't sit right."

"It's part of this arsonist's pattern. Property not people, which could mean there's a financial component involved in addition to a personal one."

"Is this personal?" John shifted in his chair as though he was unsure if he should have asked.

"Arson usually is. It can be about excitement — the thrill of the crime — but more often it's about profit, crime concealment, vandalism, or revenge. Typically, when there's a string of fires, there's one target and additional fires are set to confuse the investigation. Unfortunately, the arsonist often enjoys the chaos he's causing and keeps going until he's caught."

"What do you think these are about?"

"I can't say for certain, but I'm leaning toward revenge. My gut tells me the sites were chosen specifically, but whether the second or third site is the key target, I don't know. There's also the possibility the next fire is the focus. I do know nothing was impulsive. This person has a plan."

"What if the arsonist lost their job or business and is lashing out at the people he thinks wronged him?"

asked Lloyd. "Could mean Barrett is the target. The Northcott's are gone, and I don't think anyone in the apartments has any issues."

"Maybe there was someone Eden couldn't help with PT, and they lost their job and were mad at her," someone suggested.

"It's possible." Theo said. He didn't like the idea of her being the target, but he couldn't overlook the possibility. "I'll check with her to find out if anyone was disappointed in their progress or couldn't get help."

"My money's on Barrett. Sorry, not trying to be funny," Lloyd said, "but I don't think there's anyone in town who particularly likes the guy other than a few who've made money because of him, and even they've probably got issues. He's an easy and likely target. Maybe they hit Eden's place to upset him."

Theo considered telling them his suspicions about Keith, but not knowing if any of them were close to him, he kept the thought to himself. "He's my primary focus. If you think of anyone who's made threats or sounded serious about wanting to get back at him for something, let me know. Even if it seemed innocent at the time. Any leads would help — as would crossing people off the list."

"We're going to have another one, folks," Martin said, drawing attention to himself. "From everything Theo's told me, and given the decrease in times between fires, even if the primary target has been hit, there's another fire coming before the week is out, and we don't have enough information to catch him before it happens."

Mumbles and curses followed, and the tension in the room increased. Theo was grateful to Martin for delivering the news. Martin's acceptance of what was to come made the truth sink in quicker. No one doubted him.

John was the first to speak. "So what do we do?"

After a pause, Lloyd spoke. "I'm going to put a call out to the closest stations and tell them we're likely to need their help. They should also be alert to any suspicious fires in their towns. I've been reading up on arson. If someone in Fable Notch is the target, the arsonist isn't likely to hit elsewhere, but better safe than sorry."

There was more silence until John asked, "Is there any chance we could find him before he strikes again?"

Theo knew everyone hoped this was a possibility, but he knew better. "Not likely. I have a list of suspects but no standouts, several unconnected victims, and not a lot of helpful evidence. We could get lucky, and the accelerants could be unique, which would point us to the perpetrator, but chances are he used common items which won't narrow the search, simply give a signature."

"That kind of sucks," Dylan said. Theo listened for snark in his tone but heard only sympathy.

"No argument," Theo said. He wanted to give them some reassurance but didn't know what he could say. "Unfortunately, fire is its own forensic countermeasure. I'm going to do everything I can to find the person responsible as quickly as possible." Theo ran his hands through his hair and waited. He readied himself for comments on what good was his experience if they had another fire or if more people got hurt. He watched for — expected — expressions of irritation or disappointment.

And then Dylan spoke again. "Then we prepare as best we can, keep our ears open for rumors or some idiot bragging, and hope if there is another fire, this guy slips up so we can find him." The others responded with words of agreement and support.

"Okay, I'm new at this, as you all like to remind me" John said, "but from everything that's been shared.... It's someone we know, isn't it?"

Theo felt the weight of every pair of eyes. They knew the answer but needed to hear it. "Most likely."

"Well, shit."

That summed up the situation.

When there was nothing more to say on the fires, Theo sat and grabbed a slice of cold pizza, not feeling hungry but needing something to do. He didn't realize how nervous he'd been about the meeting until this moment when he could take in their acceptance and understanding. His shoulders relaxed, and he managed a small smile. Good people, Martin had called them. Maybe he was right.

The volunteers talked for a while longer and the conversation moved from fires to families then to the Founder's Day Festival, which was a few weeks away. When the coffee ran out, the meeting broke up.

"Thank you all for coming. I know this is rough, and it seems like all we can do is wait for the next fire, which I'm afraid is true, but I appreciate your support and ideas. Any thoughts you have, please get in touch."

Everyone offered smiles and versions of "No problem," and then John said, "Hey, one Wednesday a month, a bunch of us get together, whoever is available, to hang and relax. It's tomorrow. Come join us."

"Sounds great." And it did. These were a good bunch of guys, and it could be nice to get to know them. It would also help when the next fire happened if he were more a part of this team.

"Great, we meet up at around 5:30."

"What do you know? I'm free. Where are we going?"

"The Varnum Bar and Grill. Do you know where it is?"

Theo's stomach dropped, and the room got quiet. He kept his eyes on John , not daring to look at Martin, Dylan, or anyone who knew him. He knew where the Varnum was all too well. It was his mother's favorite place to go until she stopped leaving the house and did all her drinking and passing out at home. If there was any place in Fable Notch he didn't want to visit, that was it.

"You okay?" Lloyd put a hand on Theo's shoulder, which was when Theo realized he hadn't responded.

"Yes. Fine. Yes, I know it."

"Great," John said. "We'll see you there."

After everyone left, Martin came up to Theo. Theo knew what he was going to say. "You sure about going to the Varnum?"

"About as sure as I am about anything else right now." Which was pretty minimal. "I'll manage." Maybe he could convince himself before tomorrow night.

Martin looked as though he were about to say something but decided against it. When Theo was alone, he put the incident board back and moved papers around on his desk, trying to think about anything but what he'd agreed to do. If he could tell the arsonist where to hit, the Varnum would be the spot he'd pick. No, he didn't blame the place for the things that happened there or the memories he had, but he had no desire to see it again.

Tomorrow was going to start with interviewing Patrick Barrett and end at the Varnum. His mind was already trying to come up with reasons not to go.

As he headed out, his first thought was that Eden might be waiting at the house. She wasn't exactly waiting for *him*, but she was the one person who would understand what it was like to see Dylan again and how shocking his apology was. She'd also understand why the invitation to the Varnum had him in knots. It would be good to talk to her.

Be careful, man.

Adam's words echoed in his head, but he shook them off. He didn't need to worry. He could care for her and still leave town when the arsonist was caught. There was no way he would subject a woman as wonderful as Eden to the challenges of being with a man like him.

Chapter Twelve

♥

By the end of the day, Eden was exhausted. Tuesdays were normally busy on the weeks when she had therapy, but besides having to face her father, she had to deal with problems from the insurance company, a client showing up at the wrong time, and three voice messages from Keith telling her they needed to talk. Not even her final jazz dance class completely lifted her mood, so as soon as Eden got home, she went for the one thing that never failed to make her happy — chocolate.

She took out the box of Ghirardelli brownie mix, then added her own ingredients as she assembled it — cinnamon, a splash of vanilla and extra chocolate chips. And since brownies took a while to bake and cool, she grabbed a Lindt truffle. She needed something immediately. She popped it in her mouth and closed her eyes as the chocolate slowly melted.

Sated for the moment, she retrieved her book and snuggled under a light blanket on the living room couch. The growing scent of chocolate and the sexy story helped to ease the lingering stress of everything going on around her. Needing a new place to live. Seeing Theo again. Wanting to kiss him.

Again.

She shook her head to clear her thoughts. She could handle this. She was stronger and steadier than she'd been in years. Right?

Thank goodness her marriage was over. Leaving Keith had been Eden's first step in standing on her own. She hadn't even known it was what she wanted until the words tumbled out one day at Janelle's store.

Eden had bought a light blue dress from Janelle and had been trying it on when Keith walked in and saw her. He'd hated everything about it, from the color to the cut and insisted she return it the next day or he would. She'd gone to the store with the dress and receipt. As she fumbled over a story explaining why she was returning it, she'd burst into tears. Janelle walked her to the back room, closed the store, and made them tea. Over the course of the next few hours, Eden poured out the sadness and loneliness of her marriage.

When she was done, she was exhausted from crying and raging. Janelle asked one question. "What do you want to do?"

"I want a divorce." Eden blinked hard at hearing her own words. This wasn't the first time she'd thought it, only the first time she'd said it out loud.

"Then get a divorce," Janelle said.

"What would my father say?" The words came out so quickly she couldn't deny the truth. She was nearly thirty and worried over her father's reactions to her decisions. He'd dictated her life when she was in school, and when she'd come back for her mother, it was easier to do as he said than risk his anger. When she married Keith, she'd shifted responsibility to from father to husband.

Hearing the words — the fear — out loud changed something for Eden. For years, she'd been told by her father she needed to be helped and supported, like her mother. Because Keith had come into her life when she was at a low point, the lie had been exacerbated. It had been easy to let him take care of everything from the bills to choosing where they'd lived. She'd gotten used to doing what he said, seeing the people he liked and, as the dress proved, wearing the clothes he preferred. She was in this marriage for other people, not for her.

As she sat with Janelle, Eden couldn't see a reason to stay with Keith. Her work at Maximum Results brought in more than enough income to live on her own, and because Keith saw it as her little hobby, he'd never known what she earned. She'd put her income into savings which had grown substantially in the last few years. She didn't need him financially or want him emotionally. Realizing she stayed with him to keep from upsetting her father made the whole situation more intolerable.

"Now what?" Deciding to end her marriage was one thing. Knowing what to do next was different. Janelle found a notepad and together they made a list of things Eden needed to do. That had been the easy part. It took several more weeks before Eden was willing to look at apartments and take boxes of her things to Janelle's for safekeeping. A few weeks later, she found a place to live and the courage to tell Keith she was leaving. It hadn't taken long once she put things in motion. She suspected Keith kept agreeing to things and signing them because he didn't expect her to go through with it. There had been nothing to disagree on, nothing to fight over. No kids to worry about hurting. She'd let him have the condo they lived in because she never liked it. *It's perfect until we start a family. Then we'll buy a house and use this place as a rental property.* His plans, always his. She would never let anyone do that to her again. It was time for her plans, whatever they might be.

The divorce was final the week after the fire. She'd been too upset by the turmoil in her life to celebrate and had yet to tell her father. Millie had provided her with a place to live, but without Janelle, Eden would be wearing the same outfit every day. Janelle gave her clothes from the store, then made sure Eden's days had structure and purpose and weren't filled with streaming *Gilmore Girls* while hiding on the couch. Which is what Eden wanted to do.

But if Janelle got her going that first week, it was Eden's job that kept her going. She had clients who needed her, students who were signed up for her classes, not to mention Courtney, the student she taught privately who had more talent than almost any dancer Eden had ever met. Each day, work gave her something to look forward to.

Eventually, she'd tell her father the divorce was final. After she had a new apartment. After Theo left.

Again.

"Chicken," she said to herself.

"Really? I thought it smelled like brownies."

Eden squealed and jumped, the book falling to the floor. She'd been so wrapped up in her thoughts, she hadn't heard Theo's truck pull up or the door open. Harlow came over and whether that was to comfort her or get scratches, she didn't know. Or care. Petting the beautiful dog gave her something to do and helped her heart stop racing. She could see the appeal of a pet.

Theo walked over and sat on the arm of the couch. "Sorry about that. I guess today was my day to sneak up on you," Theo said.

"So tomorrow it's my turn?"

"Could be. If it makes you feel any better, Adam Stewart scared the hell out of me yesterday."

Eden laughed as she picked up her book, found her place and inserted her bookmark. "Where did you see him?"

"He came by the station. With ice cream," he said sliding down to sit on the couch.

"His ice cream is heavenly." Eden tucked her legs under her to give him more room. And herself a little distance? "He makes a double chocolate brownie swirl that is worth every calorie."

"And we're back to brownies."

"Hey, no matter what else is going on, chocolate never lets you down."

There was a pause before Theo said, "Yeah, sorry."

"It wasn't a reference to you."

"Why shouldn't it be? I know you didn't want to me to leave. You were willing to defer going to school and spend a year figuring out scholarships and loans. You would have fought for us."

"And you wouldn't let me choose between my dream and you." She fiddled with the charms on her bracelet finding the double hearts automatically and drawing on her mother's love for strength. "Yes, I was furious with you for not staying with me to find a solution, but I never thought you let me down. I was upset because you made leaving look easy when I was falling apart."

"It wasn't. Not at all."

"I know that now. Then, I was hurt and alone and scared." The oven buzzed, and she went to check on the brownies. She stuck a toothpick in to see if it came out clean and when she got the results she wanted, she put the pan on top of the stove. She set the timer again to let her know when they'd be cool enough to cut, then drew in the heavenly scent and let out a happy sigh.

She turned to see he'd followed her into the kitchen. "It's nice to see they're still your favorite."

"I guess some things haven't changed."

"Especially when so much has?"

Her first reaction was to brush his words aside with a joke or dismissal, but something stopped her. Theo wasn't like her father or Keith, and even if his leaving had been one of the hardest moments of her life, he'd done it out of love and the hope she would have what she most wanted. Maybe that was what hurt — the loss of someone who'd believed and accepted her without asking for anything other than her love and acceptance in return. Her eyes filled with tears and within a heart-beat he'd come around the island pulled her into a hug.

"I'm sorry." His voice rumbled in his chest, and she put her arms around him, breathing in his unique scent, the outdoors mixed with something she couldn't name. "I didn't mean to upset you. I've had a rough night, and I'm making a mess of things."

"It's not you or what you said. It's everything in the last year." She stood there in his arms and took in his warmth and strength. When was the last time someone had held her with no expectations? She didn't know how long they stood there before he kissed the top of her head. She pulled back to look at him, and in that moment, she needed his lips on hers. Not wanting him to wonder, she pushed herself up on her toes bringing her face closer to his.

When their lips met, every worry from the day disappeared. There was nothing but the feel of him, the taste of him, the complete joy of being close to him. Familiar, yet new.

She skimmed her tongue over his lips and his arms tightened around her as he opened his mouth. This was the part of the roller coaster she liked — the breathless thrill.

Everything about being in his arms was wonderful. The strength of him against her, his obvious desire for her displayed in his quickening breath and the moan that escaped when she ran her hands down his back. She wanted more, and she wanted it now. Her fingers tingled with desire, and she ached to put her hands under his shirt and touch him.

When his mouth moved from her lips to her jaw and then back by her ear, all she wanted was for him to keep kissing her and never stop.

And then what?

Was she ready to take this further? Even knowing he would leave her again?

As if sensing her change of thoughts, he stopped and pulled back to look at her. Her conflicting thoughts must have shown on her face because he said, "It's going to take the brownies time to cool. As much as I'd like to stand here and keep kissing you, I don't want to take advantage."

"I initiated this kiss."

"You did, and I am ten kinds of glad, but as I said, I had a rough night and if you're making brownies, you had a difficult day, too. We're both shaky, so what if we take a small step back. Will you tell me what's on your mind?"

Twelve years they'd been apart, and Theo could read her better than her father did after a lifetime. She missed this more than his kisses. She nodded and said, "Only if you tell me what made your night difficult."

"Deal."

They walked to the couch, and she hoped he didn't see the tears which threatened. Allowing herself to accept and express her emotions around others was new, but she wasn't sure if it was a good idea to show Theo so much. Around her father and Keith, she kept a tight rein on her emotions and made certain they never showed to avoid being criticized or mocked. Then again, Theo wasn't staying, which meant the risk wasn't as great. Maybe this would be good practice. If nothing else, he couldn't hold it over her head later since he'd be gone.

She sat with her knees bent toward her chest. There was space between them, but he was close enough that she could touch him if she reached out. "My dad came by the gym today. He told me to go back to my husband where I belong."

"He said that?"

"Not in so many words, but that was the gist of it."

"He always was charming. Doesn't he know divorce means the marriage is over?" She didn't say anything. Theo's eyebrows shot up when he understood. "He doesn't know the divorce is final."

"I haven't gotten around to telling him. No, that's not the truth. I've been avoiding letting him know. I got the papers a few days before the fire, and I need to get through one crisis before I head into the next one."

"It's always better to be prepared where Patrick is concerned. He's good at finding a weakness and exploiting it."

"Don't I know it." And Patrick had always been able to do that to her, which was how she ended up staying home longer after her mother's death, then going out with and ultimately marrying Keith.

"I've got a meeting with him tomorrow. I can't wait."

"I heard. He got a call from his assistant while he was with me. As Janelle likes to quote from *The Devil Wears Prada*, 'Gird your loins.'"

Theo nodded. "Sounds about right."

"He's going to give you a hard time."

"I wouldn't expect anything less."

"He told me to stay away from you."

Theo crossed his arms over his chest. He may not be surprised, but he wasn't pleased. Eden understood the response. "Oh look, something else that hasn't changed. You didn't mention our living arrangement, I assume."

"No, I may need therapy, but I'm not crazy."

"Therapy? Physical therapy?"

Clearly, her ability to keep things from Theo was nonexistent. She wrapped her arms around her knees and braced herself for his response. "Not in this case, although I've had that, too." Looking down at her hands she said, "My morning appointment was with a psychologist."

There was silence. Finally, she looked at him.

"If you're waiting for me to make a negative comment or smart-ass remark, you'll be waiting a while. I was stateside for almost a year before I realized I wasn't coping. I got into a VA program which included therapy. Probably saved my life. Certainly, turned it around."

"It's helped me, too. Last summer I was talking to Janelle and realized I didn't want to stay married to Keith." She told him the story of the blue dress and the revelation that followed. "Even once I decided, I dragged my feet. It took Janelle coming over and packing some of my things to keep at her place to get me going. She constantly checked in with me, asking me what I'd done. She even helped me to make a budget and went with me to find an apartment. Once I moved out, I started divorce proceedings."

"That's a lot of changes in a short period."

"Don't I know it. Maybe not the smartest move, but it felt great. At first. One day during a meeting with my lawyer I fell apart. I couldn't stop crying. When I'd calmed down, she suggested the names of a few therapists. I found one out of the area."

"Smart move. Nothing happens here without everyone knowing about it."

"And always the things you don't *want* people to know. I've been seeing her every other Tuesday morning since November. When I saw her the week after the fire, I don't know if I've ever been so grateful to have to get up early in the morning. Change is hard. I'm glad to have her to talk to."

"I won't ask if I came up in today's session, although from your blush, I don't need to."

"That's not fair. Why is it I can keep things from my dad and Keith, who've been with me for years, but you're back barely forty-eight hours and you read me better than they ever did?"

"Because I'm looking."

And he was. Her dad and Keith looked for the answers they wanted, got mad when they didn't get them, then bullied her until they did. Theo was different. It was unnerving — it had been a long time since she'd let someone see her — but it was also welcome. She needed to remember this is what it should be like between two people in a relationship. Then maybe after he was gone, she'd be able to find that with someone else.

The thought made her stomach flip, but it was a worry for another night.

She reached out and took his hand. "Thank you for looking, for noticing."

"Would it make you feel better to know I brought you up plenty in my time in therapy?"

"A little." She wondered what he said about her, but she didn't ask. It didn't matter. What did matter was he was willing to share something personal, take a risk with her. It was almost as wonderful as the kiss.

Almost.

She considered moving closer to see if they could start the kissing again when the buzzer went off at the same time she heard the ring of an old-fashioned rotary phone.

"That's the Captain's phone," he said. "Martin gave it to me since I'm in charge while he's recovering."

They both got up. She to cut the brownies, he to find out where he was needed. He was done before she was.

"Is it the arsonist?"

"No, people call the fire department when they lock themselves out of the house. I have to help break down a door. Or jimmy the lock. Who knew that talent would come in handy?" Eden smiled at the memory. Theo used to sneak into her house during their senior year by picking the backdoor lock. "I'll call Martin for back up."

As they got up, she said, "You never said what made your night rough."

"Dylan Cioni is one of the volunteer firefighters. I saw him tonight, and he apologized for what he did when we were in high school." She stared at him and blinked. "Yeah, didn't see that coming either."

"You may win understatement of the night. How about a brownie for the road?"

"Sure." He had keys in one hand and phone in the other, so she held it to his mouth and he grabbed it with his teeth. It was silly and intimate and made her stomach tingle. "Thanks," he said with his mouth full. "Shouldn't take too long, but who knows. Harlow will keep you company. I'll see you later."

For a second, she thought he might kiss her goodbye, like an old married couple. They stared at each other a moment too long, but before her heart could speed up, he turned, grabbed his keys, and headed out.

"It's just you, me and the brownies, Harlow. Sorry I can't share, but I think there's chicken in the fridge, and I'll sneak you a little of that. Another thank you for finding my bracelet."

After feeding the dog a treat, Eden went upstairs with her book and two brownies. If she stayed near the pan, she was in danger of eating them all. She'd shut her light off before Theo came back but didn't fall asleep until she heard his car in the driveway. Two days and she was listening for him, hoping he was safe. She was going to be grateful for therapy once he left again.

Chapter Thirteen

♥

There was fire everywhere. The roar of the flames and the cracking of wood burning engulfed his ears. The smoke was clawing its way into his mouth and drying out his tongue. He couldn't breathe with the mix of sooty air and heat filling his lungs. Where was his equipment? Where was his team? Then he heard the scream.

Eden.

Eden was in the fire, and he had to find her, had to save her.

He ran into the flames, felt their heat licking his skin. It didn't matter if he wasn't protected. He had to get in there. The longer the fire burned the harder it would be to find her. He'd lost a teammate to fire and thought nothing could be worse, but knowing Eden was in danger was unbearable. He wasn't going to lose her, too.

"Theo, it's okay."

It wasn't okay. He couldn't find her. Where was her voice coming from? Why was she in this building?

"Theo, can you hear me?"

He could, but the smoke was making it impossible to see. She must be yelling if he could hear her above the noise of the blaze. How bad was the fire? How much of the building had already been consumed? He tried to listen for her voice and the sound of beams breaking. There was no way the building was going to last. So many things to worry about, nothing he could control. The fire had all the control.

Something was shaking. Something was shaking him. Was the building collapsing? If it was, they would both be killed or trapped. He'd never get to her, never see her again. He had to see her again, hold her, tell her....

"No," he screamed, and the sound woke him from the dream. He sat up fast and reached out, grabbing whoever was near him, hoping to get a grip on his altered reality. His heart was beating as though he'd been running. Sweat covered his body.

"Theo, it's me. It's Eden. You were having a nightmare. You're safe. Please, wake up."

He stared at her but didn't see her. Instead, he smelled the smoke, heard the flames crackle. Slowly the dream faded, and he could see her clearly, make out the worry in her eyes. It took him a few more seconds to be present to his surroundings and notice he had both of her upper arms in a tight grip.

"Eden," he breathed her name on a sigh. She was here. She was safe. He let go of her arms and pulled her into his embrace. He was probably scaring her to death, but he had to assure himself she was real and not trapped somewhere he couldn't reach her. It took several tries before he could manage a deep breath, taking in the scent of her hair and letting it wash the smell of smoke from his brain. Letting go, he looked at her and then at the red marks forming on her upper arms. "I'm sorry. I hurt you." He should have known better. When he got close to people either they got hurt or he did.

Her eyes followed where his were looking. "I'm fine. I didn't even realize you grabbed me so hard."

"I can't believe you heard me. I didn't think our rooms were close I must have been loud."

"It's okay. I understand getting nightmares. Several of my clients have them if an accident is what brought them to me. Memories and fear all mixed together. I didn't know if I should let you come out of it on your own or wake you."

"I'm surprised you were able to. And I can get violent. Oh God, I didn't hit you before I grabbed you, did I?" He'd done that once before.

"No, Theo, of course not. This is nothing." She put a hand to his cheek and the brief touch helped him relax.

Until he noticed the red marks again. Seeing the bruises made his stomach flip. Theo knew it was likely he'd have a nightmare while he was here. Too much shit coming up for him. But he expected to be alone. The last person who had been with him during a nightmare was a woman he'd been dating for a few months. He'd stayed overnight in her apartment and accidentally hit her when he thrashed in his sleep. She'd woken him by yelling. Granted, Eden hadn't been in bed with him, so there wasn't the same danger, but he needed to remember to keep a safe distance. "I'm sorry," he repeated.

She took his hand and gave it a squeeze. "I'm fine, and now you are, too."

"I didn't mean to scare you. Living alone, I only bother Harlow." At the mention of her name, the dog jumped on the bed and snuggled close. After nightmares, he usually found her waiting nearby. She wouldn't come up until he acknowledged her, as though she knew he needed space. He put an arm around her, letting her warmth soothe him. "She doesn't mind."

"That explains it."

"Explains what?"

"Your yelling didn't wake me. It was Harlow. She was pawing at my door. I guess it was her way of knocking. I opened it to find out what was going on, and I heard you call out."

"Were you here long?"

"No, I didn't know if you'd calm yourself and fall back into a better sleep, so I waited. But then the yelling got louder, and you called my name. Do you remember what was happening?"

Her question made it clear she understood these nightmares. Sometimes he woke with no memory of what caused the fear. Other times, like today, the images were vivid after he woke. "There was a fire. You were in it. I couldn't find you." He scrubbed a hand over his face, then ran it through his hair. "Lloyd and I took care of a kitchen fire that got out of control yesterday. I'm guessing the was part of the trigger."

"Was it bad?"

"Not at all, but the smell and the heat were familiar, if smaller. I haven't had to help with a live one since the army."

She moved further onto the mattress, so she was closer to him. "I'd heard that was your specialty. How did you end up there?"

She was trying to distract him. He appreciated the effort. "After boot camp, I scored high on the Armed Services Vocational Aptitude Battery tests I took. I think it's one of the first tests I've ever done well on. On the list of recommended jobs was firefighter. Thinking of Martin and all he'd done for me, it seemed like the right choice."

"Did you see a lot of fighting?"

"Not in the way you think. We were stationed near the action to be close if they needed us. There were fires resulting from artillery, some after explosions or and sometimes we managed blazes set to create natural cover. We also inspected buildings and vehicles for hazards and explosive materials. There are private companies over there doing this work, but we filled in the gaps."

"Stressful and dangerous work."

"And unpredictable. We could have days of quiet followed by a week of action where we lived on adrenaline, training, and teamwork. It didn't always end well."

"You lost people, friends."

"One. His name was Michael." He turned his right shoulder toward her so she could see the phoenix tattoo on his back. "His initials are in the wings. Two others were sent home with serious burns. I guess I'm luckier than most. I met plenty of guys when I came back who'd seen and lost more."

"That doesn't make it easier."

"No, it doesn't. The nightmares started after Michael's death."

"Do you have them often?"

"Not as often as when I first came home or after my accident. That lost me a lot of sleep. PTSD is a nasty thing. As you said — memories and fear. Can't control it. I was expecting it to hit, coming back here and all, but knowing doesn't make it easier."

"Last night you mentioned you've had therapy. Is that one of the reasons?"

He nodded. "The main reason. I almost waited too long. Me and a few of the guys on my team always said shrinks were for the weak. We could go back and be fine, no problem."

"You thought that before the army. I remember our high school guidance counselor suggesting you see someone when your mother went into the hospital. You, um, turned them down."

"I'm sure I said something a bit more colorful. It was hard to accept that needing help for what I was going through was no different from seeing the right medical doctor for an injury. But, as I said, I tried to handle it on my own. I never drank the way some of my friends did — mom set a powerful example against that. But after I got back, I worked as a roadie again with Cole, like I did after high school. We were always up late, and I'd wait to go to bed until I couldn't keep my eyes open. I tried prescription sleep aids hoping they'd help prevent the nightmares. Each time they came back, I'd up the number of pills I took. Cole noticed and got me help."

"He dragged you to therapy."

"He dragged me to therapy."

"He always was a good big brother."

"And practically a father." Martin and Millie played a big part in keeping Theo from ruining his life as a kid, but it was Cole he first trusted and looked up to. Cole had driven him to the appointments in part for support, in part to make sure Theo went and stayed. Six months later, one of his army buddies reached out to him about the position at Prometheus. Without Cole's support, he wouldn't have been in any shape to take the job. Theo knew how lucky he was. He may have drawn the short end of the straw with parents, but his brothers were gold.

Eden reached out and took his hand in hers. "I'm glad he was there for you so you could be there for the people you've helped. And now for Martin."

Her smile melted his heart. Eden saw the best in others. She knew how to make people feel good about themselves. He imagined it helped her as a physical therapist. When they were together, it was something he valued as much as her love, and he'd missed it often over the years.

"Thank you for waking me." He brought her hand to his lips, giving it a kiss. And noticed what she was wearing or, more accurately, what she wasn't wearing. Apparently, Eden slept in a nightshirt that, because of the way she was sitting, barely came to the middle of her thigh. It was baby pink, with three little buttons at the neckline he ached to undo so he could touch and see if her skin was as soft as he remembered. He snapped his eyes away from her chest and found her staring at him. Was she thinking the same thing? "I want to kiss you," he said.

No guessing, no confusion.

"Do it. I want to be kissed."

He moved forward, then stopped. Seeing her, being near her, was bringing back old desires. But was it a good idea to act on them? "What if I want more?"

"How much more?"

"I'm not sure. Possibly a lot."

"I don't know if I'm ready to say yes to that yet," she said.

"Then I'm only going to kiss you until you know what you want."

He pulled her close, and she melted into his arms. Before today they'd been dressed, and their surroundings helped to keep them at a distance. But all she had on was that flimsy shirt, and he wasn't wearing a shirt at all. Her hands were on his chest, her breasts pressed against him and his "possibly a lot" moved swiftly into "everything, definitely."

Dragging her more onto his lap, he kept her on top of the blankets that covered him from the waist down. He hoped the material would be enough of a barrier. It was bad enough he could see her nipples harden beneath the fabric of her shirt. He kept kissing her and let his hand graze over her breast before he rested it on the small of her back. Her sharp intake of breath pleased and excited him. Good. He wouldn't push her farther than she was ready, but knowing she wanted and ached too told him there was a possibility of sharing more.

More became her nails raking across his shoulder blades, sending shivers of delight through his body. The simplest of touches from her brought the most intense responses. He couldn't imagine what might happen if they were both under the covers.

Actually, he could imagine all too well.

Her tongue teased his, and he sucked gently, pulling it deeper into his mouth. She gasped at the sensation, and the sound thrilled him. He'd never allowed himself to imagine she'd be in his arms again, but for however long she was, he would savor it. He ran his hands through her beautiful, blond hair, loving the feel of the strands through his fingers as he remembered pulling her hair out of her dance bun.

He kissed his way along her jaw, then down her neck as her head fell back. He breathed in the scent of her skin, finding it both familiar and changed. She used a different soap, but underneath was her unforgettable scent. It enveloped him like a sweet smoke he was happy to be trapped in.

His hands moved from her back, down over her ass and then to her leg, where he was distracted by a familiar sensation, but one he'd expect on his leg, not hers. Breaking away from their embrace, he looked down at her right thigh. The angry scar spoke of something violent.

"What's wrong? Why did you stop?" She followed his gaze to her leg.

"What did this, Eden?" She tried to pull away, but he held her closer. She grabbed for the blankets to cover it up. "Stop, you don't have to hide it. Hell, I have scars and burn marks all over, but because I do, I can tell something terrible happened. What was it?"

He watched as emotions changed her expression. He could see she considered distracting him with more kisses before she surrendered and spoke. "The reason I stopped dancing."

Chapter Fourteen

♥

"I know it's an ugly scar. A turn off." Keith had told her many times and never touched her leg. It was part of the reason he insisted she wear longer skirts. She'd considered plastic surgery at one point to put an end to his comments and her embarrassment. She tugged at the too short nightshirt, but Theo put his hands on hers and stopped her.

"If that's a turn off, then you're going to run for the hills when you see mine," he said and pulled the blanket to the side, showing his leg. When she saw him at the gym, he'd worn long pants, and although she could imagine what the scar would look like given the injury, seeing it was different.

"You're right. Yours is worse." Unlike hers which had faded, his scars were red. She could see where the bone had ripped through the skin and the careful stitching of the surgeon. "You're lucky you can walk."

"So I've heard. Looks like the same might be true for you. What happened?"

It had been a long time since she'd told the story. She looked at him, then back to her leg. As she leaned against him, staring at the scar, she let the memory return. "It was a few months after my mother died. I was having a hard time, grieving. My father called it moping."

"He always knew how to be supportive."

"Right? That summer, Keith was interning at dad's office. His way of helping was to invite Keith over for dinner and suggest we go out. It was easier to agree."

"Anything to get Patrick off your back."

"A quiet Patrick is a happy Patrick," she said. Her father hadn't yelled, thank goodness, but he was uncomfortable with her emotional state. It was easier to say yes. "We started seeing each other several times a week. One day in August, we were out with Keith's friend Rob Russo and his girlfriend, Monica, for dinner and a movie. No big deal. Until the drive home."

"There was an accident."

"A bad one. Someone cut us off at an intersection. Keith was driving and lost control of the car. We went off the road and smashed into a tree, passenger side first. There was no guard rail. Glass shattered. Metal crumpled. Rob ended up with a concussion that gave him headaches for years. Monica was sitting behind me, and we were both trapped. It was an older car, so no side airbags. The door was wedged into my leg, and I remember being able to feel I was bleeding. There must have been a lot because I could smell it too, sort of metallic. When they pulled me out, the wound gushed, and I passed out."

"The door was holding you together, keeping the cut from gaping."

"So I was told. I woke up in the hospital in a cast and attached to all sorts of IV's. The doctors explained that besides a broken leg, the door sliced through muscle and nerves causing severe damage. There were a few scary hours when they were considering amputation. Afterward, they weren't certain I was going to gain enough muscle strength in the leg to walk again unassisted. Dancing was out of the question."

"I can't imagine how awful it must have been."

"I cried until I couldn't anymore. I wore myself out. I've hardly cried since, emotional moments of the last few days to the contrary."

"Clearly their prognosis on your walking was wrong."

"I'm as stubborn as you sometimes."

"I prefer determined."

"So do I." She put her arms around his waist, able to relax after talking about the worst of the experience. "It was a long rehabilitation—you understand—and took the better part of a year. I tried dancing again, hoping that if they were wrong about walking, they could be wrong about dancing, but the leg isn't strong enough. I left the Conservatory. The next year I reapplied to schools and went to college closer to home."

"And became a physical therapist?"

"I was out one day and rolled my ankle, which strained my leg. I went to see the PT who'd helped me after the accident. We got to talking, and she thought I'd be a great therapist since I understood the body. I laughed it off but couldn't stop thinking about it. I was working in my dad's office and hated the tedium and routine. I think my dad was glad to see me go. I'm a lousy secretary."

"But an excellent PT," he said.

"I hope so. When Maximum Results hired me, it was part time, but when they found I could teach dance classes, too, it became a full-time job."

"How did Keith end up hanging around?"

"He claimed he felt terrible for his part in the accident. He was attentive and kind, visiting me regularly during my recovery even though he was finishing college. For too long the only voices in my head were my dad's and Keith's and, as hard as it is to say, it was as if I forgot how to be strong. I don't think I even wanted to be."

"You're doing better now," he said, giving her a gentle squeeze.

"I am. I've had setbacks, as you know, but it's been worth it. My friends have been an immense help."

"And therapy."

"Absolutely."

"I'm sorry for all you went through, for all you lost. And even though I don't know if I could have helped, I'm sorry for not being there."

She swallowed past a lump in her throat. So much for not crying. She whispered, "Thank you," then leaned back to look at him, hoping he could see how grateful she was for his understanding. She looked into his blue eyes, the soft light of daybreak streaming in through the window making them a shade lighter. She sat up and pulled away from him, then straddled his waist. No covers between them. She was willing to take the risk. Before she put any of her weight on his legs, she asked, "Is this okay?"

He nodded, and she cupped his face, needing to touch him. Her other hand snaked into his hair as she dipped her lips to meet his. She wanted to thank him for listening to her story and not judging her — for letting her take her time with whatever this was. She felt him between her legs and wanted more, but knew she wasn't ready. Yet. For now, she'd enjoy his tongue licking her lips open so he could suck on her bottom lip. She moaned as the insistent tug that sent a shiver down her spine and between her legs.

In this moment, she couldn't imagine how she ever believed he had turned his back on her.

A soft woof made them reluctantly end the kiss, although Theo held her gaze and kept an arm around her. "Can't you see I'm busy?" Theo said to Harlow. She barked again.

"Maybe she doesn't like seeing you with another woman."

"Then she and I are going to have to have a long talk later. What is it, girl?" he asked, finally turning to the dog. Harlow cocked her head to the side. Eden laughed at the clear signal. "Right, morning walk. Something's can't wait. Sorry."

"Duty and nature calls."

He laughed. "We woke you up early. I think that deserves something to say thank you. Can I take you to the diner?"

"It sounds wonderful, but do you think it's a good idea for us to be seen in public together? First thing in the morning?"

"Good point. Okay, rain check on the diner, but when Harlow and I get back, I'm making breakfast. Deal?"

"I don't have Pop-tarts," she said, referring to the staple of his childhood.

"Very funny. I can do more than toast things." He kissed her again as they got out of bed. Part of her didn't want to get up.

She stopped in the kitchen to make coffee in the pot rather than the Keurig so there would be plenty for them both, and when he came out wearing sweatpants, hoodie and sneakers, she handed him a filled commuter cup. "Fuel."

"You're a goddess," he said, taking the mug from her and giving her a quick kiss. "See you soon."

She stood there sipping her coffee, taking in the last hour — learning of his nightmares, telling him of her accident. Learning she could be vulnerable with Theo. Discovering how intensely she still desired him. It was a lot for one morning. Emotions long dormant were waking up and making her feel alive. It was wonderful and scary.

And when he left?

She didn't want to think about that, although she wasn't in denial either. He wouldn't stay once they caught the arsonist. This wasn't his home. They had this time, and she'd have to enjoy it. After he was gone, she hoped to stay open to taking risks. Because after this brief reminder of what it felt like to be seen and heard, she knew she didn't want to live without it.

Chapter Fifteen

♥

After he and Harlow got back from their walk, Theo made a simple meal of cheesy scrambled eggs and toast and presented it to her with a flourish. They laughed, realizing this was the first time either of them cooked for the other. They both had long days planned, so breakfast was quick. Theo didn't tell Eden about the planned meet up at the Varnum. He was hoping to get out of it. They said goodbye with a kiss when he headed out. It was easy and comfortable, which Theo appreciated in the moment but concerned him once he'd headed for the station.

It was dangerous to fall into a routine with Eden. It would make it harder after he left. Given how quickly things heated between them this morning, however, Theo gave up the possibility of not getting hurt. It was too late from the moment he first saw her again. The best he could hope for was happy memories to take back to Baltimore.

His meeting with Patrick wasn't until eleven. Theo used the time to make a list of the things he wanted to ask the man and chose pictures to bring if Barrett gave him any problems. Theo knew Martin wouldn't consider suing over getting hurt during the fire, but Theo wasn't above making a few threats if it got him information he could use.

Before he left, he heard from the laboratory where he'd sent the samples from the first and third sites. They confirmed what he assumed — the accelerant was kerosene, easily acquired in any local shop. No help there. He also got a return call from Keith's secretary who confirmed a ten o'clock appointment the next morning. As much as he wanted to get it over with, he was glad not to have to do both on the same day. Barrett and the Varnum were enough.

Prepared as possible, he and Harlow arrived at Barrett's office fifteen minutes before the meeting was planned. He knew Patrick would make him wait, but he wanted Barrett to know he was early. As expected, the woman at the front desk made a call, then told Theo to take a seat. Harlow sat at his feet in the sparsely but expensively decorated reception area. Theo ran a hand through her fur to calm himself.

Theo wanted to pace but stayed seated. Part of him was a teenager who couldn't get over where he was sitting. He'd made an appointment with Eden's father and the old man had to keep it, had to talk to him. Since the last time he'd seen Patrick, he'd gone from being the troublemaker forced out of Eden's life to a senior member of a nationally recognized organization. Barrett was going to have to show Theo's job, if not Theo himself, some respect. It was surreal.

Then again, so was seeing Eden.

Nothing and everything had changed between them. Their time together was already better than any fantasy he'd ever conjured, and they hadn't done more than kiss. Sitting here, he could recall the smell of her hair when her chest was on his shoulder, the softness of her hands in his, the sound of her laughter.

Theo gave his head a quick shake. He had to get himself under control. He was not walking into Patrick's office sporting a hard-on for the man's daughter.

Fire. Arson. All the different ways he'd like to pin this on Patrick and see the man in prison garb and out of

Eden's life once and for all. That calmed him down. It even put a smile on his face, which was still there when the secretary told him to go in.

Theo walked into an office designed to impress and intimidate, decorated in dark woods and leather. There was a time in his life when it would have affected him, but after being in the company of generals and other men who earned respect instead of demanding it, he wasn't fazed.

"Good morning, Mr. Barrett. Thank you for taking the time to see me."

"Cut the false niceties, Hanson," Patrick said, placing both hands in front of him and knitting them together. "I agreed to see you because someone burned my building. Since I don't want more of my properties destroyed, I'm cooperating."

If this was cooperating, Theo would hate to see hindering. Knowing he'd never get an invitation, Theo sat in the chair across from Patrick and made himself comfortable for what would likely be a short meeting. He released Harlow and let her walk around the office. He got a perverse kick out of seeing the man's nostrils flair at the liberty.

"What is he doing? Why did you bring a pet with you?"

"*She* is an arson dog, and she is getting familiar with your scent. That way, if she picks it up at any of the fire sites, she'll recognize it." Theo didn't add that if there was even a trace of accelerant on Patrick, she'd pick that up, too. Instead, he pulled out his tablet and opened the notes app.

Patrick gave short, clipped responses to every question. It was like a tennis rally, back and forth. No, he didn't have trouble with any of the tenants. Yes, everything was up to code. The building was older and didn't require sprinklers because of the size and age. It was what Theo expected and was not helpful. Only one question got him an interesting answer.

"When was the last time you were at the Dunstan Street building?"

"Months. Maybe a year ago. Keith Peters manages and leases that site." Keith again. Interesting. But important? No way to know yet.

Theo braced for the reaction his next question would get. "You don't need the insurance money on the building which burned, right? Business is good?"

Patrick's lips thinned. "I will not answer that."

"No problem. I can have someone from our company investigate your finances. I'm sure, given the insurance claims you and your tenants put in, we could get a court order to review them if necessary. It might hold up the insurance checks, but that wouldn't be an issue, would it?"

Patrick's face grew red. Theo couldn't help but enjoy it. Ah, the little things. "I did not burn down my own building."

Theo waited in case Patrick wanted to elaborate. He didn't. "I ask because when I was reviewing the cases with Chief Sinclair, he said your buildings are well maintained. "

Patrick blinked at the compliment. "I take care of my business. Losing this one is a little bittersweet. It was one of the first I bought, but it's older, and I can't say I'm sorry it's gone."

"Why is that?"

"Smaller buildings have smaller rents." Barrett's tone suggested he thought Theo was an idiot. "This area doesn't have a lot of developable land because of all the National Forests. Tearing down the building was a needless expense, but since it's a pile of rubble, I can build something bigger."

Could Patrick have had the place torched for the opportunity to build a larger property? Maybe in partnership with Keith? Maybe they each wanted a property destroyed, and they created this plan. It was something to consider. There was another possibility Theo wanted to discuss. "One last thing, can you think of anyone who would want to hurt you or Eden?"

"Eden? Why would Eden be involved?" Now the man showed concern. He may not know how to offer love, but Theo never doubted he cared about Eden.

"Her apartment, your building. It's a connection. I can't overlook anything."

"You think someone wants to hurt me and is trying through her?" Theo heard genuine worry. The man may be a lousy father, but he loved Eden.

"It's one theory. I'm working on finding proof."

"I know there are people who don't like the way I do business or the way my properties look."

"What's wrong with how they look?"

"Business buildings and strip malls aren't cute and quaint, no matter how many false windows and awnings you put on them, Mr. Hanson. They're functional. Some residents think this detracts from the... scenic beauty of our town." His tone made it clear what he thought. "But when their quaint businesses fail, and I build something that gives people jobs, they don't complain."

"Any names come to mind?"

"No," Patrick answered quickly.

"I'd appreciate it if you'd take the time to consider my question, Mr. Barrett."

"And I'd appreciate it if you wouldn't take my time at all, but we can't always have what we want."

Several choice phrases ran through Theo's head, followed closely by Martin's voice telling him to be the better man. Still, he didn't have to be too kind. "I understand. And if another one of your properties is hit, you can explain to your insurance carriers how you didn't cooperate with the investigation when you were given the opportunity."

Patrick growled. It was a satisfying sound. "Fine, I'll make up a list and have it sent to the station." Patrick broke eye contact with Theo and shifted his focus to the files on the desk. The meeting was over.

"Thank you again for your time." There was no answer. Theo got up and motioned for Harlow to come with him.

"One other thing, Hanson," Patrick said.

As he turned, Theo braced himself. He knew what was coming. There was no way he was getting out of here without Patrick mentioning what bothered him most about Theo's being back. "Yes?"

"I have power in this town. Stay away from my daughter."

For a moment, he considered saying nothing, then changed his mind. "You don't have any say over me or Eden. She's a grown woman and free to make her own decisions."

"She is not free. She's married."

"I heard her status changed a few weeks ago."

Patrick slammed a fist and bellowed, "What?"

Oh shit. Theo kept his features schooled but internally cringed. Eden may not be happy that he let that information slip. No backing out now. "Sorry to be the bearer of bad news, but I've spoken to Eden, and she told me her divorce was final. She's an excellent physical therapist, by the way," he said. *And a great kisser*, he thought. Patrick said nothing. He made a mental note to let Eden know she was off the hook. "You'll need to speak to her or your son-in-law, sorry *ex*-son-in-law, for more details. As you said, it's none of my business."

"The last time I saw you — which should have been the last time I saw you — I said you wouldn't amount to anything. I don't care what you've done or what your job is. I was right to pull her away from you then, and if I wasn't sure you'd be gone soon, I'd do it again. You can't change what you come from. You're no good for her."

There was a time when those words would have made Theo react violently with either words or actions because he would have been afraid the person saying them was right. Today, he recognized them for what they were — the beliefs of one man who made a decision a long time ago and couldn't be swayed. It had nothing to do with Theo. It was a powerful realization and as Theo let it sink in, he watched Patrick grow uncomfortable with the silence.

After considering a dozen responses, Theo said, "Thank you for your time." When he got to the door, he stopped and turned around to add, "Personally, I don't think birth parents determine much about us. You are a hard ass and a bully, yet your daughter is one of the most loving and thoughtful people I've ever known. If you're right, she must get that from her mother."

Chapter Sixteen

♥

Theo spent Wednesday afternoon getting through to the rest of the people on the tenant's list and pacing around the station. He also did a lot of running his hands through his hair and pulling on it. When he was at Prometheus there was always something to do. If he wasn't part of an active case, he was supporting other staff members or working with attorneys and insurance companies to confirm their findings on other cases. And when he was at a location, he was part of a team with at least two other investigators and specialists. Here he was on his own.

Not that he needed help to sit around and do nothing, but the lack of progress and work was driving him crazy. There were only so many walks Harlow wanted to take. People kept dropping by the station claiming to need to file reports or pay tickets, but Theo knew it was to check him out. They'd be "surprised" to see him, then ask about his brothers, if he'd seen Eden, what he'd been doing, what kept him away. His jaw ached from tension, false smiles, and from having to say, "No, I don't know who is behind the fires" more times than he could count.

He was exhausted and pissed.

He didn't think he'd have this wrapped up in three days. He'd known before he arrived there wouldn't be enough evidence to point him clearly to a suspect and the lab results weren't in yet. But other than Patrick and

Keith, he didn't know where else to look. If he didn't catch the person responsible, he'd confirm to everyone he was the family screw up. Cole had his band. Nick had his finances. What did Theo ever do?

He should have told Martin to reach out to the State Fire Marshall and have them send someone to investigate.

But after the parade of people Theo saw today, he understood the reason Martin called him. Chances were the arsonist was someone Martin knew, and he wanted this handled as quietly as possible. This way, once the person was caught, it would be easier for people to move on. Martin loved this town and would do anything to protect it, just as he'd once protected Theo and Nick by becoming their legal guardian when their mother died, and Cole was already on the road.

And Theo would do anything to help Martin. Even visit the Varnum Bar and Grill with the volunteers, so when the next fire came, they worked well as a team.

Theo delayed leaving the station as long as he could, then brought Harlow over to stay with Martin and Millie. She could be on her own at the house, but she'd been with him and bored all day long and with the Duncan kids around, she'd have fun. One of them should have a good night.

The minute the dog saw Millie, she perked up, but when the kids stepped out onto the porch, she was through the rolled-down window like a shot. "Traitor," he said, although he'd stay there, too, if he didn't feel the need to conquer this old demon. Afraid he might not leave if he got comfortable, Theo waved to Millie and drove off.

His mouth went dry when he pulled into a parking spot at the Varnum. For a few minutes, he sat there staring at the building. He didn't love the house where he grew up, but he had some good times there with his brothers and Eden. He couldn't say the same about this place.

The bar hadn't changed. He was in seventh grade the first time he came here. It was the first time his mother didn't come home before Nick went to bed. Cole had been a sophomore in high school, and the Sinclairs had been in their lives for a little more than a year.

They'd ridden over on Cole's bike and found Susan nearly passed out. Rick, the bartender, had been preparing to call to see if anyone could get her before he got her a cab. That news would have spread through town in no time — Susan Hanson was finally too drunk to get herself home. Theo and Cole carried her to the car. They put the bike in the back and Cole, with only a learner's permit, drove them home. Technically, a licensed driver had been in the car with him. It had been awful. He hadn't seen the place since sometime early in his junior year since by then Susan stayed home to drink until she succumbed to a stroke a year later.

Sitting in the car wasn't going to change the past or make this easier, so Theo gave himself a mental shake and headed in. As his eyes adjusted to the yellow lights of the restaurant, he took in the old space. If anything had changed, other than an increase in the availability of alcoholic seltzers and a flat screen television, he couldn't see it. The bar was to one side, the open dining area to the other. Servers in tight black t-shirts brought food guaranteed to not be on your diet. He could picture his mother in her customary seat at the corner of the bar, hunched over a beer and a shot, both usually empty. Nothing there now but ghosts and memories.

"Theo, over here," Dylan called, and Theo turned to see five guys sitting around tables that had been pulled together. Everyone was facing the television — and him. As if being here wasn't odd enough, socializing with Dylan was going to take getting used to. Someone asked, "What are you drinking?" and for a moment he didn't know how to answer since his first thought was he wasn't old enough to drink.

You're thirty-one, not eighteen, Hanson. Martin was right. He would never be able to move forward unless he stopped looking back on the kid he'd been. He'd made it through a meeting with Patrick Barrett. He could get through this. The bar didn't have to change. He did.

He took a steadying breath and grabbed an empty chair. After ordering a beer along with a burger for himself and a bucket of wings for the table, he joined everyone in rooting for the Red Sox. He was relaxing and waiting for his food when a familiar voice caused the hair on his neck to stand up.

"What a surprise. Figures once a Hanson was in town, you'd find him here. How many of those empties are yours, Hanson? Planning to close the place down like your mom?"

His reaction to the voice must have been visual because suddenly all eyes at the table were on him and then looking past his shoulder to the person talking. The universe had a sense of humor and wanted Theo to see Keith before their appointment. He wasn't looking forward to it, but at least he would have been prepared. Now, and especially in this setting, he felt off-kilter. But he wasn't going to let Keith know.

He stood to face Keith and took in a quick appraisal of the former high school football hero and Eden's ex. Time hadn't been good to Keith. He looked heavier both in body and mind with his stomach showing the beginnings of a paunch and the exhaustion in his eyes noticeable even in the dim light. Theo didn't envy anyone working for Barrett, but he figured Keith deserved any agony that came his way. Theo had trouble imagining Eden married to this guy, but he wasn't going to hold her past choices against her. No one knew better than he did how unfair that was.

Keith took a step closer to him and said loudly. "Are you as good at holding your liquor as your mom? I'll bet your time in the army taught you a thing or two even she didn't. You're lucky they took you. Didn't you once have to repeat a grade?"

Theo could hardly believe Keith was bringing this up. A severe case of pneumonia kept him home for almost a full school year, so he repeated seventh grade. Theo and Keith had been in the same classes before that. The back of his neck got hot as he wondered how much the guys at the table could hear. He raised his chin and slowed his breathing. "That's the best you've got?"

Keith gave a dismissive flick with the back of his hand. "I know bad apples don't fall far from rotten trees."

Theo glanced over his shoulder to see everyone at his table watching them. He turned back to Keith. "And I know no amount of dredging up history or pretending to live there will get you Eden back." Okay, low blow, and he probably shouldn't have gone there, but since Keith was trying to hit him in the soft spots, Theo didn't see any reason not to return the favor.

"Don't you dare mention my wife." The guys definitely heard that.

"Ex-wife," Theo said. Keith's nostrils flared. If the place were brighter, Theo was certain he'd see the man's face had gone red. "What's the matter, Peters? My past is fair game, but yours isn't?"

"I've got nothing to be ashamed of. My dad stuck around, and my mother was a fine woman."

"Which makes the fact you turned out to be such a shit so much harder to understand."

Keith stood taller and changed tactics. "Perfectly understandable why you'd never want to show your face in this town again. Last time you were here, didn't Patrick Barrett run you off?"

It wasn't exactly true, but it was close enough. Theo's muscles tightened. The urge to clench his jaw and fists was overwhelming, but he kept his face and body neutral using everything he'd learned about staying calm under pressure. He could be as angry as he wanted as long as it didn't show. "At least the best part of my life didn't happen before I turned twenty."

"Keith, are you joining us or not?" Keith waved to the person who spoke without taking his eyes off Theo. *Good, he's on edge*, Theo thought. The knowledge helped bring his heart rate down a beat. "This isn't over, Hanson."

"If there's something more you need to say, I'm sure you'll tell me. Unless, of course, you have to get Mr. Barrett's permission first. Wouldn't want to do anything to piss off your boss now that you're no longer his son-in-law."

Theo took pleasure in the scowl Keith couldn't hide. He'd found a soft spot. Keith looked as if was about to say something else, then squinted at the men Theo was sitting with and backed off. Theo should have let Keith go, but as he turned away, Theo called out louder than necessary, "Don't forget our appointment tomorrow to talk about your involvement with these fires. I appreciate your cooperation with the investigation."

Keith stopped. Theo braced himself for the scathing retort, but the man took a breath then kept walking. Theo may have gotten in the last word, but by not saying anything, Keith had come out on top.

Theo sat down heavily and took a long drink of his beer. The exchange had been pointless and frustrating. It was as if the years had peeled back, and every fighting instinct Theo had honed came roaring out. There was a moment Theo hoped Keith would take a swing at him so Theo could slug him. It would have felt great, but solved nothing.

There was silence at the table until John asked, "What was that about?"

"Old news," and "Before your time," Dylan and a few of the other volunteers chimed in. It was good to remember not everyone knew his past — or cared.

Theo was grateful for their understanding and tact, but decided he wasn't going to avoid talking about what happened. It didn't change anything. "My mom was the town drunk when I was growing up, and back in high school I dated the woman Keith married. She also divorced him, which I know is bugging the shit out of him. I shouldn't have let him get to me, but old habits die hard."

Once he spoke the situation as simple truth, not as something needing to be defended or his fault, the tightness in his chest eased. Drinking was his mother's choice, leaving was his father's. Their problems, their decisions. He had made different choices and could make different ones now. Theo could picture Martin's smile.

As if to emphasize his thoughts, John said, "Jeez, what a jerk. Like we all didn't fuck up as kids or think our folks were idiots. He could never do what you do, Theo. Clearly, the guy can't deal with anyone being successful if it's not him."

He smiled at John and clicked bottles with him in acknowledgment. As he drank, Theo let the' words sink in. Keith's comments still rattled, but he was a little steadier. "Next round, I'm buying," he said.

Theo's time with the volunteers was fun, more enjoyable than he expected. He'd had a good time and a conversation about the military with Dylan, but the longer he stayed at the bar, the more memories filled his thoughts. Most of the group was still there when he said his goodbyes.

He got into his truck and headed to the Sinclair's to get Harlow, then changed his mind. He was restless and needed a way to get rid of the building aggravation. He made a three-point turn and changed directions.

There were a good number of cars in the parking lot at Maximum Results, even though it was nearly eight. He didn't mean to, but he looked for Eden's Mini Cooper. He didn't find it, but given how small it was and how large some vehicles people drove were, his included, he wasn't surprised. Besides, he didn't come here to see her.

He rolled his eyes at the lie.

He pulled a t-shirt and a pair of joggers out of a duffle he kept in the car because walking through fire sites was messy work and headed in. At the front desk, he bought a visitor's pass which would allow him to use the gym equipment, then went to change. A woman called to him as he got to the locker room. "Hey, handsome. Don't look like you need a workout to me."

"Rosie, you gorgeous creature, what are you doing here?" he said, bending to give her a quick kiss on the cheek.

"Darlin', how do you think I keep up my energy and my girlish figure?" She bumped him with her hip, knocking gently into him.

"I figured you let Helen chase you around her work-space a couple of times a day." Besides running and teaching at the Artist's Coop, Rosie's wife created over-sized paintings and sculptures in her garage studio next to their multicolored Victorian house.

"Yes, that too, but a woman needs a little downtime. Your Eden is around somewhere. She led our yoga class."

"She's not my..."

"Oh, yes, she is," Rosie interrupted. "Once you accept what you want, you'll see I'm right." With a wave of her hand, she breezed out before he could say anything.

Her words stayed in his head as he changed. When he got to town, all he wanted was to solve this case for Martin and get back to the life he'd built in Baltimore. Less than an hour ago, what he wanted most was to meet Keith in the parking lot and beat the hell out of him. How was he supposed to know what he wanted? He couldn't even come up with a solid lead on a small-town arsonist.

He headed to the free weight section where he stretched before doing basic upper body lifts. He switched between lighter weights and higher repetitions and heavier weights with fewer reps. By the time he moved to the barbells, he'd worked up a sweat, but still hadn't worked out his aggravation toward Keith and his questions about Eden. Maybe he needed a punching bag. Or heavier weights. He loaded up a bar and lay back to do some slow bench presses.

When he reached for the bar, Eden was smiling down at him. "Need a spotter?" She got into position, standing by his head. Damn, she looked hot in a white tank top and light blue leggings, which was not what he needed right now.

"This habit we have of surprising each other needs to stop," he said. "You shouldn't sneak up on a man who's raising nearly two hundred pounds over his head."

"Don't you remember? It was my turn for sneaking. Are you ready?"

"I don't need any help. I can do this on my own." It came out harsh, but he meant it. On his own was how he did things best.

"Just because you can, doesn't mean you have to."

"No, but it might mean I want to. If you'd go back to whatever you were doing before and leave me in peace, I'd appreciate it."

"What's wrong?"

He sat up and looked at her. "Nothing, okay. Everything is absolutely great. I'm exactly where I want to be doing exactly what I want to be doing. Can't you tell? This case has been the easiest of my career. I'm only moments away from figuring out who's been setting these damn fires, and when I do, I'll make Martin proud and glad he called me."

"Of course you will and, of course, he'll be proud. He always is. And maybe it won't be 'any minute' but you'll find who's behind this."

"What makes you say that?"

"What do you mean?" She looked puzzled.

"What proof have I ever given you or Martin that I can be successful? Martin has the blind confidence of a loving parent, and you haven't seen me in over a decade.

Any minute I could decide all of this is too hard and leave like my father did." A voice in his head said shut up, but once the rant started, he couldn't stop. He kept going, his voice getting louder, his tone more hostile. "But why would I want to solve the case so fast? Not when I can stay here where everyone is so happy I've returned. I can't image why I stayed away."

"Theo..."

"This place is everything I remembered and more. Everyone wants to know everyone else's business, and memories and the past are never forgotten. Have you ever considered maybe your father and everyone else are right about me?"

"First of all, outside of business, my father is almost never right. And second, who is this 'everyone' you're referring to?"

"I know what people think of me and my family."

"You know what *some* people *once* thought based on the limited information they had and their own narrow-minded filters. And, yes, people here have long memories, but there are plenty of people who have good memories of and with you."

"Yeah, right."

"I don't know what got you into this mood, but you will not yell at me since I have nothing to do with it."

"Which is why I asked you to leave in the first place."

This time, she didn't argue. Instead of going back to lifting, Theo watched in the mirror as she walked away. Her head was high and her stride purposeful, but he knew if he saw her face, he'd see her distressed.

Damn, he should have kept his mouth shut. Should have let her help him and hoped by the time he was done, this lousy mood would have passed. Better, he should have gone to the house, shut himself in his room and been alone with Harlow where he couldn't see anyone. Hurt anyone.

Hurt Eden.

He was an idiot. He tried to continue his workout but minutes later he put the barbells back with a bang, which earned him a look from one of the other patrons. Yeah, he was doing a lot of things wrong tonight. At least there was one he could correct immediately. He was not letting Eden go to bed thinking he was an asshole.

He was delayed at the Sinclair's by two kids who didn't want to give up their new pet. Since he needed to talk to Grace Duncan about the fire, he agreed to come over for dinner the next night and bring Harlow with him.

When he walked into the house a few minutes later, Eden was in the kitchen eating a brownie from the night before. He took off his work boots and went directly to her, taking her hands in his. "I'm sorry. Especially for yelling. I know you hate it. You didn't deserve it. You were the first person to get in the line of fire." She handed him a brownie. "A peace offering?"

"Can you think of a better one?" He could, but now wasn't the time.

"Do you want to tell me what's going on?"

"It's been a rough day."

She put a hand on his chest. "I figured."

"It started with an interview with your father and didn't get better. I sat at the station for hours looking at pictures, writing questions, talking with people who had offices in the third building, and not getting any closer to figuring this out."

"Do these things usually get solved quickly?"

He ran his hands through his hair before answering. "No, not serial arson. It's generally — and unfortunately — a slow process, and I'm worried on two fronts. One, someone else is going to get hurt when the next fire happens — which it will. And two, the arsonist is going to go bigger the next time. Arsonists tend to escalate. I need more information and damned if the only way to get it is another fire." She handed him a bottle of water he hadn't noticed her get. He opened it and took a swig. "This sucks."

"So, my father pissed you off — he's good at that and you expected it — and the case is moving slowly, which you also expected. I'm guessing there's more."

"I had dinner tonight with some of the volunteers at the Varnum."

Her eyebrows shot up so fast he laughed. "You went there? Willingly?"

"It gets better. I ran into Keith."

She gave him a quizzical look. "Define run in."

"Words were exchanged, insults thrown. General male stupidity. He brought up my family. I brought up you. We didn't take out rulers and measure, but it wasn't far off."

"And when all was said and done?"

"I felt as though I was eighteen again with a lifetime of proving myself to people still in front of me. Real mature, right?"

Eden shrugged. "I don't think it has anything to do with maturity. It has to do with where we hurt, what upsets us. It doesn't matter how much time has passed. The wrong comment at the wrong time can hurt like hell. All someone has to do is make a passing comment about remembering me dance, and isn't it a shame about the accident, and I'm back in the hospital bed finding out my dream is over." She stepped closer to him and put her hands on his chest. "You have nothing to prove to anyone, Theo. Certainly not to Keith. And never to me. I've always known how great you are."

The heat of her hand seeped through his t-shirt and warmed him, as did her words. "When did you get so smart?"

She smiled up at him. "Therapy helped, and experience is such a wonderful teacher, isn't she?"

"She's a bitch, but one thing *I* am smarter about is not running away from tough or uncomfortable situations. I'm sorry."

"Guess we both grew up. I was waiting here for the same reason. I thought of going to my room, not talking to you tonight, but I knew that wouldn't be good for either of us. You're not here long, and it's not worth letting a misunderstanding ruin whatever time we have."

"So smart." He opened his arms, and she stepped into his embrace. As he held her close, he took his first easy breath since that morning. It would have been better if she hadn't had to see him in this mood, but the fact it didn't make her pull away went a long way to healing old wounds.

"There is something you should know about Keith," she said, her head against his chest.

He pulled back to look at her. "What's that?"

"If you had taken out the rulers? You'd win. No contest."

He laughed out loud both at her candor and the information. And then he couldn't resist, didn't want to. He leaned down and kissed her passionately. Her immediate sigh of pleasure was all the encouragement he needed.

When he decided to apologize, he imagined a short, brusque conversation and a quick goodnight. He didn't expect her compassion and humor would relax him and touch his heart. She reawakened everything he once felt for her by the way she opened him up.

And with her kisses.

The feel of her lips, the play of her tongue against his. The way her hands moved from his cheek to his shoulder and then to his back as she pressed against him. There was nothing like kissing Eden. There never had been, and he accepted that there never would be. But since this couldn't last, he would do what he could to memorize everything about her so he could take it with him.

He moved his mouth to her jaw, her neck, and worked his way to her ear, nibbling and licking, loving how she shivered. He ached for her. "Come to my room," he whispered in her ear. "I have to touch you. I want you in my bed."

Chapter Seventeen

♥

For the briefest of moments, she hesitated. She and Theo had sex once– on their high school graduation weekend, ironically in the room where she was staying. Since then, she'd only been with Keith, and she could never please him. What if she couldn't please Theo?

"I'm aching to touch you everywhere," he said, kissing a sensitive spot behind her ear. She shivered with pleasure and with awareness of his desire. No, this would be nothing like being with Keith.

He pulled her to him, grabbed her hips, and lifted her easily off her feet. She wrapped her legs around his waist as he walked them to the bedroom. "You are so light, so fun to carry." He put her on the bed, then turned and let her go to on the nightstand light.

"Concerned you may lose me in the pillows because I'm so skinny?" Damn, old fears were slipping out. She needed to control them.

"Never, why would you ask...?" He must have seen something in her eyes, because he said, "Someone else made that comment. Someone suggested you were too thin." She knew he was avoiding saying the name.

"Yes," she whispered, glad she didn't need to explain. Keith used to tell her there was hardly anything to screw. It made her want to disappear. It wasn't long before sex was something she worried about rather than looked forward to.

As he moved them both to the center of the bed, he said, "You are," he kissed her neck, "and always have been," he kissed her jaw, "beautiful and desirable to me." With each word, he peppered her skin with kisses, giving her goosebumps. "Let me show you," he whispered, staring into her eyes. And with a deep kiss on her lips, her fear disappeared — as did every thought of her ex-husband.

Eden arched up, pressing her chest into his, and loving the heat of his body against her. She could feel the obvious sign of his arousal against her hip and loved that he wanted her so badly. She ran her hands through his hair and over the back of his neck as their kisses heated, tongues and lips exploring, enjoying.

She wanted more, and she pulled at his shirt to free it from his pants. When he figured out what she was doing, he sat back, took it off himself. The PT and the woman inside of her both admired his body. His pecs and abs were more defined than they were when he was a teen. She ran her fingers through the hair on his chest, then down to where it disappeared into his pants, noticing small scars that weren't there the last time she saw his skin. Some things had changed. Some things hadn't.

"Your turn," he said, leaning back far enough to find the edge of her top, then worked it up and over her head before tossing it to the floor.

As he traced the lace cup on her bra, she was glad she'd taken the time to change out of her sports bra before coming home. "Very sexy," he said as he licked her skin at the edges of the cup's material, then undid the front clasp. "And I like how easily these open."

He slipped the straps off her shoulders, bearing her to his touch, then sucked a nipple deep into his mouth. She moaned as his hand played with her breast. The warmth, the sensations. Having him close. She called out his name as she ran her hands over his shoulders, encouraging him, bringing him closer.

Her hands roamed his body with growing need, and when she got to his ass, she said, "Too. Many. Clothes."

"Good point," he said, releasing her breasts.

She didn't want him to stop, but being naked was more important. He stood and kicked off his shoes. She slipped off her leggings and underwear, not able to take her eyes off his as his clothes joined hers in the growing pile on the floor. The moment his last sock was off, she reached for his hand and pulled him onto the bed. "That took too long."

"You're so greedy," he said with a throaty chuckle.

"Yes, I am," she said unapologetically. "For you. For this." She kissed him deeply and wrapped her hand around his hardness. Now it was his turn to moan. She loved how it sounded, how she had the power to please him.

The last time they'd been together they'd been young, naïve and believed they had forever. Tonight there was need and years of fantasies. She was going to live out as many as she could and enjoy it all.

His body was muscular, thrilling. With a professional's understanding, she appreciated the muscles in his arms, back, and legs. With a woman's desire, she reveled in the feel of him under her fingers as she discovered and rediscovered what pleased him, what made him catch his breath, what made him lean into her.

As her hands explored his body, he reached between her legs to tease her. He broke their kiss to say, "You're so wet. So ready." His fingers stroked her swollen entrance, and he slipped first one and then two fingers inside of her. She arched her back and gasped at the pleasure, digging her fingers into his shoulders. He covered her mouth in a searing kiss.

God, how she ached. Her body was ablaze, and she couldn't wait. They'd waited long enough. There would be a time, she hoped, to enjoy him slowly, but not tonight. As he continued to stroke and tease her, she said, "Please tell me there are condoms nearby."

"Good question. Don't go anywhere," he said.

"I don't intend to."

He slipped off the bed and hurried to the bathroom. The view of his naked ass was tantalizing, almost worth the pause. She heard the medicine cabinet open and close, then drawers. "Found some," he called and walked back in holding a strip.

"Planning a long night?" She couldn't help but tease. With Theo, being playful came easily. She never had to worry about saying the wrong thing, and after their discussion tonight she knew even if she did, they could talk it through. It wouldn't become a win-lose battle like it did with Keith.

He put the condoms on the night table, got back into bed with her, and said, "Planning a wonderful night. Come back here." She moved into his arms again as they resumed touching and tempting each other. "I want more."

She wasn't certain what he meant until his kisses moved down her body, first to her breasts, then lower to her stomach and lower still, until his mouth joined his fingers in an explosion of ecstasy that had her crying out and clawing at the sheets.

Eden remembered the first time he'd kissed her there. She'd heard about oral sex — wondered if Theo would ever pressure her for a blow job the way she heard other girls talk. Instead, he went down on her first. She'd been embarrassed and nervous until excitement made those concerns irrelevant, and her body reacted completely and without control.

Nothing had changed. Theo's touch was magic, igniting her from within.

His tongue stroked her outer lips as his fingers continued to slide in and out of her slick pussy. The combination was exquisite. The pleasure may have been focused between her legs, but the sensations traveled through-out her body. She tingled everywhere and craved more.

When he focused his attention on her clitoris, her hips rose as she offered herself to him, and she threaded her hands in his hair. He moaned at her touch and slid a hand under her ass as if to make certain he could feast on her the way he wanted. She felt devoured. Taken. Wanted.

It was an intoxicating combination, to be naked and open in the arms of the man she'd never stopped fanta-sizing about and knowing he wanted her as much as she wanted him. She hoped he could tell the same was true for her.

Years of longing unfolded in an orgasm that hit her so quickly she thought she might stop breathing. And didn't care if she did. She called out his name as she came, her back arching off the bed, his hands gripping her hips, not losing contact.

While her body continued to shudder, his kisses moved to her inner thighs, then her stomach. When he pulled away, she nearly protested until she heard the condom wrapper ripping. Eden watched as he sheathed himself, then moved between her legs.

He paused and looked into her eyes. He wanted her consent. His consideration made her heart swell. More certain than she'd been about anything in years, she reached between them and guided him inside her.

Her body stretched to accommodate him — it had been so long, and she hadn't been kidding about the ruler comment — and she lifted her hips to ease him deeper inside.

"Eden, my Eden." His voice was hoarse with need. It thrilled her.

As they moved together, she couldn't tell where her desire ended and his began. It was as if they fed off one another. They each gave; they each took. And the sensations they created were beyond every fantasy she'd ever had. Nothing compared to the reality. She couldn't touch him enough, couldn't be touched enough. Her hands moved over his chest then down his back. His fingers stroked her breasts, teased her nipples. They kissed feverishly, gasping. She didn't know how long it was before another orgasm built.

"Please, I'm close," she said, barely recognizing her voice.

"I am, too," he said. She loved how breathless he sounded.

He inched back and before she could protest, he brought his hand between them to find her swollen clitoris. He used her wetness to stroke her, intensifying the experience as he drove his length into her, filling her deeply.

It was all she needed. Her second climax overtook her body, and she dug her nails into his shoulders. She screamed his name as they rode each other into wave after wave of bliss. He caught her next moan with his kiss. Never had she felt as connected to someone. He shuddered with his orgasm, calling out her name again, and she reveled in the knowledge she'd given him that pleasure.

As her orgasm ebbed, she wondered vaguely if her nails left marks on his skin and decided it didn't matter. They lay there in silence, their heavy breathing the only sound in the room. She loved the weight of him on top of her, the way he stayed inside of her.

"That was," he started. "You were...."

"Absolutely." She was having a little trouble thinking coherently herself, let alone speaking. His hand came under her chin, and he lifted her face to his. Then he kissed her so tenderly it nearly brought tears to her eyes. She stroked the side of his face, tracing the edges of his jaw, looking into his fathomless blue eyes, and feeling as though she could fly. Rediscovering her passion was wonderful. Discovering someone could desire her the way Theo did? For that, she had no words.

They said nothing for the next few minutes, simply lay there kissing and touching. He caressed her skin, letting his hands go where they wanted, and she did the same. Eden allowed herself to be happily lost in her thoughts and emotions, not letting them scare or overwhelm her. It didn't matter what happened before or next. Tonight was perfect, and she would remember it always.

Eventually, he rolled to the side, bringing her with him. "I'm going to crush you if I stay in this position too much longer."

"What a way to go."

"But difficult to explain to the authorities. I also don't want to hurt your leg." His fingers traced the scars around her knee. "We almost match."

"I don't wear shorts or short skirts anymore because of it."

"Too bad, you have great legs."

"This — what we did — wasn't a strain for you, was it? I'm not the only one with an injured leg, and yours is more recent than mine."

"This was a lot of things, but a strain wasn't one of them." He pulled her closer, and she snuggled into him, putting her head on his chest, and breathing in the scent of his skin, hoping she could always remember it. "I love how responsive you are."

It wasn't how she'd describe herself for recently, but tonight she believed it. It was an enticing thought. "I think my ears are ringing."

He laughed and kissed the top of her head. "God, you feel good."

"At the moment I feel great, thank you very much."

"You're welcome?"

It was her turn to laugh. The sex was intense, their renewed connection was wonderful, and that was all she needed. She wasn't going to think about what the future held. To push the worry away, she moved up and kissed him, loving how he reacted by wrapping his leg around her. For now she would stay in the moment and let what was coming work itself out.

Chapter Eighteen

W hen Theo woke and realized Eden was next to him, he had a moment of panic, followed by relief. He hadn't had a nightmare and hurt her. It was a small miracle, and he was grateful for it. Grateful for the night which preceded it, too. They'd lost their virginity to each other in this house. That had been a perfect night, even if everything had gone to hell soon after. But last night was better. He put his arm over her shoulder and kissed her forehead.

"Good morning," she mumbled.

"I didn't mean to wake you. Should I get coffee?"

"Want something else more."

He smiled, drew her close, and gave her what she wanted. What he wanted as well.

An hour later, they made it out of bed and to the coffee. When he got to his truck after kissing her goodbye, he thought it was the best way he'd started a day in years. He could get used to it.

He shouldn't get used to it.

Theo couldn't ignore all she was stirring up in him, emotionally and physically, but he couldn't let himself get carried away. *You're no good for her*, a voice in his head told him. More voices followed. *You're a rebound from her marriage. She needs more than you can give her or anyone. She doesn't need a man who could hit her in her sleep. This is only for now.*

Was sex with Eden a mistake or the best thing that had ever happened to him? Probably both. Every moment had been wonderful, more amazing than anything he remembered or thought possible. But, God, it confused things.

He took Harlow for a walk by the river behind the Kinsman Diner, then got a breakfast sandwich and coffee to go. While waiting for his order, he chatted with Rosie's wife, who was sitting at the counter. Helen and Rosie had been together almost as long as Martin and Millie. They'd gotten married the Valentine's Day after same-sex marriage was legalized in New Hampshire. They were one thing he hoped never changed.

Food in hand, he headed to the station and jumped on Prometheus' Zoom staff meeting. Because the company had offices in Atlanta and Chicago and investigators on active sites around the country, biweekly staff meetings were held virtually. Sometimes Theo found them a waste of time, but today he was glad to see people outside Fable Notch, to contribute where he could, and to commiserate on the slow process of apprehending an arsonist.

Theo must have been more energized than usual because Oscar Stanley, the Baltimore Senior Partner, commented, "Even with the frustration of a short suspect list and not enough evidence, it sounds like you're in a good mood. New England agrees with you."

Eden agreed with him. There was a difference. "It's weird being back, but I'm trying to help."

"Do you expect the next fire soon?"

"In the next day or so," Theo said, and his breakfast sat like a lump in his stomach. Unless something happened to the arsonist, it was coming. "This part never gets easier."

There were nods of understanding in all the Zoom boxes. "Hopefully, you'll get what you need. You know, we've thought of opening a branch in the northeast. Interested?"

Theo laughed instead of answering. He didn't know why "no way" didn't roll off his tongue the way it would have a week ago. Sex was making him stupid.

The call broke up a few minutes later. Theo had enough time before leaving for his meeting with Keith to call Adam and suggest they have lunch together. He needed something to look forward to. When Adam suggested the Just Right Café, Theo said, "Another business with a cute name."

"Hey, easy on the sarcasm. I resemble that remark. Besides, the woman who runs it has the last name Behr, so it's appropriate."

"Does she have golden locks?"

"Very funny."

"Sorry, I've got a meeting with Keith Peters in an hour and I'm on edge." *And I slept with Eden last night.* Yeah, he wasn't ready to say that out loud.

"Maybe we should find a place serving alcohol. Wanna meet at Seven Brothers?"

"No, we can go there another time. And I don't think it's a good idea for anyone in this town to see me drinking in the middle of the day." There was a pause, and Theo knew Adam was going to make a supportive or kind remark. Before he could, Theo said, "Where's the cafe? Is it a cabin in the woods?"

"More jokes. It's on Main Street across from my place. Great sandwiches and dog friendly."

"Sounds good. Will 12:30 work?"

"You'll be done that fast?"

"Do you really think Keith and I are going to spend a lot of time talking?"

"Good point. 12:30 it is. See you then."

Once again, he and Harlow arrived early for their appointment. Keith's office was in the same building as Patrick's, but on a lower floor. Theo knew this was Barrett's way of keeping the other man in place. The waiting area was less expensive looking, but equally stark. Would Keith be willing to set the fires to move up a floor?

Especially since he'd lost the leverage of being married to the boss's daughter. It was something to consider.

The receptionist showed Theo to Keith's office a few minutes after the appointment was scheduled to start. Keith wasted no time letting Theo know where he stood. "This is a waste of time. There's nothing I can do to help you."

Oh yeah, this was going to go well. "Great, now that we've gotten that out of the way, do you mean nothing you can do or nothing you will do?" Theo said, sitting without being asked, as he had with Patrick. As he opened the notes app on his tablet, he released Harlow, who walked to Keith and circled him, giving him the canine once over.

"What the hell is this dog doing here? Get him away from me."

"I'm sure you've heard about Harlow around town." He wanted Keith to know he was a suspect. It would be interesting to see the man's reaction. "She's learning your scent, so she'll be able to detect it at the fire sites or to see if there's any lingering accelerant on you. I'm guessing she'll recognize something since you have a connection to all the fires."

"What are you talking about? I have no connection to them."

"Not true. Several months ago, you bid on the Northcott Estate, the first fire site. Your association to the second site is through Eden, and you work under Patrick, who owns the third site, and he tells me you manage that property." He used the word 'under' deliberately and was pleased when Keith scowled. "What I want to know is if you're the reason these buildings are being destroyed."

"Why would I want to destroy the Northcott place? I pulled my bid because I decided on a different investment."

"That's not what my sources say. My understanding is your bid was turned down by the owners for being insultingly low. However, a pile of ash is something the owners are more likely to want to get rid of cheaply. Were you trying to acquire it for Barrett?"

"No. He has no idea I made the offer." Keith sat up straighter with the admission. Theo could see it wasn't something he talk about.

"So this was something you did without telling your boss?"

"There isn't anything to tell," Keith said, clearly trying to decide how to proceed. "It's been for sale for years, and I was considering buying it to demolish the carriage house and possibly the main house to build something new. There's a lot of under-used land on the site. It was a good investment. I made a bid for what I thought it was worth. The owners disagreed."

"That's all?"

"Yes, and I have nothing more to say on the subject."

Theo made a note on his tablet. Time for a new tactic. "So who do you think would want to hurt Eden or Patrick, or both?"

"No one. Why? You think they're the targets?"

"It's possible." Theo wasn't sure how much to say. If Keith was the arsonist, Theo didn't want to offer anything that might make Keith change plans for the next site. "We always look at who was affected by a fire when we look for suspects."

"I can't imagine anyone having a grudge against Eden. As for someone who might harbor ill feelings towards Mr. Barrett, all I can say is there are always people who resent the success of others."

Including you? Theo said nothing, but he wondered. "So you have no idea who might be behind these fires."

"Absolutely not. Besides, I'm not convinced there's anything suspicious happening in the first place. Sure, you've found a flimsy connection between the properties and the three of us and, yes, the town has never had so many fires in such a short period, but..." Keith's voice trailed off. as if he heard what he was saying and realized how it sounded. He finished quietly, "It might not be arson."

"Since I'm the expert, why don't you let me decide?"

A knock at the door had both men turning as a woman of medium build with brightly dyed blond hair entered before she was invited. She looked familiar, but Theo couldn't place her. All he could think was her smile was too bright, her skirt too short, and her makeup too heavy. He preferred a more natural look. And leggings with a tank top.

Stop. This was not the time to think about Eden.

"Hi, Keith, I came by to review the... Oh, I didn't know you were in a meeting. Your secretary wasn't at her desk." Theo couldn't explain why, but he didn't believe her.

"Monica, you may remember Theo Hanson. He's here at Martin Sinclair's invitation to investigate the fires we've been having."

"Hi, I'm Monica Russo," she said, holding out her hand. "I remember you, but you would have known me as Monica Gibson."

"Hello," Theo said. He vaguely remembered the former head cheerleader, but what struck him was that this was the other woman in the car when Eden had her accident.

Harlow, who had perked up at the arrival of someone new, walked over. Monica bent over to pet her. "And what a cute dog. You'll find lots of friends in this town." Theo noticed she didn't suggest *he* would be welcome in Fable Notch. Harlow gave a short bark, startling Monica. She stood up and fixed her hair, which hadn't moved. "I don't mean to interrupt, but Keith, I'd appreciate your input on some new properties I'm showing." She turned to explain to Theo, "I sell and rent residential real estate, and sometimes we exchange leads to help each other. Keith, I can leave these for you and come back later. Nice to see you again, Theo," she said, giving a little waggle of her fingers as she left.

"Likewise," he said automatically. He could have sworn he saw something pass between her and Keith, but he let it go. If Keith was seeing someone else, it was better for Eden.

"So, Keith, nothing to confess?" Theo asked once they were alone again.

"You wish. You'd like nothing better than to create trouble for me and Eden."

"There is no you and Eden. Your divorce was final weeks ago." Before Keith could answer, Theo stood to leave. "Since you apparently know nothing, I'll be going too, but this doesn't mean you're off the hook. I'll find out if you're hiding anything."

"There's nothing to find. You and your dog can go," Keith said. Theo walked to the door waiting for the final remark. He had his hand on the doorknob when Keith called, "One more thing, Hanson. Stay away from her."

He had a sense of déjà vu. He had no more intention of listening to Keith than he did Patrick. Theo turned and looked at the man who made Eden feel less desirable, less capable, and all he wanted to do was punch him. Unfortunately, he'd regret it the moment he acted. It wasn't worth it. Thinking about it was nice though. Instead, he answered, "You should know better than to say that to me. I don't exactly have a reputation for doing what I'm told."

Chapter Nineteen

♥

Five days. Theo had been back less than five days, and Eden's emotions were turned upside down. Eden admitted she was both shocked and thrilled by how fast everything happened. How emotions she'd thought locked away were as strong as before. How desires she'd thought forgotten came rushing back.

Last night had been beyond wonderful. In the days since she'd first seen Theo, she'd imagined what it might be like to be in bed with him. And when they'd kissed last night, she knew where it would lead. She didn't know which was better — how much he excited her or how much he wanted her. Both were exhilarating. His obvious pleasure was a balm to years of Keith's near indifference. Eden didn't admit it until she'd decided to leave him, but Keith had never wanted her, in bed or out. He wanted proximity and access to her father.

With Theo, *she* was his focus — in bed and out.

Maybe she shouldn't be surprised by the speed things were moving. They were living under the same roof, and it wouldn't be long before he was gone again. She wasn't going to kid herself. If it weren't for Martin's injury, Theo never would have returned. No matter how she cared, no matter what happened between them, she wouldn't hold him somewhere he didn't want to be. She knew what that was like. She would enjoy what they had as long as she could.

And hopefully it would include more nights like last night.

She couldn't say she'd slept well. It had been almost a year since she'd shared a bed with anyone, so she woke several times during the night. She'd been tired today, but she had no complaints. Having Theo nearby all night had been its own kind of wonderful. She'd slid closer to him, not touching because she didn't want to wake him, then match her breathing to his, falling back to sleep easily.

She was already looking forward to seeing him tonight. He mentioned he was going to the Sinclairs for dinner to let the Duncan kids have more time with Harlow and to find out if Grace remembered anything about the fire in the apartments. He invited Eden to join him, but she had a full day of clients and classes that would have her busy until at least eight.

After her morning PT clients, Eden had some free time, and she had two errands high on her priority list. First, she made a quick trip to the bank to retrieve the ballet slippers charm from her safe deposit box, then went to Prince's Jewelers. As a child, she thought it was called Princess Jewelers, not knowing it was the last name of the owners. A bell tinkled sweetly as she went in and was greeted almost immediately by Beverly Prince, who ran the shop with her husband. Eden never shopped here, but Beverly had slipped on ice last winter and had come to Eden for several weeks for the torn Achilles tendon in her ankle.

"Eden, my sweet. What can I do for you today?"

"I have a charm I'd like to put on a bracelet," she said, placing both of them on the counter. "Can you help, Mrs. Prince?"

"Beverly, dear, and of course I can." She picked up the bracelet and held it as though she knew it was precious. "I haven't seen a bracelet like this in ages. Most people like those bead ones nowadays. Is this the one your mother gave you?"

"How did you know?"

"Where do you think she bought it?"

"I never considered it. All that mattered was that it was beautiful and grown up."

"Which is how she described you." Eden was moved by the woman's memory. "It won't take long to get this on. If you can wait a few minutes, I can do it for you now or you can come back to pick it up."

"I'll wait." She'd waited long enough.

"Feel free to look around and see if something catches your eye."

"Thank you," Eden said.

It would be wonderful to have Theo's charm back on the bracelet. After Theo left, she'd taken it off with an angry twist and gone to Silver Lake to toss it in, but as soon as she tried, the pain of loss overwhelmed her. Instead, she'd put it in a small box, hoping someday she'd be able to look at it without her heart aching. She'd peeked at it the day she put it in the bank vault, and not again until today. Now she'd be wearing it again. Even when he left, she knew she'd be able to look at the charm and feel love.

Wait? Love?

"Eden?" A familiar voice broke into her thoughts. "What are you doing here?"

She looked up to see Monica Russo coming over, arms open for a hug, which Eden barely had time to return uncomfortably before the other woman pulled away. "I'm having a piece of jewelry fixed. How about you?"

"Oh, I'm such a magpie. I love anything that sparkles, and whenever I'm about to close a big sale, I peek at what's here to find myself a little something as a reward. A girl can't have too much jewelry, right?"

"Of course." It was easier to agree than say she couldn't imagine why someone would need a lot of jewelry, but then noticing the earrings, necklace and wrist full of bracelets Monica wore, she could see it was the other woman's preference. Keith gave her jewelry when they were dating and proposed with a classic diamond engagement ring which impressed her father. After they were married, all his gifts were money tucked in a card. "Buy yourself whatever you want." He didn't know her well enough to know what she might like or care enough to find out. She'd buy a few books or a new sweater and put the rest in the bank. Ironically, five years of gifts supported her ability to leave him. These days, there were plenty of things she wanted. Dinners out with friends, furnishings for a new apartment, clothes she enjoyed wearing.

"How have you been since the fire?"

"Fine, thanks." She didn't have anything to say to Monica. They weren't friends, and had only hung out together because Monica's husband, Rob, was close to Keith. After Monica and Rob split two or three years ago, the weekly double dates ended, and Eden never saw Monica.

"I hear about you all the time from my niece, Courtney, and my sister. They've been worried about you."

Eden had forgotten that connection. Courtney was Eden's most promising student and the only one who took private lessons. "She's a lovely girl, and one of the best dancers I've even known."

"High praise coming from you. Weren't you almost a professional?" Eden remembered another reason she didn't stay in touch with Monica. Monica had a way of asking questions which made Eden either uncomfortable or defensive. It was like the former cheerleader never left her mean girl stage. Before Eden could respond, Monica was talking again. "I was at Keith's office dropping off some files a little while ago, and I saw Theo Hanson. I'd heard he was back in town because of the fires. Was he always this cute?"

"I thought so."

"No wonder you two were so hot and heavy back in high school. Have you seen him? Oh, what am I saying?

Of course you have. He'd need to talk to you about the fire. Must be odd to have him in town."

Eden was glad people didn't know she and Theo were living together. Monica was the type to spread gossip. "It was at first, but we got past it."

"Oh good. Now tell me, anything new happening there? Or perhaps something rekindled?" Monica blinked rapidly, as if to be flirty. Eden didn't usually have the urge to roll her eyes, but she did now. "With you and Keith being separated, there's no reason not to enjoy yourself."

"It's not that simple." Eden wanted this conversation over.

"No, of course it isn't. After all, he's not planning to stay."

Monica's blunt statement had a chilling effect. It was one thing to think about Theo leaving, another to hear someone else say it. "Not as far as I know," she confirmed, fiddling with the charm bracelet and willing Beverly to show up and end this conversation.

"And speaking of Keith, how are you doing without him? Must be hard to be on your own."

It was harder to be with him, she thought, but wouldn't share that with Monica. "I'm managing."

"If things heat up between you and Theo, you could always leave with him."

"Leave?"

"What's keeping you here? You and Keith are separated, and your job could be done anywhere. Patrick would miss you, naturally, but if you go with Theo, you'd have someone to take care of you, then you won't have to worry about making enough money from your little classes."

Someone to take care of her? Is that how people saw her? "What do you mean?"

"You've always had people to help you. Your dad has plenty of resources, which I'm sure made things easy, and Keith was there for you for years. If you and Theo get together, you won't need to be alone. I wish I was that lucky."

Eden didn't say anything. It wasn't the thought of leaving with Theo that bothered her; it was the worrisome truth to Monica's other comments. Whenever Eden was struggling, there was someone to catch her before she fell. It was one of her biggest fears since leaving Keith. Could she manage on her own? Her father had given her a place to land after her mother died and after the accident. Her marriage to Keith had never been what she'd hoped for, but in those early years it gave her security. And when her apartment burned down, the Sinclairs were there with help. Janelle and Dani, too. Was she capable of managing on her own?

"Eden?"

"I don't know," she said.

"You don't know what? Where did you go?"

Damn, she hadn't heard a word Monica had been saying. "Sorry, I've got a lot on my mind."

"No problem. Wasn't important. I need to be going. These houses aren't going to sell themselves. Good to see you."

"You too," Eden said. Monica waggled her fingers goodbye and left the store. Eden took a deep breath and let it out on a sigh. That was kind of awful.

"All set, Eden," said Beverly, reappearing at the perfect moment. Eden didn't want to think about Monica's words. "Let me help you put it on."

"I can do it myself." The woman pulled back, and Eden realized her tone was harsh. "I'm sorry, that was unnecessary."

"Are you okay?" Beverly looked concerned as Eden held out her wrist.

"Yes, thank you. Monica Russo stopped in. Some things she said bothered me."

"Oh, her," Beverly dropped her voice to a whisper, even though there was no one else in the store. "I don't much like her either. She comes in to look at engage-ment rings but never buys anything."

"Engagement rings?" Not the reason Monica gave for being in the store.

"Yes, for the last six months she's stopped by regularly. I keep expecting her to come in with her boyfriend, but no one yet." She shrugged. "Some women are hopeful long before the man knows what's happening."

"I suppose." Eden remembered more about the day she took off her engagement ring than the day Keith put it on. "What do I owe you?"

"For putting a charm on a tiny ring and hooking it onto your bracelet? Nothing, of course. It's my pleasure. It's a beautiful charm, well made and designed."

"Thank you. It was a gift."

"Clearly from someone who cares about you very much, yes?"

There was a period where she wouldn't have known how to answer, when the pain of the question would have brought tears to her eyes. Today the response was simple. "Yes," she said. "Yes, he does."

Chapter Twenty

♥

After leaving Keith's office, Theo took a drive with Harlow, enjoying being close to the mountains. Whatever mixed opinions Theo had about this area, the setting was beautiful. He'd done a lot of traveling since leaving and there was no place quite like New Hampshire's White Mountains.

When he came back to the center of town, he had no trouble finding a place to park since it was Thursday afternoon, and the weekenders hadn't arrived yet. As he and Harlow walked through the downtown area, Theo noticed both the changes and the places that remained. A Thousand Lives Bookstore was new. He saw the sign for Lloyd's accounting business.

Not every business on the main street had a cute name, Adam was right, but plenty did. If it helped bring in customers, who was he to criticize? And unlike living in a city, many of the places had out bowls of water for dogs. Harlow got lots of attention from people they passed, and a peanut butter dog biscuit from a specialty store called Significant Paws. Some folks looked famil-iar, but it had been so long since he'd been here, he couldn't be sure. The wife of one volunteer introduced herself and thanked him for coming to help, but he was waiting for someone to recognize him and make a nasty crack. All these feeling had him on edge.

Feelings about Eden. Feelings about Fable Notch. This was more than he expected. Life in Baltimore was simpler. Go to work, hang with coworkers he considered friends after hours, quiet nights at home. He laughed to himself. Wasn't that what he'd complained about here? There was nothing to do but the same things with the same people. He'd gotten away but ended up creating a similar life. It wasn't like he took advantage of city living other than going to an Orioles game occasionally. He might have to change things when he went back, although he couldn't imagine what that might mean.

Adam waited on the bench outside Just Right when Theo and Harlow walked up. He gave his friend a hug, then they went in and the smells of fresh bread and other things cooking hit him. Theo stopped and took a long, deep breath.

"I do that every time I come in here," Adam said.

"And the day you don't is the day I know I've done something wrong." A beautiful woman with a riot of brown curls held back by a headband and a hint of the South in her voice greeted them. "Good to see you, Adam. Who's this?"

"Sheridan, this is my old friend, Theo Hanson. He's come back to help find out who's been setting the fires. And this is Harlow, his arson dog."

"Well, even though the circumstances suck, I'm glad you're both here. Take a seat anywhere."

As they walked to a table near the window so Harlow could sit by the wall, Sheridan said, "Menu's up on the chalkboard. Which reminds me, we're almost out of your PB&J Swirl ice cream."

"Making another batch today," Adam said.

"Great. Bring me over a tub as soon as you can. The special today is beef stew."

Adam did a fist pump. Theo assumed that was a good sign. "With homemade biscuits?"

"Absolutely, darlin'."

"Then that's what I'm having."

"Shall I make it two?" Theo nodded. "Be back in a quick shake."

"She is not from around here," Theo said, stating the obvious as he put the plastic menu back in the holder.

"Alabama, if you can believe it."

"Winter must have come as a shock."

"She loves it. You'll never meet a bigger snow bunny or a worse skier," Adam said with a smirk.

"And she serves Bright Spot Ice Cream."

"One of my best sources of customers. I stock her cookies at my place and make ice cream sandwiches with them. There are eight or nine of us in food service who support each other by carrying one another's products."

"The ultimate word of mouth," Theo said.

"Exactly. It's made a big difference. I hope if I open another store, I find the same support there, too." More praise for their hometown. Theo was glad his friend was finding success here. It clearly made him happy. "How was your meeting with Keith?"

Theo gave Adam the basics. "I want to pin this on him, but I've got no hard evidence."

"If he did it, you'll find it." Theo appreciated Adam's confidence since he wasn't feeling it at the moment.

Sheridan came back carrying a tray with two big bowls of stew, one small one, and a basket of biscuits. "The small one's for the puppy. Hope that's okay. There's nothin' in here she can't have as long as it's all right by you."

"Thanks, she'll love it." Sheridan put down the bowl for Harlow before serving Theo and Adam. He liked her priorities. Curious about this newcomer, he asked, "How'd you come to live in Fable Notch?"

"I was college roommates with Laurel. We studied culinary and restaurant management together and became good friends despite the fact I'm a morning person, and she isn't human before noon. I went home after school, but two years ago, I was between jobs and didn't know what to do. The brewery was new, and Laurel needed help, so she invited me up. I fell in love with your town, and when I talked about starting my own business, the Stewart's convinced me to stay and helped out."

"That sounds like them." Roger and Valerie Stewart may have a big family of their own, but they were always ready to welcome more.

"I couldn't ask for a more supportive community."

Theo almost made a derisive remark, but before he could, he remembered afternoons at Adam's house after Valerie had given them apples, which they barely ate, and peanut butter cookies, which they devoured, Sunday dinners with the Sinclairs, cross-country team victory parties. Not to mention countless hours with Eden. Then he thought of things that happened since he'd come back, like Dylan's apology and the way his old nemesis stood up for him the other day. Why was all the bad — and especially the shit his parents did — what he usually focused on?

Since he didn't have an answer, he picked up a spoon and dug into the stew. He couldn't have stopped the moan if he tried.

"Ah, music to my ears," she said. "Enjoy, y'all."

Needing a safe subject, Theo asked, "So you make a PB&J ice cream?"

"It's one of our biggest sellers." Adam talked about how he created flavors and what he did for each season, but soon stopped talking. "What is it?"

"What's what?"

"Dude, you're nodding at what I'm saying and pretending to be interested in ice cream, but something's clearly bothering you other than your meeting with Keith."

"You think you can still read me?"

"Time apart doesn't mean you don't know a person anymore. I may not know what you've gone through since you left, but who you are? That hasn't changed. It's Eden, right?" Theo stopped chewing. "I'm not surprised. You two had something special when we were kids. Don't think I realized it then, but looking around, and having a poor dating record myself, I can see your connection with her was rare."

"Never have found anything like it again. Not that I've been looking."

"I've looked, and I haven't found it, my friend. I told you to be careful, but I guess it wasn't an option."

"She's always been everything I've ever wanted and everything I can't have."

"What's that supposed to mean?"

"When I thought we could get out of this town, I figured we had a chance. No one looking at me funny and no interference from her father. But even after all this time, I'm not good for her. I wake up violently from nightmares. I have no history of being able to handle a relationship long term, not to mention the fact she's got a life here, and I don't want that."

"So Patrick was right? She's better off without you?"

"She deserves someone better than me."

"You're probably right. After you go back to Baltimore, I'll have to ask her out. Laurel told me her divorce is final. I'll wait a few weeks, then see if she'd like to go to a movie or for coffee."

Theo knew what his friend was doing, but it didn't stop the pang of jealousy. Once the arsonist was caught and he left, Eden was free to see whoever she wanted. No matter how great last night was, he didn't see himself staying here, and he wasn't so callous as to hope she'd be alone for the rest of her life. She should have love and a husband and children and....

Adam broke into his thoughts. "Look, I haven't seen you in almost a decade, and even if I had, this wouldn't be my business. But be careful."

Theo sat back. "I'm not going to hurt her."

"Her? I'm worried about you, old friend. Remember, I saw you before you left town the last time. I thought you might go bald from the way you pulled at your hair."

It had been one of the worst days of Theo's life, ranking up there with the day his father split and the first time he'd gone with Cole to bring his mother home from a bar. After Theo left Eden, he called Cole to thank him for the graduation gift — a car — and told him what had happened. Cole offered him a job as a roadie for his band, Emporium, and Theo jumped at the chance to put as many miles as possible between him and this town. Adam included. "I remember."

"You were wrecked. I'm glad seeing her is giving you clarity or closure on what happened, but are you sure that can be it?"

"What are you saying?"

"You should be careful about anything that happens between the two of you."

Theo put down his spoon, surprised to see the bowl was empty. "You think I'm vulnerable where Eden's concerned?"

"Got someone waiting for you?"

"No," Theo said.

"Break many hearts or had yours broken since her?"

"No, not really," he said and crossed his arms over his chest. "I see where you're going."

"You two had something special and intense. I think distance made things easier for the last twelve years, but now you can't avoid her."

His friend had a point. The last time he left her had been hard enough. "I get it. Thanks for having my back."

"Old habits."

He'd missed Adam. He hadn't realized it or hadn't allowed himself to. He'd left this town behind and didn't let himself have any regrets. Cut himself off from everyone. "Did I say goodbye when I took off?"

"You came by the lodge to tell me what you were doing and managed a 'See ya', which I didn't believe."

Theo hadn't allowed himself to think about anyone after he decided to go. Maybe that was a mistake. "I've got a question."

"Ask away."

"Are you pissed I didn't stay in touch?"

Adam thought for a minute. "I was at first. I mean, I couldn't understand what you were going through losing Eden, since I was happily unencumbered, and I didn't share your dislike for this town, but we were friends. Other than a few of my brothers, I was closer to you than anyone. I remember when Martin told me you were headed to Afghanistan. I figured that was it. You'd rather put a half a world between yourself and this place. Even risk your life. All I could do was hope you'd be happy with whatever choices you made and that you'd make it back."

Adam was a good friend, no matter how long it had been since Theo saw him. "Thanks for the honesty."

"No problem. In my family, you learned if someone asked for your time, thoughts, or help, consider it important. And maybe it's not my place to say this, but if I'm reading you right, you have some things to figure out beyond who's been setting these fires."

Theo filled his mouth with a biscuit so he wouldn't have to respond.

Eden stared at the little ballet slippers hanging from her bracelet as she walked back to her car and almost tripped over Janelle because of it.

"Someone's on another planet. Hope it's a happy place."

"Sorry, I wasn't watching where I was going."

"I noticed. Would this have something to do with Theo?"

"Some, but not entirely."

Janelle gave her a quizzical look and said, "Sounds like you could use coffee and girl talk. Do you have time?"

Eden glanced at her watch. "A little."

"Great. Help me bring this thrift into the store, and we'll talk."

Janelle pulled a dozen hangers of clothes out of the trunk of her Outback and handed an armful to Eden, then grabbed so many bags she could hardly walk. "I wasn't able to carry in all the new stuff when I got here this morning. Follow me."

As they went in, Eden smiled and breathed in the scent of lavender. Janelle told her simple scents made people want to linger and shop more. She followed Janelle to the back room where there were several empty racks and at least twice as many filled ones. Eden hung the clothes up and glanced at the piles everywhere, including the couch where she'd spent the night not long ago. "Where did you find all of this?"

"I took the day yesterday to hit at least a dozen thrift stores along the Massachusetts border, then went to an estate liquidation where I bought all the clothes they had for next to nothing. I'll likely end up discarding or donating a good chunk of it, but I've already seen several pieces ready to sell and a few for me to revamp for YouTube. I'm still determined to find something to make for you."

Janelle started two pots of coffee — she always made a separate one for other people because she drank her coffee notoriously strong — and Eden walked into the store to look through what was available. After leaving Keith, Eden had donated half of her closet to Janelle. Every dress Keith picked out, every button-down shirt he'd made her wear. In exchange, Janelle helped her find clothes that made her feel comfortable and beautiful. After the fire, she'd been heartbroken to lose those clothes, but Janelle assured her there was always more. Which was a relief because otherwise Eden would have had nothing to wear. She was fingering a blue silk blouse and thinking how it would feel if Theo took it off her when Janelle handed her a mug. Pulling her thoughts away from Theo, she said, "Every time I'm here, I am amazed by the size of your inventory. It's like a big, messy closet belonging to your favorite fashionable aunt."

"I know. I love it. I get to play dress up as part of my job." Eden followed Janelle back to the workroom.

"You always had flair." Eden envied her friend her bright style and the way she seemed to not care what others thought. True, this came from being raised by a disinterested stepmother who was more focused on her own daughters, but Janelle had a way of turning loss to her advantage.

"What can I say? Seeing Mollie Ringwald in *Pretty in Pink* had a lifelong influence on me. But that's not what you're here to talk about. Come. Sit. Talk." Janelle tossed clothes off some chairs, giving them space to sit, and Eden talked about her run in with Monica.

After hearing the story, Janelle asked, "Which of her comments is bothering you — the one about Theo not staying or you needing a big, strong man to take care of you?"

Eden considered before answering. "I never expected Theo to stay."

"So it's the big strong man issue."

Eden sighed. "I don't mind the idea of loving someone, and leaning on them for strength and comfort. But I don't want to be dependent on them. I can stand on my own."

"Of course you can," said Janelle with all the confidence Eden wished she felt. "Last time I looked, you were handling work, finalizing a divorce, and living on your own without help from anyone."

"Not including my therapist." Eden had told her friends months ago.

Janelle brushed off Eden's comment. "Everyone needs that kind of help at some point."

"You didn't."

"Yes, I did. How do you think I got clear about leaving New York and moving back? I was falling apart and about five minutes away from a nervous breakdown, total burnout, or both."

The mug stopped an inch from her mouth. She and Janelle had had some long and late- night talks since Eden left Keith, but her friend never mentioned this. "Why didn't you tell me?"

Janelle pulled an errant thread from her shirt. "It didn't come up."

"Not even when I told you I was going to see one?" Did Janelle think Eden wouldn't understand?

Janelle shook her head. "My stepmother's way of showing support was to center the conversation around her. It was always 'Well, when I was...' or 'Let me tell you what happened to me....' She made sure I knew that whatever I was going through, it wasn't as important as she was. I made myself a promise that I wouldn't talk about myself when someone was looking for support. I assume either the time will come to tell them — like now — or I'll bring it up when we're discussing me. Which isn't now. From what I've seen, you've been doing great on your own. Better all the time."

"But when my apartment burned down, I needed so much help."

"Who doesn't need someone — or several someone's — when catastrophe happens? Eden, who told you being strong means doing everything on your own?"

"It's more like people telling me for years I wasn't strong enough to be on my own."

"By 'people,' you mean your father and Keith."

"They were very convincing." The two loudest voices for the longest times. They made sure Eden knew how much she needed them. How many times had Keith told her, "You're lucky I'm here. You're like your mother. You need a man to take care of you,"? It wasn't until she was considering leaving her marriage that she noticed she earned enough to live on her own. And it took the fire, when several former PT patients reached out to offer food and other necessities, for her to notice how she'd made a difference in people's lives. Maybe getting support when she needed it was different from being needy.

As if she knew what Eden was thinking, Janelle leaned forward and put a hand on Eden's knee and said, "No matter what those two tried to get you to believe, you are more than capable of managing your own life, and I'll bet it drives both of them crazy that you're doing well."

He only has the power you give him. Eden remembered Theo's words again. "I'm not doing well at the moment."

"Moments pass. And you got walloped — first with the fire and then Theo showing up."

"You've been awesome. You and Dani."

"We're here for you, like you've been there for us. No one gets through entirely on their own."

Eden gave a small nod. She could hear the truth in Janelle's words. "I guess needing people isn't a bad thing."

"As long as you're going to the right people."

"An important distinction." Eden was glad her life finally had the right people in it. She finished her coffee, hugged her friend, and headed out. As she walked to her car, she heard a familiar bark and, moments later, Harlow was at her feet. "Hey sweet girl. What brings you here?"

"We had lunch with Adam." She looked up to see Theo. Her body flushed at the memories of their night—and morning—together. Part of her wanted to step into his arms and kiss him, but not knowing who might see them, she thought better of it.

"I want to kiss you, too," he said, leaning close. She wasn't certain she was glad he could read her so easily, but she was glad he understood. "But my being here already gives people something to talk about. We won't add to it."

Especially since if people saw them together romantically, she was going to have to explain things after he left. Still, starting the day in bed with him and then having to stand here in public as though there was nothing between them was tough. Too much of a seesaw for her heart. Hoping her concern didn't show, she said, "I'm glad you and Adam have had time together."

"Me too. He and I turned out okay."

"How did your meeting with Keith go?" She was proud of herself for being able to manage a simple conversation given the knots of her emotions.

"Like you'd expect. He was difficult, argumentative, and gave me as little information as he could. He didn't like that I knew about his interest in the Northcott Estate or about your divorce being final. Which reminds me, I forgot to tell you I let that information slip to your father. I hope you're not mad."

"Are you kidding? That saves me from having to deal with it. It's interesting he hasn't called to let me know he heard, but I'm sure he's waiting for the 'right' moment. Thank you. I owe you one."

Theo leaned in and whispered in her ear, "I'm going to collect on that."

She certainly hoped so. There was no way to know how much longer he'd be here, but she could enjoy as much of that time as possible. And there were so many ways to enjoy him. To keep from kissing him, she asked, "Do you think Keith could have done it?"

"He's at the top of my list until I can rule him out. He has motive and a selfish streak combined with ambition that makes him think he can do whatever he wants to win. When he's threatened, he could make dangerous choices. But I need proof."

"Then you'll get it."

"Not before the next fire."

She saw and heard his frustration. She rested her hand on his arm in comfort. He covered her hand with his and for a moment she was ready to throw caution to the wind and kiss him. Who cared who saw them? As she took a step closer, her phone alarm went off, reminding her there were other things in the world beside her and Theo. She took out the phone and silenced it. "Real life interferes."

"Appointment?"

"The first of several, along with three classes. I'm not going to be home until after eight."

"And I don't know how long I'm going to be at the Sinclairs," he said, reminding her of his plans to talk to Grace Duncan about the fire. "I suspect Grace's twins will want to play with Harlow until they go to bed."

"Then I'll see you later. Bye, Harlow." She gave the dog several rubs between the ears. At least she could show affection to one of them.

She got into her car and let her head fall on the steering wheel. She'd thought the fire had turned her life upside down. But it was nothing compared to the storm of emotions Theo caused. She had no regrets about sleeping with him. It had been wonderful and, truthfully, she couldn't wait for it to happen again, even knowing she was opening herself up to a world of hurt. It's a good thing Janelle reminded her she could ask for help, because after Theo left, she was going to need her friends.

Chapter Twenty-One

♥

At the station, there wasn't a lot to be done. Theo was going to end up with a bald spot on the floor from his pacing or in his hair from pulling at it. Needing to do something, he and Harlow left for a drive through the White Mountains and a long walk on the trails. He passed other hikers, plenty of dogs, and thought about Eden more than the case. He didn't have good ideas for either. Being in bed with her was wonderful, but that didn't mean it was a smart idea. He'd been wrecked when he left her the first time. How was he going to protect his heart so that he wouldn't fall apart when he said goodbye again?

Maybe she'd like Baltimore.

Theo stopped walking, and Harlow barked when her leash tugged. "Sorry, girl," he muttered. He found a bench and sat, Harlow making herself comfortable in the shade nearby.

He and Eden had made plans to leave Fable Notch once before. Could this be their second chance? He wondered if she'd like Baltimore. She'd been excited about being in Boston so clearly she didn't mind the idea of city living, but that was a long time ago. They could find a place in one of the suburbs, if that worked better for her. He pictured a house where the two of them shared coffee in the mornings—assuming she was awake—and talked about their days at night. His mind conjured images and ideas, dreams and....

What if you hurt her?

And there it was. This wasn't about her father's conviction that Theo was a poor bet. There was a real possibility his issues could injure her. Yes, people with PTSD had relationships. Two of the men in his old unit were married with children, but Theo had familial problems on top of the psychological ones.

When Harlow bumped his leg, Theo looked at his watch. He'd been lost in his thoughts for over an hour and wasn't any closer to knowing what to do with his feelings for Eden. He wasn't a fan of 'wait and see', but he couldn't come up with an alternative yet. At least it was time to head to the Sinclair's for dinner.

Lunch with Adam, dinner with Martin and Millie. He couldn't remember the last time his days were this focused on food and who he ate with. When he wasn't traveling, lunch was usually at his desk, dinner was whatever he could grab on the way home or leftovers. He knew how to cook, but rarely did. Occasionally, he went out with people from the office, but he already had more of a social life here. He didn't entirely hate it.

Today, when Theo pulled up to the brick red colonial, he recognized that Nick's renovations to their old house made it look more like the Sinclairs'. It wasn't surprising. Not only were most of their happy childhood memories here, but as the youngest, Nick spent more time here than Theo or Cole did. Nick had only been nine when the Sinclairs came into their lives. Theo was barely twelve.

Standing there staring at the house, he could admit, at least to himself, he was sorry it had been so long since he'd spent any real time with Martin and Millie. He made a mental note to apologize, even if they understood his reasons.

A squeal of "Harlow's here" brought him out of his thoughts as an eight-year-old girl came barreling toward them. Harlow gave a short bark and went to greet the child, who was joined by her twin brother. Theo couldn't help but smile as he watched the three of them run around the front yard. Harlow got plenty of exercise with him, but it was nothing like this. She'd be exhausted tonight.

Millie met him at the door, and he gave her a quick kiss on the cheek. "Thank goodness you're here," she said. "They've been asking when Harlow was arriving for the last hour."

"It's understandable. She's more fun than I am."

"Come on in. Grace is in the kitchen helping me finish the salad."

He stepped inside the house and even though his lunch at the Just Right with Adam had been more than satisfying, his stomach growled. "Do I smell...."

"Lasagna, yes. The kids love it, and it's easy to make a lot." Theo knew Millie didn't have trouble making a lot of any of her meals. Growing up, there were always leftovers for him and his brothers to take home. It was the best food they ate all week. All three of them could cook, but with limited ingredients, they couldn't come close to what Millie made.

"Great, I'm starved."

"You always are." Theo grinned. He knew to her he would perpetually be a teenager, growing right before her eyes and eating everything in sight.

When he stepped into the house, the first thing he noticed was how little had changed. The same furniture, the same overstuffed bookcases. What was different was the pile of boxes and bags in the corner. "What's all that?"

"Donations people have been bringing by for Grace and the kids. Toys, games, books, clothes. Things for the kitchen. There's even furniture, but we're keeping that in the garage. By the time she finds her new place, she'll have almost everything she needs."

"Great," Theo said without any enthusiasm. Just because he'd been remembering some of the better times he'd had growing up, didn't mean he'd forgotten how little outside help his family received when they needed it.

He followed Millie into the kitchen where she introduced him to Grace Duncan. The woman looked young to have eight-year-old twins, but, as he understood, sometimes life threw you curveballs. "It's nice to meet you, Theo. I've heard so much about you from Millie and Martin. I assume you've met Connor and Sophia."

"I can't say I met them since they headed straight for Harlow, but I saw them."

She laughed. "Sorry, I'll introduce you at dinner. I hope it's okay that they hang all over Harlow. They've both wanted a dog, but between living in an apartment and having to manage on my own, it's not an option. I keep hoping my sister will get a dog for her family and that will be a temporary fix. I'm glad I didn't give in to my idea of getting them something smaller and caged, like a hamster, or it would have died in the fire, and I don't think I could have dealt with that."

Theo nodded. Over the years he'd spoken with people who'd lost pets in addition to property. It was awful. "Can I ask you a few questions about the fire?"

"Sure, although I don't think there's much I can tell you I didn't already tell Martin. The kids and I came home after their art class, and I remember thinking the back of the building was glowing. When I pulled into my parking spot, I saw smoke coming out of the windows and it hit me. I drove across the street for safety, facing the car away from our apartment so the kids couldn't see what was happening, and called 911. By the time the fire department arrived, the flames looked like they were coming from everywhere. I spent most of my time holding Connor and Sophia, consoling them while not falling apart myself. It was one of the worst nights of my life."

Helplessness, loss, no control over a situation. Theo understood what the victims went through. "I'm glad the Sinclairs could help."

"In more ways than I can say. I heard you used to be a regular here, too, when you were a kid."

"They have a knack for being there when people need them."

"I don't know how we would have gotten through those first few days, or even these last weeks without them. Not to mention all the people who have brought things to help us out."

Her experience of Fable Notch residents differed from his. He remembered the last time he went grocery shopping with his mother. She hurried through the aisles, not making eye contact, and putting only what was necessary into their cart. He saw people turn away when he tried to look at them. No one spoke to her, no one asked how she was doing. They were invisible and alone.

Grace and her children were getting the help they needed. He hated the sting of envy it brought up, but didn't let the pain of his past show. "Is there anyone who might want to hurt you? Someone at work? Ex-husband?"

"I work at the White Mountain Credit Union managing the tellers. Maybe if I were in mortgages and loans, there might be something, but not my department. And there is no ex-husband."

He wondered if she was going to elaborate, but Connor, Sophia, and Harlow interrupted them. The kids wanted to know if it was time for dinner, and Harlow looked as though she was asking the same question. They were told to wash up, then help Millie set the table. As they rushed out of the room, Grace called, "Use soap." Theo laughed. He'd heard the same thing countless times in this house.

"It doesn't sound like this fire has a personal connection to you, but if you think of anything, please let me or Martin know."

"Absolutely. I'm glad you're here. The night Martin got hurt, I was here. I've never seen Millie so worried. The kids and I took her to the hospital to be with him. She was very relieved when she heard you were coming."

"Sounds like your being here has been good for her, too."

"I hope so. I'm grateful I can do something. It's hard to be in a position of needing so much, especially after working for years to prove to everyone that I'm fine on my own. Being able to give back has been nice."

Theo was saved from responding when Millie came in to take the garlic bread out of the oven. Needing so much. That's what it was like. It was why he was always willing to help Martin around the house, and it was one of the best things about his relationship with Eden. With her, he had a place to give to someone else. With her, he was strong, not stubborn. Supportive, not needy.

His thoughts were a jumble as they ate dinner, but the twins soon distracted him. He wouldn't have brought up his work at all, but the twins hammered him with questions about Harlow and loved the fact that he had a dog for a partner. Both kids insisted they wanted jobs where they could take a dog to work. He kept his answers simple, watching Grace's face to make sure he wasn't saying anything that might upset them.

They were clearing the table and putting dishes in the sink — the rule of no dessert until the table was cleared still held — when Sophia came up to him. "Thank you for looking for the person who burned down our house. My mom's been sad and scared since it happened, and I want her to be happy again."

"She wants the same for you. Have you been doing okay?"

The girl looked thoughtful for a moment, and Theo was almost sorry he asked. "I was sad, too, and I missed all my things, but my friends have been awesome and so have Millie and Martin." Theo wasn't surprised she called them by their first names. "I had a hard time sleeping the first nights we were here, and Millie gave me warm drinks and read me stories."

"I'll bet that helped."

She nodded. "A lot."

Millie knew how to make children feel safe and supported. It was one of the things which made her an excellent piano teacher. Truth was, she made everyone feel good. No matter their age.

As they were finishing dessert, the Chief's phone in Theo's pocket rang at the same time as he heard noise from the squawk box Martin had in the kitchen. His stomach clenched. Ten days since the last fire. Early evening.

Theo knew what he'd hear before answering. He jotted down the address on a notepad. When he hung up, he looked at Martin and said, "It's him."

Theo put his Bluetooth headset on, called Lloyd, and started alerting the volunteers. In minutes, he and Martin were in Theo's car and heading to the station, then suiting up and driving to the fire. The volunteers would meet them there. He saw smoke when they were a few minutes away and the glow from the flames when they were less than a mile out. "Call in the next two towns, Martin. We're going to need help."

Chapter Twenty-Two

♥

Eden heard the sirens in the distance when she stepped out of Maximum Results. Was it the arsonist? As she waited to pull out of the parking lot, a string of fire engines from the next town passed, answering her question. Without thinking, she changed the direction of her turn signal and followed them. Only a few miles later she saw them turn into a nearby shopping plaza. The stylized PB logo at the top of the entrance sign told her it was another of her father's properties.

The place was ablaze. She took a parking spot as far from the building as she could, got out of the car, and watched from a distance as the volunteers worked. It had been less than four weeks since the fire at her apartment, but she'd forgotten how loud a raging fire could be. That night, she'd been overcome with heartbreak and loss. Tonight, her heart thudded with worry.

As the crowd of emergency vehicles and people grew, she knew it was a mistake to come. More people wouldn't help, but her own concern had her stomach flipping so much she thought she might be sick. She needed to glimpse Theo, reassure herself, and then she would go.

Eden tried to distinguish him from the others battling the fire, but the uniforms and helmets made it impossible. Finally, she saw Martin giving orders near one of the engines.

Running over to him, she asked, "Where's Theo?"

"Honey, you shouldn't be here."

"I know, but I need to see him before I leave. Please, Martin."

For a second she thought he was going to send her home, then he nodded and scanned the people working to get the fire contained. She jumped when he said, "There," and pointed.

Eden didn't know where to look, but then she recognized Theo's build and movements even though the visor of his helmet obscured his face. As if he felt her eyes on him, Theo turned. She was going to wave and leave, but Theo shouted something to the person next to him and ran over to her.

He raised his visor, and she took in the strain on his face. "You shouldn't be here," he said.

"So I've been told. I panicked. Sorry. I wanted to make sure you were all right."

"I am, but we have a long way to go."

Her mouth went dry. "It's bigger than the last one."

"As expected, and there's a dentist's office on the end with flammable products, which could be a real disaster. We can't let the fire get there. You have to leave. I can't be worried about you and the fire."

"I'm going. Promise."

"If you want to help, you could go by the Sinclairs' and pick up Harlow. I was there when we got the call. You'll save me a stop. Keep Harlow company. She wasn't happy with the way I ran out the door and left her."

"She's not here?"

"No, there's nothing for her to do. She's not a good firefighter." He gave her hand a quick squeeze, letting her know he was trying to make a joke. The thick gloves he wore reminded her of the work he needed to do. "Gotta get back."

"I'll see you later."

"Thank you for understanding." He gave her cheek a smoky kiss and went back to work.

She took a deep breath in relief and coughed from the smell of smoke. The air was thick with it. She stepped away but couldn't resist turning back to watch Theo for a few minutes, drawn in by his focus and determination. He worked with the volunteers, checking to make sure each fighter was holding up, backing them up where they needed it, adding support when the fire blazed up in a new area. She may have been graceful when she danced, but here, too, there was a grace and rhythm.

As she headed back to her car, she saw Monica near an ambulance, wrapped in a blanket and crying. Eden walked over to offer comfort but stopped when Monica got up and ran to a familiar man. Monica threw her arms around Keith in a gesture which suggested more than friendship. Curious, Eden moved closer to hear what they were saying.

"I don't know what happened. I was working late, putting some new listings onto the website, when I smelled something burning. I opened my door and tried to get to the center stairs, but the hall was filled with smoke. I went back, grabbed my phone and jacket, and ran to the side stairs. As soon as I got outside, I called 911. Then I called you. I guess I wasn't the first to call because firefighters got here just a few minutes later."

"It's going to be okay," Keith said and kissed her forehead.

"How can you say that?" she said hysterically. "Everything I've worked for is in there. I don't think these idiots even know what they're doing." She gestured to the firemen and Eden bristled on their behalf. "There will be nothing left. What am I going to do?"

"You'll figure it out, baby." If the endearment didn't make their relationship clear, the way Keith pulled Monica closer did. "I'll be here for you as much as I can. You'll get through this."

"Can I stay with you tonight? I don't want to be alone."

Eden didn't stick around to hear the answer.

Eden and Keith separated less than a year ago. If things were serious between them, how long had this been going on? Was Monica expecting an engagement ring from Keith?

Eden left the fire site in a fog of jumbled thoughts. When she pulled into the driveway at the Sinclair's, she sat in her car for a few minutes trying to reestablish a level of calm, but between what she'd learned and thinking of Theo at the fire, it wasn't possible.

Eventually, she gave up, got out, and went to the door. A few moments after she rang the bell, Millie greeted her with a smile. "Eden, what a lovely surprise. What brings you here?"

"Theo asked me to come pick up Harlow."

"You heard about the fire."

"I saw the engines drive by the gym as I was leaving. I followed."

"That explains why you smell of smoke. Your timing is perfect. Grace is upstairs putting the twins to bed. If you'd arrived ten minutes earlier, you would have heard loud complaints about taking Harlow away. Come into the kitchen. I'll get us lemonade and sugar cookies. Or would you prefer coffee?"

Part of Eden wanted to take Harlow and go but being alone with her thoughts didn't sound appealing. "Lemonade sounds nice."

She followed Millie and watched in silence as the other woman poured their drinks and plated the cookies before joining Eden at the table. "You're worried," Millie said, stating the obvious.

Eden bit into a cookie and nodded. "It was like my car turned and followed the engines of its own volition. I had to see Theo and make sure he was okay." She held up a hand before Millie could say anything. "I know it wasn't a good idea. I could have been a dangerous distraction."

"But you couldn't help yourself. I understand. I followed Martin to more fires than he knows the first year we were together."

"You did?"

"I'm not good at standing by and doing nothing. At first, I thought there might be a way for me to help, but, like you, I learned my being there was a bad idea. After that, if I went, I made sure he couldn't see me. It took a while before I understood that if I was going to have a life with this man — and I had no intention of letting him go — I had to accept his work and the potential danger that went with it.

"I guess you're used to it by now."

"I thought I was, but with Martin's injury and the size and frequency of these fires, it took all my willpower not to do what you did tonight."

"How do you let him go into a potentially scary situation?" She brought the glass to her lips, determined to listen to whatever advice Millie offered.

"Vodka."

Eden almost spit out her drink. "What?"

"Vodka for the nerves, hair dye for the grays. Want me to spike your lemonade?"

"Really?"

"No," Millie said with a smile. "My liver would have been shot decades ago if I drank every time I was worried during my marriage. I will admit I dye my hair."

"It was hard?"

"Was? It still is. Loving someone, committing to a life together, means accepting years of worry. Doesn't matter if they have a nine-to-five desk job or something more dangerous."

"You're saying it's a risk no matter what."

Millie nodded. "It's a risk to love someone deeply. It makes a person vulnerable. It's why it took me so long to say yes to Martin in the first place. I said no the first time he proposed."

"You did?" Mille nodded. "I would never have guessed."

"I don't think I told Theo or his brothers. Or even Ryan. When I was younger, I was petrified of all that marriage means — my parents didn't set a great example — and I was right to be scared. The things Martin and I have been through. It's a wonder I don't drink." She paused and took a bite of her cookie. All Eden saw was a happy couple. She'd never imagined what that happiness required. "And it's not the fires. It's the little things combined with the big things. Tough financial times, times when Ryan was in trouble, when our parents passed," she paused for a moment. "When I miscarried."

Eden put her hand on Millie's and said, "I'm sorry. I had no idea."

"You don't broadcast the moments that make up a marriage, that build the bonds or break some relationships apart, but everyone goes through them. There's no planning. No warning."

"Like Martin's heart attack."

"Absolutely. After he came home from the hospital, I didn't sleep for weeks. If he turned over, I woke up. If he snored or stopped snoring, I woke up. I'm so thankful he made it. For all the hard times I've gone through, I'm glad to have gone through it with him by my side."

"That's love."

"That's commitment. It gives as much as it takes. No, I'm wrong. It gives more."

Eden sensed Millie had an ulterior motive for telling her this. She wanted to remind Millie there was no longer a possibility of her and Theo being together. Instead, she said, "Thank you for sharing this with me."

"You're welcome." Millie stood, then gave Eden a hug. It had been years since Eden experienced a motherly hug, and she relaxed into Mille's arms as tears came to her eyes. Ah, the joy of experiencing all her emotions.

A few minutes later, Eden collected Harlow and headed to the house. She took a shower and sat down with a book, but couldn't focus on reading, so she watched a sitcom on Netflix until she dozed off in the living room with Harlow's head on her lap. When Theo came in, waking her up, it was after ten. Over three hours. She and Harlow went to him as he toed off his shoes. Harlow sniffed around him, but Eden kept her distance, knowing she'd need another shower if she got too close. "Everything all right? Everyone all right?"

"As all right as we can make it. No injuries. The few people in the building when the fire started got out quickly. Took three departments. My guess is he used more accelerant. We didn't lose the whole place, but a substantial portion is gone."

"The dentist's office?"

"The only thing functional after this. We kept most of the volunteers focused on it and that worked. I've got a shitload to do, but there's nothing more to be done tonight. I'm not sure how effective Harlow will be, but I'll bring her in the morning, and we'll see what she can discover."

"It's another one of my father's properties."

"I noticed. Wonder if he'll call me this time. I should leave him a message in the morning. More joy." She could hear the list of to-dos he was making in his head.

"You must be exhausted."

"That's an understatement. Fighting a fire is different from investigating one after the fact. I need a big glass of water and a shower. I can't relax when I smell like this."

Eden went to the kitchen, got a glass, and filled it. "Ice?" He shook his head and took it from her, finishing more than half before stopping. "Is there anything else I can do?"

He stared at her without speaking, and she couldn't figure out what he might be thinking. Before she could ask, he said, "Nothing, thanks. I'm getting out of these clothes."

She waited, hoping he'd say more, her own thoughts racing. She knew he wasn't mad at her even if he'd been abrupt. He'd spent the last several hours facing down a fire and his own fears. When she heard the shower, she went into the bedroom and found his clothes in a heap on the floor at the foot of the bed. She scooped them up, the acrid smell stinging her nose, and brought them to the laundry room. One less thing for him to do. One small thing she could do to help.

She stood at the washer, letting the sound of rushing water calm her and thought of something else which might help. Smiling, she went upstairs, brushed her teeth, and put on her nightshirt. For the first time, she wished she had something sexy to wear, but he'd liked the shirt last night, so she didn't worry. She gave her hair a quick brush, dabbed on the tiniest touch of perfume — a new scent might be exactly what he needed — and went back to his bedroom.

Waiting for him to be done took forever. She almost left to go to her room to get a book when he came out, towel around his waist, skin damp from the shower. Desire rushed through her at the sight of him. She would make him forget all about the fires, at least for tonight.

He stared at her, not stepping closer, not saying a word. It lasted long enough for her to squirm then move to the center of the mattress, in case he wasn't clear on what she wanted. She knew she'd made a mistake when she saw his hand ball into a fist.

"Eden, you need to get out of that bed. Now."

Chapter Twenty-Three

♥

W alking into a room to find that the woman you never stopped wanting was waiting in your bed would be most guy's idea of heaven, and Theo's heart leaped at the sight of her. But as she smiled at him with hope and invitation, another image came to mind. He could see her afraid and shaking, her lip bleeding and looking at him with horror and hurt.

Theo was dangerous for her. He was a bad bet on a good day, and tonight was not good. This wasn't about what the town or her father thought of him. This was about accepting who he was — and who he wasn't.

The fire tonight had been out of control, and keeping it away from the dentist's office meant sending four men into the building. As much as Theo dreaded going in, he hated men going in without him even more, but when he tried to suit up, another captain stopped him. They needed Theo outside to continue to manage the whole situation. Staying behind went against all his training. For hours they beat the fire back as he'd battled his own demons, using all of his training to keep his focus on the blaze and away from memories. Everyone had been exhausted after and, Theo hoped, too relieved the fire was out to notice his anxiety.

And here was Eden, waiting for him with her soft lips and willing body. He didn't want her to leave, but he had to do what was right for them both. And that was to be apart.

"I don't understand," she said. Did her voice waver? Didn't matter. He wouldn't think about that.

"You can't stay there. You can't be here."

"But—"

"No, Eden. Chances are good tonight's fire will unleash a horror movie in my head. I almost left bruises on you the other morning. I will not risk hurting you when I have no control over my actions."

"You'd never hurt me."

"Not intentionally — leaving all those years ago notwithstanding. But when I'm in the middle of a dream, I thrash around, flail my arms, even punch things, people, too, if they're close."

"How do you know?"

"How do you think? I've hurt people. I had to have my own room when I was on the road with Cole because I woke up my roommate and slugged him. I hurt someone. when he tried to help me. Not to mention what I did to a woman once." He didn't want to tell Eden any of this, but if got her out of his bed, it would be worth it. "I don't remember the dream. I do remember the sound of her screaming and the split lip I gave her." It had been awful. The blood. Her tears. And worse, the way she looked at him. They'd broken up by the end of the week. "I can't stand the thought of doing that to you."

"When did this happen?"

"The last time?" Eden nodded. "Three or four years ago."

"Maybe things have changed." She looked so damn hopeful. He wanted to fall into that hope and hold on to it, but he knew better.

"I'm not willing to take a chance. Please, go." He wondered if she could hear the longing in his voice because no matter what he was saying, what he most wanted was to climb into bed and hold her all night. He wanted to believe being with her would change everything, somehow heal him. But it wouldn't, and if by giving in to his own needs he hurt her, he'd never forgive himself.

He waited for her to try to change his mind. He didn't know if he had the strength to turn her down again. Finally she said, "Okay," and got up. He did his best to keep his focus on her eyes, not her gorgeous legs or the light coming through her shirt as she walked toward him and gave him a quick kiss on his cheek. When she got to the door, she turned and said, "I put your clothes in the wash, in case you're looking for them in the morning. I hope you get some sleep."

"I'm sorry," he said.

She looked at him and said, "I know." Then she was gone, and he was alone.

He stood there, his thoughts racing. When the door opened again, he was about to yell until he saw it was Harlow. He appreciated the dog's awareness of his mood and need for comfort, but he wasn't in a place to take it. "No, girl, not tonight. I need you to get out, too." When she didn't move, he raised his voice and pointed. "Out. Now." She gave him a look and padded out. And he felt more guilty than before, something he didn't think possible.

Alone, he sat heavily on the bed and put his hand on the indentation Eden left on his pillow. "Fuck this," he said, grabbing it and throwing it across the room. It didn't go far and landed with an unsatisfying and silent plop. He took the other pillow, covered his face with it and screamed, letting loose his rage and fear.

Tossing the pillow back in its place, he got up and paced, grateful there was enough space to move. So many whys. Why tonight of all nights had she chosen to be waiting in his bed? Why couldn't she have gone to sleep while he was in the shower? Why did she still have to be in this town? Why did he still have to have so many feelings for her?

He didn't have a good answer. This was why it was better for him to be by himself. He couldn't allow his shit to damage anyone else. It didn't matter that he sent her away before something else could go wrong. He hurt her anyway, and everything about it sucked.

He should have known if he got close to Eden it would turn out badly. Again. It was one thing if he got hurt, but he had to protect her. She needed to accept he was too broken to care for. She deserved a relationship where she could be safe, and he couldn't give her that.

When he finally turned out the light, he knew there was a possibility he wouldn't have a nightmare because with everything going on in his head, he doubted he was going to sleep at all.

The bedside clock glowed four thirty when he woke tangled in the blankets. He didn't remember much, but the images he did recall were enough. Flames, heat, screams. He sat up, appreciating the cool air on his sweat-soaked skin.

He had no luck getting back to sleep. When the sky brightened, he got out of bed, made coffee in a to-go mug and got in his truck with Harlow. Today, he took a short drive to Silver Lake, a place he and Eden used to spend hours together. They'd find a secluded area and forget the rest of the world existed.

The morning was already warming up, and there was no one around. He let Harlow off her leash as he walked and remembered. Most New Englanders claimed fall was their favorite season with its cool air and colorful foliage, but he preferred spring when it looked like they were finally done with snow and things bloomed again.

Fresh starts. They weren't always possible. He'd unwillingly let Eden back into his heart, but after last night, and knowing all the baggage he brought with him, he was where he was twelve years ago, thinking she would be better off without him.

When his stomach growled, he headed back to town. He considered going to the diner, but since Rosie was too good at reading people, he decided against it. Instead, he went to Just Right and stared out the window as he drank another coffee and ate what was put in front of him, which he barely remembered ordering.

After breakfast, he headed back to talk to Eden. It was early, and he didn't know if she'd be up, but he could wait. He didn't want this hanging between them. He bought her two blueberry muffins as a peace offering. It wasn't chocolate, but hopefully it would do.

Chapter Twenty-Four

♥

Mornings weren't something Eden was good at navigating. She'd had a poor night's sleep and finally stopped fighting it and get out of bed. She wanted to talk with Theo before he left for work and was upset when she saw his car gone. Deciding to make herself something to eat, she put bread in the toaster oven. Then she'd gotten lost in her thoughts and didn't realize what happened until she smelled the toast burning. She'd opened the oven door seconds before he'd walked in. Great, as if he didn't have enough smoke the night before.

The expression on Theo's face almost broke her heart. The circles under his eyes told her he'd slept as poorly as she did, but it was the look of hopelessness that got her. It reminded her of how her patients reacted when they weren't making the progress they wanted. The past and the present were tangled in sadness and frustration. She didn't know why people — herself included — thought they could get "through something" and leave it discarded behind them with no chance of it returning. Life didn't work that way.

He as he joined her in the kitchen, she said, "And I thought I was up early."

"Guess neither of us had a good night."

"I don't think either of us expected to." Last night Eden stared at the ceiling and considered calling Dani to see if she could stay in Dani's second bedroom after all. Being near Theo and knowing she couldn't be with him felt too hard. It wasn't his anger. It was his pain and knowing there was nothing he would let her do about it. She couldn't stay if her presence made a difficult situation worse.

He held out a plain white bag. "I brought blueberry muffins from Just Right. They may still be warm."

She took the bag, opened it and stuck her nose in, breathing in the warm sweetness. "Heavenly, I haven't had these in ages." Putting muffins on a plate, she decided to treat herself. She got a knife and uncovered the butter dish before cutting the muffins in half and giving each a swipe. She took a big bite and, with her mouth still full, said, "So good. Thank you."

"You're welcome. I needed to find an extra way to say I'm sorry. I was a mess after the fire and knew I wasn't going to sleep well, if at all."

"I understand. Even our bodies don't heal in a straight path. There are always unexpected setbacks."

"So let's work through them." He came over and put his arms around her waist. "I handled things badly last night. Seeing you in bed short circuited my brain. You have to know how much I wanted you, but I couldn't have you stay with me. It was too risky."

"I appreciate you wanting to keep me safe."

"I had to. Had to do something right." He gave a frustrated groan, let go of her, and walked into the dining room. He sat down heavily at the table, running his hands through his hair. She hated seeing him upset. "Who am I kidding? This whole trip has been one setback after another."

She didn't like the sound of that since she was a part of the whole. "What makes you say that?"

"This arsonist has gotten away with four fires, and all I have is a short list of suspects and no hard proof against any of them. If I can't find this guy, we have less than a week before the next fire. I came here to help Martin, and not only haven't I done that, but I've also upset you and frustrated myself. Nothing's changed."

If she didn't think it would be a terrible waste of the muffin, she would have thrown one at him. As she looked for an alternative, she noticed her bracelet and the ballet slipper charm. Twelve years of frustration, loneliness, and decisions she regretted broke through the dam that usually made her hold her tongue or try to say the right thing to keep a situation calm. She was done with calm. He needed comfort, but he wasn't going to get it. Not yet.

"And what's changed the least is you." He looked at her as if she'd sprouted wings. Maybe she should have thrown the muffin after all.

"What does that mean?"

"Did you expect to have this case solved in less than a week?"

"No, but—"

"Has Martin told you he's disappointed in your progress or your work?"

"No, but—"

"Has anyone made any comments to you suggesting you don't belong here?"

"Other than your father and Keith?"

"You're going to tell me you care about their opinions? Or that you're surprised by their response?"

"Of course not, I—"

She held up a hand to stop him. "Have you noticed that no matter what, you assume the worst about Fable Notch? Even when good things happen. Your old bully apologized to you. You reconnected with a good friend, and until last night, you and I were having what I thought was a wonderful time."

"We were, but..."

"I am not saying you should stay here or even visit after this is over. You need to make the right decisions for you, but you have got to stop thinking this place and the people in it are against you. Yes, some lousy things happened here, and your family was treated poorly, but not by people who knew you or who mattered to you. You reminded me my father only has the control I give him. Why do you let this town have control over what you think of yourself?"

"That's not what I'm doing." His voice rose. Good, he was angry.

"It's not?" Instead of the usual fear she experienced around anger, Eden felt empowered. They needed to have this discussion and if it happened as a fight, then so be it. Turns out there were some things worth raising your voice for, some things that deserved a fight. "I know you as well as you know me, no matter what we've been through since we saw each other last. You think everyone needs to see you're not the screw up you once were, but you don't acknowledge that the person who is hardest on you — is you."

"I'm trying to get things right and not hurt anyone. Especially you."

"And I think you're just as worried about getting hurt as you are about hurting me. You have a nasty tendency of deciding for both of us in a situation. You did it last night, and you did it when you left me. What about what I want?" She was proud of herself for the strength in her voice. She kept her hands firmly on the island counter so he couldn't see they were shaking.

"I always care about what you want. I've never cared about anything more."

Strong words and they made her heart swell, but the two of them had to break this pattern in their relationship. "When my father made his terrible ultimatum, I wanted to find other solutions, but there was no talking to you. You decided how *we* would handle things, and I had to go along with it."

"It was the right thing to do." She hoped the skepticism was clear in her features. "I thought it was the right thing. I didn't want you to give up your dream."

"No, you didn't want me to give up my dream for *you*. There's a difference. I wanted to have both, but you decided, and there was no swaying you."

The pain of his final goodbye came rushing back. After a three-week graduation trip in Europe with her mother, Eden couldn't wait to see Theo. While she was gone, she and Donna had done research into the possibilities of grants and loans to pay for school. It would mean starting a semester later, maybe even a year, but it was worth it. She could have dance and Theo.

Then she found the package on her bed with Theo's handwriting. Her heart had skittered with joy, hoping this meant he reconsidered until she found his cell phone. No note, no explanation. She'd rushed to the Sinclair's thinking he might be there. Instead, Millie sat her down on the porch swing and said Theo had left two weeks earlier to work as a roadie for Cole's band. When Eden showed her the phone, Millie's eyes filled with tears.

"Now things make sense. He bought a new one before he left. Said he accidentally broke the other one. He got a new number and said...." Millie paused, unable or unwilling to finish. When she could finally continue, she said, "He said not to give it to anyone."

If Eden pressed, Millie might have given her the number, but knowing Theo didn't want her to have it was enough to keep her quiet. She'd been so hopeful, and he'd taken away their future. When she came home at Christmas, she learned he'd joined the army.

As Eden came back to the present, old pain mixed with new frustration. She looked at Theo and said, "You walked away, closed the door behind you, and locked it."

"I wanted what was best for you."

"And made a decision I had no say in." Staying angry, staying true to her feelings felt good. She was definitely going to keep doing this.

"You make me sound as bad as your father."

"Maybe you two have more in common than you'd like. He tried to control the situation one way. You did it another. He thought he was protecting me. You thought you were supporting me, and neither of you thought my opinion mattered at all."

Theo looked as though he were getting ready to yell again. He stood, took a step toward her, and his chest inflated with an intake of breath. She braced for the outburst. She'd asked for this, and she was ready for whatever he said.

But he stopped. When he spoke, he was quieter. "My father made my mother give up her dream."

She didn't know what he was referring to. "What dream?"

"She painted and drew. She loved it. He thought it was a waste of time. It didn't make money, and it didn't take care of him. He belittled her constantly. She tried to teach me and Cole. If we came home from school, and she was working on a project, she'd give us supplies so we could join her. One day we were sitting around drawing and having fun when my dad found us. Said she was making his boys weak. He grabbed every piece of art we'd done, everything of hers, made a fire, and burned it all. She was different afterward. He did that to her. I couldn't do that to you."

"You've never mentioned this."

"I didn't make the connection back then. All I knew was your dad could help you go for your dream. I couldn't. So I left. I didn't see another option."

Eden couldn't stay away for another second. She crossed the room to him, and he pulled her into his arms. She could hear his heart pounding where rested her head on his chest. Eventually, she pulled back to look at him and put her hand on his shoulder. This time, he was the one who noticed her bracelet. He took her hand in his and saw the charm. "You put it back on."

"I told you I would."

They stayed there, fingers entwined. She thought she might burst all she was feeling and what she wanted. She put her hand on his cheek, and his eyes closed at her touch. Then he turned his head and kissed her palm. "Even after all this time, you still find ways to amaze me," he said.

She reached her arms around him, raised herself on her toes, and kissed him. Opening her mouth, she licked his lips with her tongue, telling him she wanted more. He responded in kind as she let herself melt into the feel and taste of him. Her nipples hardened under her t-shirt, and she ached for his touch. He stroked his hands through her hair, then down her back to rest on her ass. When she shivered with delight, he grabbed her harder, pressing her against his erection. He was as needy as she was.

She'd experienced more desire — and more emotions—in the last few days than she had in the last several years. Yes, since leaving Keith she'd let down the wall she'd build around her feelings, but since Theo had come back, more had come rushing out. She couldn't decide if it was overwhelming or wonderful. Probably both. She wouldn't kid herself. He wasn't staying. But she wanted him now, and now was what they had. If this was their only chance, she would enjoy every moment she could.

Chapter Twenty-Five

♥

"Tell me you don't need to get to work early," he said as they continued to kiss.

"I don't need to get to work early."

He took her hand and hurried to the bedroom. Taking off each other's clothes took a little longer than he wanted because they kept stopping to kiss and touch one another, but he couldn't complain. Before long, they were naked and entwined. One hand cupped her breast while the other palmed her between her legs. She was so wet he could have taken out a condom and slid into her without any other preparation.

Before he could decide what to do first, her hand wrapped around his erection, and she stroked him. He couldn't stop the moan. The warmth of her touch combined with a need he didn't know he was capable of feeling.

"Last time you drove me crazy," she said. "Today it's my turn."

"Your turn to...." He stopped talking as she pushed him back, so he relaxed against the pillows. She gave him a deep kiss then sinuously moved down his body until her mouth joined her hand. "Eden, oh my god..."

He was lost.

Lost to the sensations she was creating. Lost to the feel of her hair as he ran it between his fingers. Lost to everything she did and who she was. He'd laid himself bare before her, his fears and his past, and she accepted it all.

Her mouth worked with her fingers, driving him insane. As she took him deeper, he moaned and grabbed her shoulder with one hand, keeping the other in her hair. This wasn't something he usually let women do for him. It required a level of trust and intimacy he wasn't comfortable with. Pleasing a partner was one thing. Accepting pleasure was different.

But with Eden, it was easy. Comfortable.

Incredible.

She continued to build his arousal with her mouth and hand until he couldn't stand it anymore. "If you want more from me... you... are going to... need to stop soon. Because I'm... not going to be... able to..."

"That," she said, moving her mouth away, but swiping him once more with her tongue, "was the sexiest thing anyone has ever said to me."

Theo sat up and put his hands on her waist, then brought her to him so he could kiss her. When he was finally willing to take a breath, he said, "You drive me wild."

"You make me bold."

"You deserve to be." He reached into the nightstand, took out a condom, and handed it to her. "You do it."

The smile she gave him was hungry and filled with promise. She unwrapped the condom, rolled it over his length, then straddled him. She glanced at his leg and asked, "Are you sure?"

He loved that she asked about his injury. This was the woman who knew all the places where he hurt and never took advantage. "Absolutely."

With her hand wrapped around his erection, she guided him into her, and they both moaned as he filled her. Her eyes went wide. "Oh my goodness, this is.... I mean.... It's... different."

"You've never been on top?" She shook her head. There was something exciting knowing that once again he was a first for her. He looked up at her and saw the confusion on her face. "Is something wrong?"

"I don't know what to do," she said with a little laugh.

"Whatever feels good to you will be wonderful for me."

She moved her hips, and he almost laughed when he saw her expression change from surprise to delight. "Will you help?"

"It would be my pleasure." He put his hands on her hips and raised her up, then brought her down. Clearly liking how the movement felt, she did it herself. She raised herself to where he almost slid out of her before sliding to sheath him inside her once more. "Do you like that?"

"Very much."

"Then find your rhythm and go for it. I'll be with you, every stroke."

And he was. She was hesitant at first, but grew bolder as each movement brought pleasure. When she found a consistent pace that had her arching her back, he reached up to grab her breasts, teasing the nipples and relishing her moans. Her pleasure was the sexiest thing he'd ever seen.

"I think I'm..."

"I'll help," he said and moved his hand to her swollen center. The moment he touched her, she cried out. Her movements sped up, and he used his thighs to meet her every thrust.

When she screamed out his name, he was right behind her, and when she collapsed on top of him, he wished they could stay that way forever.

Last night he was fighting a major fire, then sending Eden out of his room. Hours later, she was in his arms, and he was happier than he could remember being. So much for things changing slowly in small town New England.

Sadly, they had responsibilities which couldn't be met by staying in bed. They got dressed again and went to the kitchen. He put his arm around Eden as they stood drinking coffee. "I'm going to need a vat of this stuff to get through the day."

"You and me both," she said.

"What I really want is to go back to sleep for a few more hours."

"You sure you want sleep?" He smiled at her sassiness and gave her a lingering kiss. "I'll take that as a no."

"Sleep, sex and then maybe more sleep. But unfortunately, Harlow and I have to get to the newest site. The tenants will want to see if there's anything they can salvage, and I don't want them walking through the debris and getting hurt or contaminating evidence."

"I couldn't believe how big the fire was," she said.

"This one was not only bigger, but more daring. It started before it was fully dark, and people were working. Everyone got out, but there was a possibility of injury."

"Speaking of people who got out, one of the businesses was the real estate office where Monica Russo works. I was going to ask her if she was okay when she threw herself into Keith's arms. They're involved, and it wouldn't surprise me if their relationship began before I left Keith."

She told him the details of what she saw and overheard. "Interesting," he said. "She stopped by when I was interviewing Keith. I got the sense something was going on between them. It gives him another link to the fires. Maybe your father, too."

"My father? How so?"

"If he knew about the affair and thought Monica was interfering with the possibility of you and Keith getting back together, this could be his way of sending her a message to stay away."

"Except it looks like it drove them together."

"And truthfully, arson — even if he had someone else do the work — isn't your father's style. He's direct when it comes to getting what he wants. And he'd never destroy his own property."

"I have a motive, too. To hurt the woman involved with my ex-husband."

"That would be true if you knew about the affair before the fire."

"Which I didn't."

"And if you cared about Keith."

"Which I don't."

"I knew that," he said with a smile and a kiss. "Four fires, but the list of suspects hasn't changed. Maybe the site will give me information to narrow things down."

"There is one other overlap."

"Which is?"

"Grace, who lived in the other occupied apartment? Her sister, Linda, runs the temp agency in the building."

"Tenuous, but I'll take what I can get. Especially since I don't like how this keeps circling back to you and people connected to you."

"As you're so fond of pointing out, this is a small town. It doesn't take a lot for things to circle back."

"That's not comforting."

"Do you want a list of places and people connected to me?"

"Not a bad idea. Keep it to the key places you go and the people you see in a week. Also, make a note if they have a connection to your father or Keith."

"I'll have that for you as soon as I can."

They reluctantly got ready for work and headed out. He couldn't help but think again about what a life with her would be like. But his daydreaming stopped when he pulled into the parking lot of the ruined building, police tape creating a barrier to keep people back.

He had to stay focused. If the fires were connected to Eden, and Theo's gut told him they were, he had more reason than before to find the arsonist. He may not be able to protect his heart, but he'd do whatever it took to protect Eden.

Chapter Twenty-Six

♥

By the time Eden got to work, she was already exhausted. She'd had a rough night's sleep and as wonderful as the morning with Theo had been — and, oh, the sex *had* been wonderful — her emotions were raw and close to the surface. After the initial awkward reunion, Eden couldn't help but notice the comfort and connection they shared. She found it easy to trust him again, to open up, knowing he wouldn't use it against her as Keith and her father did whenever she was vulnerable. She didn't have to be on guard or act a certain way with him. It was as much a relief as it was empowering.

As Eden grabbed her tote and walked toward Maximum Results, she couldn't help but smile at the tenderness she noticed between her legs. That was something dance and yoga never did for her. The smile disappeared when she heard "Edie?"

Her bag fell off when her shoulders dropped. She turned to see Keith leaning on his BMW. He was smartly dressed in pressed khaki slacks, a light blue button-down shirt, and a tie. She preferred cargo pants, boots, and a polo.

"Hello, Keith. What are you doing here?"

"Can't a man check on his wife?"

"Ex-wife." This was almost as bad as her father coming by a few days ago. She re-shouldered her bag and continued walking. Keith followed, which annoyed but didn't surprise her.

"I haven't seen you in a while."

"You haven't seen me since the divorce was official. The fact that you're here now suggests you have an agenda."

"I want to know how you're doing."

"Why? When have you ever been concerned about that?" Then she remembered. "This is because you saw Theo yesterday. You want to know if anything is going on since we're living together."

"You're what?" He almost screamed.

Oops. She cringed. This was why she needed to keep her guard up when she was around Keith. There was no reason Keith would have heard about her living arrangement. Theo wouldn't have said anything. Fortunately, by this time she was at the front desk and Keith wouldn't ask questions where they might be overheard. "Any messages for me, Leslie?"

"One. Mrs. Gelber is running a little late this morning. She hopes it won't cause a problem."

"Not at all. Send her back as soon as she arrives. No need to buzz me." Pretending Keith wasn't there, she continued down the hall to her office and studio. He followed.

As soon as her office door shut, the expected explosion happened. "How can you be living with him? He only arrived in town a few days ago."

Five, she thought, but who's counting? "He showed up at his old house not realizing the Sinclairs told me I could stay there after the fire. I didn't want to kick him out, and he felt the same way."

"Oh, I'm sure he did." Keith couldn't keep the sarcasm out of his voice. "It's inappropriate."

"It's none of your business."

"You *are* my business."

"No, Keith, that's the joy of divorce. Our lives are completely and legally separate. You may have a connection to my father, but you no longer have one to me. What is the real reason you're here? Is it because of the fire last night or because my father knows our divorce is final, and you're hoping to change my mind?"

"Why would I be here because of the fire? Wait, you told your father the divorce is final?"

Technically, Theo told him, but there was no reason to clarify. She found it interesting Patrick hadn't said anything to Keith yet. Knowing her father as she did, he was saving the information for his advantage, just as he hadn't reached out to her about it. That's what information was for — power.

"It's not as if it's a secret. It's been in the works for months. I wonder why Dad hasn't said anything to you."

"Because he knows I haven't given up on you. On us."

"Do me a favor, Keith. Give up."

"I don't know why you're bothering with Theo. He's only here until they find the so-called arsonist. I'll bet he can't even manage that."

"Theo's work and when he leaves is not your concern." Eden wasn't going to let Keith get to her.

"I'm making it my concern. No matter what you think, I care about you, Edie." She hated the diminutive nickname and wished he'd stop using it. "And I want you to know when he leaves, I will be here for you."

"To pick up the pieces," she said, crossing her arms in front of her.

He stepped forward and put his hands on her shoulders. It took a good deal of willpower not to shudder. "Yes, and whatever else you'll need."

She moved away from him and walked behind her desk, giving herself distance and a barrier. "Thank you for the offer, but I can tell you it won't be necessary. Should the time come when I fall apart, I have ways to put myself back together and none of them require assistance or attention from you."

"Damn it, Eden, I am trying to help you."

That would be a first. Keith's primary interest was Keith. She didn't see it when they were together, but she could now. "No, you're trying to control me and condescend to me as you always have. And to get back in my father's good graces."

"You're lucky I'm even making this offer."

She paused to collect her thoughts. She remembered what she'd learned in therapy, the support she got from her friends, the strength she reconnected to because of Theo. The pieces added up to someone who didn't need to depend on others but who knew how to reach out for help. She could stand on her own *and* accept support. There was, as Janelle reminded her, a difference. "As appealing as you think you make returning to you sound, I know without a moment's doubt I would be better off alone for the rest of my life than to spend even one more day as your wife. Besides, there's someone who wants to be with you. Maybe you should focus on her instead."

"What are you talking about?"

"I was at the fire last night. I saw you with Monica. You looked close. Intimate even. I'm sure she was glad to stay with you last night."

His face paled, and she couldn't help the feeling of satisfaction. Maybe her father had a point about information holding power. During her marriage, she'd never had the upper hand. It was a fun position. "It's not what you think. I'm with her because I'm lonely. She doesn't mean anything to me, I swear."

Eden thought of Monica looking at engagement rings. "I'll bet that will be news to her. I doubt either of us means anything to you. And although you think I'm stupid and clueless, I would also bet you started seeing her long before I moved out."

"As usual, you have no idea what you're talking about. I don't know where you get your foolish ideas."

Eden recognized his words for what they were. A way to redirect his mistakes onto what he saw as a failing or weakness of hers which he could then exploit. She had enough. "Leave. You are not welcome here."

"Edie, I'm sorry, that came out wrong. It's been stressful these past few weeks, and I've missed you. I want you back."

"I'm sure you do, but it has nothing to do with caring about me. And I can honestly say I haven't missed you at all. Leaving you was the best thing I've done for myself. I'm sorry I didn't do it sooner." She didn't enjoy having to be blunt. To her, it sounded cruel, but there was no other way to deal with him. "I have a patient coming. You need to go."

"We're not done talking."

She walked to the door and opened it. "Yes, we are. If you don't go, I will call someone to have you removed."

"Don't be ridiculous," he said.

"I have two words for you. Restraining order."

"You wouldn't dare." She stared at him without saying a word. "Fine, I'll go, but you'll regret this."

"I doubt it. Goodbye," she said and slammed the door. It was a satisfying sound.

She dropped onto her office couch, took several deep breaths, and tried to get her hands to stop shaking. She may have appeared unruffled to Keith, but she didn't feel that way. What if Keith was the arsonist, and these fires were connected to him trying to get her back? Did he burn her apartment hoping she'd live with him again? He'd offered after the fire, and she turned him down. Would he hit Theo's house next? She needed to let Theo know about Keith coming by. Getting up, she found her phone and called him. It went to voice mail, so left him a message giving him the details she thought might help. Her client walked in as she said finished, and Eden gave Mrs. Gelber a smile and got to work.

After saying goodbye to the last student in her afternoon hip-hop dance class, Eden leaned against the mirror wall drinking some water and thinking about how to fill the time before going to the Seven Brothers. She had paperwork on patients needing her attention, but it could wait. All day she'd been antsy, almost over energetic. It was likely because of everything going on in her life, but if she were honest, it was mostly because of Theo.

A thought came, and she knew what she wanted. She wanted to dance.

Eden almost never danced for herself. For a long time, it was too much of a reminder of what she'd lost, and then it was because she didn't have the time or energy with everything else. These days, her dancing was either choreographing group pieces for student recitals or working with Courtney McMann, a young dancer who, like Eden, was hoping to go to a conservatory for college. She loved seeing Courtney's hope and enthusiasm and understood the challenges and fears the girl was facing.

Eden left the dance room and went to her office where she put a long skirt over her leggings and changed from jazz shoes to split sole ballet slippers. Back in the studio, she flipped through music choices on Spotify and selected Aaron Copland's *Appalachian Spring*. She was already warmed up, so when the music started, she faced the mirror and let it carry her away.

She moved across the floor, surrendering to the joy of the music. Her skirt flowed around her legs as she imagined herself dancing through the woods and into a clearing. Although Copland never wrote of fairies, that's what Eden saw as she moved, darting and dashing, bending and arching. She pictured herself looking for woodland friends and hoping not to be caught by dangerous mortals.

As the music swelled, she was lost in its beauty. Without thinking, she spun, ran, and leaped, stretching her legs as far as they would go. It felt wonderful, that instant of flying, soaring. It was as if the music itself held her aloft.

Her landing was sure, but her right leg, unfortunately, was not, and before her second foot could come down to give her balance, her knee buckled, and she hit the floor hard.

She stayed there for a moment, her heart racing, her breathing heavy. *Stupid, stupid, stupid.* She'd forgotten she couldn't do those things. No matter how good she felt or hopeful or happy, she had limits.

Suppose, God forbid, you get hurt again. You're alone. Her father's voice echoed in her thoughts. If she continued sitting there, she'd likely hear Keith's voice in her head, reminding her she couldn't manage without him.

"Are you okay, Ms. Eden?" Eden turned as Courtney rushed into the room and to her side.

"I'm fine," she said. "Foolish, but fine." Carefully she stood up, mindful of the twinges in her muscles not only from the fall but from shifting from rapid exercise to none. She took a step and was relieved when she experienced no actual pain. A slight limp, but that was to be expected. She walked over to her laptop, stopped the music and let the sadness in. She hadn't magically healed. "I was in the mood to dance, but I shouldn't have done the leap."

"Because of when you were hurt."

Eden had told Courtney why she didn't dance. "I got carried away."

"Dancing will do that to you."

Eden nodded. The girl understood. At thirteen, she showed more promise than Eden ever had. "Did I forget a lesson?" It was entirely possible Eden hadn't put something on her calendar. She'd been scattered since the fire.

"No, but you said when I had free time I could use the studio. When I got here, I saw you dancing. You looked beautiful."

Eden couldn't stop the blush. When was the last time anyone saw her dance? The most she did was demonstrate small passages to show her students what to follow. Nothing had made her want to dance until today. "Thank you."

"Do you miss it?"

"All the time."

"I know it's selfish of me to say this, but I'm glad you decided to stay here and teach. My mother could never drive me to Concord or any place with a bigger dance school." Courtney was raised by a single mom with a busy work schedule. Before finding Eden, Courtney studied with someone who ran a studio out of her garage. 'Studied' was an overstatement. The instructor didn't know much beyond the basics. "I'd still be learning from YouTube videos. I would have given up if it weren't for you."

Eden quickly blinked back the tears. She'd had PT patients thank her and share their gratitude for what she did, and she was glad to make a difference in their lives, but to know her work, talent, and commitment was supporting another dancer? That was special. "I've loved working with you, Courtney."

"Everyone always talks about what a great teacher you are."

"They do?" She hadn't had complaints, but she'd never heard this.

"All the time. In the locker room, at school. Have you ever thought about opening your own place? You know, having your own dance academy? Oh my God, that would be so cool. We wouldn't have to hear gym techno-pop when we're dancing."

Eden laughed. The studio rooms were down a long hall and around a corner from the lobby, but they shared their back wall with the main workout room. It made for some interesting musical accompaniment. Courtney continued, "And you wouldn't have to worry if the gym wanted to schedule new classes when you wanted the studio."

Needing to work around the gym's schedule or wait before she could try something new wasn't ideal. "I wouldn't want to stop seeing my physical therapy patients."

"Sure, I get that," Courtney said, then broke into a smile. "Then do both, like you do here. Or more than one studio and then you could hire people to teach more classes. And maybe you could even find something with space for our recitals?"

Courtney was talking a mile a minute, excited by the idea. Eden was a moment from telling the girl to calm down when she noticed how fast her heart was going. A business of her own, like her friends. In her own place, she'd have a final say in anything she wanted to create. Something she could grow and build over time. Something to look forward to after Theo left. "You know, it's not a bad idea. I have no clue where to start, but it could be fun."

"You think so?"

"Don't you?"

"Are you kidding? I think it would be fabulous. I'm just not used to having adults take me seriously."

"Well, I am taking this very seriously." Eden could sense doubt wanting to rush in and squash the excitement, but she wasn't going to let that happen.

"This is awesome."

"I have some thinking to do, and you have dance practice to get in. Your teacher can be a bitch," Eden said with a wink. "There's no class here for another hour. And you know what? I'll give you an extra key to the studio, so you can come and practice when I'm not here. Just remember to sign in at the front desk so someone knows you're back here."

"Really? I can get here on my bike, which means I don't have to wait for mom to bring me. Thank you, thank you, thank you."

Courtney jumped around, making happy little yips, then threw her arms around Eden with youthful exuberance. Eden returned the hug. She was as excited as the girl, if for a different reason. "You're welcome. Be responsible. No inviting friends to join you."

"I promise."

As Eden left the studio, she looked back at the young dancer doing warm-ups at the barre. Once in her office, Eden thought about how crazy the last half hour had been. One minute she was feeling sorry for herself and what she couldn't do only to learn soon after how her work as a teacher made a difference. It was a precious gift.

And she couldn't stop thinking of Courtney's idea. If she planned carefully, she could hire other therapists and dance instructors. In the last few months, she'd had to refer clients elsewhere because there was no room in her schedule. She might not be strong enough to dance, but there were other ways to make a difference.

You are so much stronger than you know, my sweet.

Eden glanced around the office, expecting to see her mother. She'd heard the voice so clearly she wouldn't have been surprised to see Donna standing next to her.

Tears filled Eden's eyes as she thought of her beautiful mom. How many times, when she'd been down on herself, had Donna reminded her of her passion and commitment? There had been countless drives coming home from lessons where Eden spent most of the time crying, certain she wasn't good enough. Donna would let her cry it out, then ask questions to help Eden see what she could learn from the situation, whether it was an actual mistake or Eden being critical of herself. The only other person who'd been able to get Eden out of her head was Theo. It was too bad once both were gone, her father and Keith ended up filling the space.

But she'd changed that.

"How do you always know what I need?" she once asked her mother during the weeks leading up to her fall senior recital. Eden was on edge and convinced she'd never get into the Conservatory.

"Oh, honey, I don't. I sit here and listen to you and my heart aches for your struggle. I see how hard you're working, how much this means to you."

"But you always say the right thing."

Her mother had reached out and taken her hand. "I say what's in my heart and what I believe. I've seen you dance and, yes, I've seen you make mistakes, but I've also seen you get up, try again, and improve. I can't see the future, but I know how strong you are."

She was strong. Eden gave a short laugh. How had that happened?

Chapter Twenty-Seven

♥

Theo chugged from a water bottle and stared at what remained of the businesses in the plaza and the untouched dentist's office. He didn't want to think about how their volunteer teams would have managed if the blaze had gotten to the oxygen or nitrous oxide tanks. Which begged the question — why didn't the arsonist start the fire there? Was it because people were working? This arsonist focused on creating chaos and destruction of property. But a fire closer to the dentist's would have created a hell of a lot more damage.

And then there was the other question he couldn't get out of his head. How was he going to leave Eden again after this was over?

Telling her to leave his bed had been awful, but their conversation and her understanding this morning was a balm he didn't know he needed. Not to mention the sex. If he closed his eyes, he could see her above him, her face flushed with pleasure, his name on her lips.

This was not helping him focus. He had a job to do.

There was more property to cover with this fire and for the first time, Harlow found an origin site inside the building besides two sites at the back. As he suspected, the arsonist was getting cockier, less worried about being caught and more excited to do damage. It was a two-story strip mall with small offices above the principal businesses below. To accommodate them, in the center was an entrance that housed mailboxes and the stairwell. Something had been used there, making it difficult for the people upstairs to get out.

As Theo worked his way through the site, he discovered an additional parking area behind the building and meaning the center lobby could be accessed from the front and back. Theo could picture how the arsonist got the blaze going. He'd poured the accelerant outside first, poured more and set the fire, then left to ignite the exterior locations and leave before the fire was noticed. So much for finding witnesses who might have seen their firebug. A few minutes later, Theo learned there was one other thing the arsonist knew about this building — the location of the water valve to control the sprinkler. It was off.

It wasn't difficult to manage. It was like shutting off the water in a house. A quick turn of a knob and it was useless. Neither Eden's apartment nor the Barrett professional building had sprinkler systems because they were older and smaller. This site was newer and up to code, but someone knew their way around the safety feature, which put all the tenants on the suspect list.

The most remarkable thing about working through the site wasn't what he and Harlow found. It was the number of times they were interrupted. When he'd done the inspection of the other sites, people stopped by if they saw Martin's car. Here he was five days later doing the same work, but people were coming by to talk to him. Harlow would give a chuff, and Theo would look up to see one or two people parked by his truck watching him work. When he went over to ask if something was wrong, he would get some version of "Came to see how you were doing," or "It's great you're here to help us find out who's hurting our businesses," not to mention the offers of food. Who knew so many people loved to make and deliver meatloaves, apple cobbler, and turkey noodle casserole? Each time he'd say, "That's not necessary," the answer was something like, "Of course it's not necessary, but we want to say thank you."

To say he was surprised was an understatement. It was unnervingly pleasant, but he couldn't help but wonder where all this help was when he and his brothers needed it years ago.

After he finished everything he could onsite, he found Harlow dozing in the sun a few yards from the end of the property. He envied her ability to shut things off. Dogs didn't worry about letting people down, complicated pasts, or falling in love.

Love? Where did that thought come from?

Okay, he knew where it came from, but now was not the time to focus on his relationship with Eden or if she'd consider moving to Baltimore.

He snapped a few more photos to get back his focus and stared at the burned remains, willing them to tell him something new. He had enough pictures to wallpaper the inside of the firehouse. More evidence to send to the lab. And no answers.

The next "How's it going?" surprised him.

Theo looked up from the debris to see Dylan standing a few feet away. Great, just what he needed. A witness to his incompetence. "Fine. Finishing the first step. Evidence inspection and collection."

"I had a break in my day and thought I'd drive over to see what's left of the place. That was some fire last night. Biggest I've ever been around. Anything I can do to help?" Theo heard concern, not criticism, in the question.

"Unfortunately not. There's a lot of 'hurry up and wait' in this work." Theo whistled for Harlow, who joined him and Dylan as they walked to his truck.

"Did you find traces of accelerant again?"

"Inside and out. He intentionally caused a bigger blaze."

"Damn," Dylan said, putting his hands in his front pockets. "What does that mean for us?"

"Us?" Theo was confused. This was his responsibility.

"We're your team. We all want to catch this guy. Everyone's on edge with this arsonist doing more and more damage. We want to help you."

Theo didn't know how to respond. "I appreciate the offer, but I'm not sure what I can suggest."

"What would you be doing on a regular case?"

Theo considered the question. With Prometheus, he worked with a team, and no one shouldered the burden of solving a case alone. Here, he didn't think he had a choice. He was the only one trained as an investigator, and he'd taken it as a personal mission to do this for Martin and prove himself to everyone. Was that unnecessary? "We look into the financials of the owners, talk to witnesses and anyone who was harmed. Then we'd bring the information together, look for connections. I also wouldn't need to fight any new fires. I'd be watching the crowds."

Dylan considered this then said, "I'm a little crazy these days with after school wrestling team practice, but the assistant coach to do more work, so I could make some calls for you during my breaks or look over the new pictures if you want. I mean, I'm no expert, but who knows? Maybe I'll get lucky."

Theo fell back against the truck. He hoped it looked like he was relaxing and not like he was floored, which he was. He'd never thought to ask for help. "That would be great. Would you also be willing to call a few of the volunteers from here and the other towns? Maybe someone saw something, and they don't realize it."

"Of course."

"I could get all of you a list of people affected. You might see a connection I missed."

"We can do that. Anything to catch this guy."

"Thank you." He didn't have any new answers, but he had support. It was a start.

Dylan turned to go to his car then stopped. "Theo?"

"Yes?"

"I'm glad you came back. You're being here has been a huge help."

He wasn't back, the teenager inside of him protested automatically. And he didn't know if he could help anyone. But the thoughts didn't ring as true as they once did.

After another trip to get photos printed — they knew his name at the pharmacy already — Theo got in his truck and said to Harlow, "Let's get something to eat, girl, before we sift through all this information at the station." She chuffed in agreement.

He stopped to get gas at the pumps in front of the Triangle General Store and realized he'd done so little driving to get around the small town, this was the first time he'd needed gas since he arrived. Good thing, since there weren't many places to fill up. They named the Triangle for its location at the intersection of the main road that led into Fable Notch from the highway and another diagonal road which led into town. Tourists stopped to get gas and shop for souvenirs in the quaint general store, but locals knew they sold great sandwiches, and it was the only place they could buy Claire Fisher's pickles, which she made fresh. She and her husband, Tom, ran the Triangle, and they'd both been kind to Theo and his brothers, adding chips and salads to simple sandwich orders.

He stepped in and looked around, noticing small changes like a stand of gift cards and another which held phone chargers and portable batteries. And while they now sold vape products in addition to cigarettes, there was still a large display of maple syrup candies in funny shapes. He never liked the overly sugary treat, but outsiders bought them up like crazy. He headed to the counter to place his order, but stopped when he heard a conversation about a familiar topic.

"I drove past what was left of the strip mall this morning. What a mess. There's almost nothing left."

"No one was hurt, and the dentist's office was spared. That's important." He recognized Claire's voice.

"I heard they had to call in fire departments from two other towns. And this is after Martin called in Theo Hanson. The biggest fire yet." He thought the woman's voice was familiar, but he couldn't place it. He definitely recognized the tone. Contempt.

"Calling in other departments has nothing to do with Theo. It's about the size of the fires," Claire said.

"And did you hear? He broke into the Polk's house yesterday."

"He what?"

"Well, practically. Rita locked herself out, so she called for help. She said Theo had no trouble picking the lock."

Theo's face heated. This is how the truth became something twisted and painful. This is how people continued to think what they did about him.

"He was helping. And I heard he did a great job last night."

"I can't believe we're having this fire problem. Nothing like this has ever happened before. Do you think they're going to catch the person responsible?" The woman said 'they,' but Theo knew she meant him.

"Martin wouldn't have asked Theo to come if he didn't think he could help."

"He hasn't done much good." Theo hated the truth of that.

"Millie was in here the other day, and she said Theo is terrific at his job. If anyone can find out who's behind this, Theo can."

"She's always had such a soft spot for him. For all the Hanson's." Soft spot was code for blind spot. "Everyone knows without the Sinclairs, those boys would have ended up with child services even before their mother died. Martin and Millie took on so much responsibility."

And responsibility was code for expense. A knot formed in Theo's stomach. It wasn't until years after he'd left that he wondered how Martin and Millie managed to take care of three extra kids on Martin's salary and the part-time income Millie made as a piano teacher. He owed them. He wouldn't — couldn't — let Martin down.

"Theo turned out admirably. So did Nick and Cole."

"Oh, please. Cole may be a big rock star, but we know they're all into drugs and things."

"You shouldn't generalize," Claire said. Theo appreciated Claire's standing up for them, but the other woman held the more common opinion.

"I hear he's been seen with Eden Barrett again. I'm sure Patrick's not happy. Some things never change."

No, Theo thought. They didn't. He turned to leave and was almost at the door when Claire noticed him. "Theo, we were just talking about you and all the great work you're doing to help stop these fires. What can I get for you? On the house. Do you still love roast beef?" She must have known he'd heard the conversation. Heard the derision and suppositions made by the woman he couldn't see.

"No, nothing. Thanks." He turned toward and headed for the exit.

She called after him, "Are you sure?"

"Yeah. Just came in to say hi, but I know you're busy, and I should get back to work." He dropped the bag of chips he was still holding onto a display by the door and hurried to his truck. He got into the driver's seat, then slammed his head back against the headrest several times. Harlow gave a woof, as though asking where lunch was. He turned to her. "Sorry, girl. We'll get food somewhere else."

As Theo put the keys in the ignition, a knock on the car window startled him. Claire was standing there, a worried look on her face. He rolled down the window, and she said, "Theo, don't mind Alice. She's never had a kind word for anyone, not even her own children. Why she worked in the high school for all those years is beyond me." Now he recognized the voice. Alice Bruce, the secretary for the vice principal, was someone he spent way too much time seeing during his four years.

He couldn't remember her smiling. "Here," Claire said as she handed him a bag through the window. "It's not freshly made, of course, but you were not leaving without lunch if I could help it."

Theo looked in the bag and saw the pre-wrapped sandwich, smelled the garlic of the pickles, and the bag of chips he'd been holding. "Thank you. You didn't have to."

"Of course I didn't, but that doesn't mean I didn't want to. And like I said, it's on the house. Have a good day."

He gave her a smile and drove off. He appreciated her generosity, but Alice's words and attitude stayed with him. *Some things never change* she'd said. It was true, and he'd let himself forget. Let the changes in a few people lull him into a false sense of acceptance. He should have known better. The people in this town had long memories for old mistakes.

Fable Notch was not the place for him. It ever was.

He couldn't let himself forget.

Chapter Twenty-Eight

♥

In between clients and classes, Eden spent some time in her office doing an Internet search on nightmares from PTSD, reading medical journal articles and first-person experiences from people who were suffering from it. She also researched people who lived with people who had it. It was clear Theo's case was not as bad as some, but it would impact any relationship they had.

Okay, they didn't actually have a relationship, but in case she was around when he had another nightmare, she wanted to be prepared to give him whatever support she could.

Because you want him to stay.

She needed to shut that voice up, tell it to stop wanting the impossible. Why would he stay? For her? He had a job, a community, and things to go back to in Baltimore. Even if they did care for each other — and even if their attraction hadn't changed — it wasn't enough of a reason to relocate his whole life.

You could move. She could. She leaned back in her chair as she considered the possibility. There were phones and Zoom calls to keep her in touch with her friends and her certification as a PT would make it easy for her to find a job. But she had to consider the people she knew and saw, the things she was a part of. Even her dad was a reason to stay. They might not have the best relationship, but he was the only parent she had.

"No," she said to the empty room and closed her laptop, wishing she could close her thoughts as easily. She shouldn't move for Theo any more than he should move for her. She'd have to find a new therapist. And when Theo traveled for work, she'd be alone. Really alone. No friends close by for company. No places where she could go to see familiar faces. The only available relationship she'd have would be Theo, which was too close to what happened when she was with Keith. Not a situation she wanted to repeat, no matter how much she cared for Theo.

She took a drink of water and admonished herself for allowing her teenage dreams to rule her thoughts. She needed to stop imagining a future with Theo. It wasn't as if he'd given her any indication he wanted something more. Maybe after he caught the arsonist, they could talk about next steps. She could see him in Baltimore. He could come back on the holidays.

It won't be enough.

She stopped. That was a truth she could accept. She'd always want more when it came to Theo, but the last year made her aware she had needs too, things that were important to her, and she wouldn't give those up. She wouldn't try to hold him. Instead, she'd build a life she loved.

This thought brought her back to Courtney's idea of opening a studio of her own. The challenges of working around the needs of the gym occasionally frustrated her. It limited what she could do and the number of students she could teach. She'd thought of having her own place when she first started adding classes to her schedule, but Keith had squashed the idea. First, he'd laughed and then he spent the rest of the night discussing the risks to the point where not only did she not believe she could handle it, but he made it sound so awful she lost interest.

Now she had a good friend who ran her own business, and another who was taking over a veterinary practice. They would give her the advice and encouragement she couldn't get before. From what she saw and heard from Janelle, there would be a lot of work with unexpected backslides and frustrations, but successes and progress to balance that off. It would be worth it. She opened her laptop again and searched for sites on starting a business.

Are we on for dinner at 7BB? After her last client, the group text started by Janelle confirmed their regular Friday night get together. Laurel held the owner's table for them, and they sat for hours eating, drinking, and talking.

Dani's reply came first. *I'm done by 6, but no drinking for me. Have an early morning surgery.*

Eden glanced at her schedule and texted, *I'll be there by 7. Don't finish the nachos without me.*

No promises, came from Janelle.

We can order another, said Dani.

She loved her friends. Honest and funny, supportive without being critical. Completely different from the professional dance world — and her father. For years she heard in one way or another how she was doing something wrong, needed to do it better or do it over. Janelle and the others were a balm on an ache she'd carried most of her life.

When she finally arrived at the Seven Brothers, there were a few bites of nachos left. After hugging her friends, Eden slid onto the bench next to Janelle, then ordered a glass of Laurel's seasonal ale and more nachos. Dani was telling them about a pet owner who almost didn't let her look at her cat because Dani was "too young."

"They want Doc Wheeler, and every day there's at least one tense discussion before I can treat their pets. He can't even come in on the days I'm there or they'll demand to see him," Dani said. She took a sip of her soda and stared into the glass.

"You've barely been back two months," Janelle said. "It's going to take time for people to accept he's retiring, and you're the one in charge."

"Maybe I shouldn't be. Maybe he should hire someone else, someone older than me. Make me the part-time person."

Eden hated seeing her friend sad. "Is that what you want?"

"No. I love it there. Here," she said, gesturing wildly to take in the world. "But what if the people don't trust me? I just want what's best for the patients."

"And that's you," Janelle said, banging down the glass she was drinking from for emphasis. Eden agreed. She remembered when Dani was young and visited her aunts during the summer. Every year she'd volunteered at the veterinary clinic. Working with animals had always been Dani's passion.

Dani sighed. "I hope so."

"It is so," Eden assured her friend. "A few bad days or difficult owners doesn't change that."

"Thanks, you two. I thought taking over the practice would be easy and fun. It's much less crazy than the animal hospital in Houston where we barely knew our patient's names and our schedules were jammed, but this change has been rough."

"That's why Doc is working with you. You're not on your own here."

Laurel came over to the table and put down a plate of nachos and one of poutine drenched in gravy and said, "You're never on your own here. Haven't you noticed?"

"No fair — you grew up with seven brothers," Eden said. As an only child, Eden found Laurel's large family fascinating.

"And I can't get rid of them." She pointed a chin in the direction of the bar where her oldest brother, Gabriel, sat talking with someone. "One or two more will be by before the night's out."

"That's because your beer is the best," Janelle said, lifting her glass in a toast.

"True," Laurel said, sitting next to Dani and giving her a quick hug. Eden smiled as Dani put her head on Laurel's shoulder. The two had been as close as she and Janelle, at least in the summer. "Try not to worry. Give people time. You're not an outsider, not after all those years with Rosie and Helen. Eventually, they'll trust you."

"I'm afraid patience isn't one of my virtues," Dani said and took a bite of the poutine she'd put on her plate. "Yum. Neither is moderation when I'm here. These are so good, Laurel."

"Glad you like them. Keep eating. I'll be back in a bit."

After Laurel left, Eden took a deep swallow of her beer and said, "I could use a little help, too. A student put an idea in my head, and I want to know if it's viable. Who wants to help me create a plan to open my own business?"

Chapter Twenty-Nine

♥

Theo had pictures and notes spread on the dining room table. He hoped a new layout and location would help, but even with Dylan and two other volunteers stopping by, he had no new ideas. When he heard a car pull into the driveway, he looked at the clock, surprised to see it was after ten. Eden had a fun night with her friends.

Eden walked inside, laughing with her arm around another woman. It took him a moment to recognize her. Nick's old girlfriend. "Dani Vaughn? Is that you?"

"It is. Hello, Theo. Can you give me a hand with our girl here?"

That was when he noticed Eden had her arm around Dani. "What's wrong? Did she hurt herself?"

"Only with beers. She rarely drinks much and clearly this was little more than she could handle. I didn't drink since I have an early appointment tomorrow morning, so I drove her home. Truthfully, I think it's more excitement than alcohol that's got her flying. Ready to come down, Eden?"

"Nope, never. Isn't it great she's here again?" Eden said, looking at Dani and giving her a squeeze. Theo blinked hard at the sound of Eden's higher pitched voice. "We've had so much fun together."

"Especially tonight," he said.

"I'm celebrating."

"What are you celebrating?"

"My new business," Eden said and lifted her hand in a toast as if it held a glass. "I'm going to have a dance and PT studio."

"That's wonderful news." He looked at Dani for clarification.

"One of her students gave her the idea to open her own studio. We spent most of the last few hours brainstorming with her, coming up with next steps, and I think there may be the first draft of a business plan on some of these cocktail napkins." She pointed to a wad of napkins in Eden's hand. "With Janelle and Laurel helping, a lot of planning was done."

"It's going to be so, so, so, so, great." She twirled away from Dani and barely missed hitting the table. Harlow, hearing a familiar voice, had come in and took a step back when Eden nearly tripped over her. "I'm going to have space for classes and patients and maybe even a place to hold recitals depending on the building I find. I don't know where I'll find it, and I don't know how I'm going to pay for it all, but I know it's going to be so, so, so great."

"It sounds great." It was more than the alcohol making her loopy.

"Doesn't it? I won't have to worry about when the gym wants to hold classes or hearing the awful music they play for the people working out. And maybe I'll be able to hire other teachers who are good at the areas I'm not because students want to learn tap dance, and I don't know how." As if to prove her point, Eden attempted a few steps, tripping over her feet in the process.

He reached out to steady her, but she skirted away. "Eden, you need to take a breath,"

Dani laughed. "Good luck with that. She's a little eager about this project."

"So I see." Theo couldn't help but smile at Eden's enthusiasm. She was dancing all over the room, putting down napkins as she went. He could see drawings and numbers and stars.

"I'm looking forward to *all* of it. Even the hard work. It will be wonderful." She gave a little spin and landed in Theo's arms. "I'm going to name it after my mother."

"Name what?"

"The studio, silly. Hutchinson Studio for Dance and Physical Therapy. Doesn't that sound perfect? My father has plenty of places with his name on it. Now my mom will have one, too."

"It sounds terrific. But first you need to get some sleep."

"Do you need my help?" Dani offered.

"I've handled bigger drunks than this. I'll give her aspirin, a big glass of water, and put her to bed."

"Her car is at the Seven Brothers. Can you get her there tomorrow?"

Since the case was going nowhere, there was no need to be at the station early. "Not a problem."

"I don't think she has any morning appointments, so you can let her sleep in."

"Will do. Thanks for bringing her home."

"Anytime. Good night, Eden. Sweet dreams. Don't give Theo any trouble."

"Me?" Eden put her hand on her chest. Her dramatic look of surprise was comical. "I never cause any trouble. I always do what I'm supposed to do. Well, maybe not recently, but I think that's good, don't you?"

"Absolutely. You're our rebel. Now get to sleep." With a wave, Dani was gone.

"I'm glad she's back. She's terrific. So are Janelle and Laurel. They're good friends. I'm so lucky." She slumped against Theo, her energy waning. "I don't know if you noticed, but I've had a little too much to drink."

"So I see."

"It's because Laurel makes great beer." In an unexpected shift, Eden pulled away, a look of concern passing over her face. "Oh, Theo, I'm sorry. You're not mad, are you?"

"About what?"

"That I've been drinking. I know with your mom—"

He put a finger on her lips to silence her. "Eden, you are nothing like my mother. Getting carried away with your friends isn't even remotely related to what she did to herself and to us."

"Okay, good. This is not something I usually do. Please don't tell my dad or Keith. They'd get mad at me, and you know how I hate when people yell." She stopped and burst out laughing. "I forgot. I don't have to worry about them anymore. Maybe I should call them and *tell* them I'm drunk. Show them it's my life, and I can do what I want. I can drink what I want, stay out with my friends, start my business. I can kiss you."

And she did. She put her hand behind his head and pulled him into a kiss that was more sloppy than passionate but still ignited everything inside of him. She closed what little distance remained between them and his arms went around her of their own volition. He loved the feel of her and wanted more, but alcohol fueled her current bravery, and he wasn't going to take advantage. "You need to get to bed."

"You're going to take me to bed? That sounds like a lovely idea."

"I'm going to put you to bed. There's a difference."

"But I like it when we're in bed together. Wasn't this morning incredible? When I kissed my way down your body until I got to your...."

Theo silenced her with his mouth. Nothing too passionate, but enough to get her to stop talking. He didn't want her reminding him of how they started their day or listing all the things she enjoyed about their lovemaking. Tonight, he would be a gentleman. He had a strict rule against sleeping with a woman when she'd been drinking, even if she'd previously consented. He'd seen how his mother's inhibitions changed when she drank. More than once, when he and Cole had gone to the Varnum to bring her home, they had to pull her off a guy who was more than willing to take advantage of her inebriated state.

"You need sleep, Eden. Let me help you." He walked them to the stairs, but she pulled out of his arms.

"No, no, no. I don't want to be in my bed. I want to be in yours. Then I can tell you about my new business, and you can tell me about your day, and it will all be wonderful."

Wonderful, he thought, as he followed her into his room. If this is what it took to get her to sleep, fine. He sat her on one side of the bed. Like an actual couple, sharing their lives. Except they weren't, and they couldn't.

He slipped off her shoes, then her leggings, doing his best not to be distracted by the exposed skin, the curve of her hip. As quickly as he could, he covered her with a blanket and gave her a kiss on the forehead. He took a step toward the door, but she grabbed his hand. "You're not coming to bed?"

"I'll be there in a minute. I'm going to get you some water or you're going to have a whopper of a headache in the morning."

"You always know what I need," she said, releasing his hand.

If only that were true.

After making sure she took the aspirin he gave her, Theo turned out the lights in the bedroom and went back into the great room. He walked around collecting the napkins she'd strewn about, putting them in a neat pile on the kitchen island so she'd be able to find them in the morning. There were sketches of a building layout, lists of possible costs, and even a hastily drawn logo. He stared at them with a mixture of sadness and pride. As soon as she'd mentioned the business idea, she took a step away from him and into a new life. Even when the alcohol wore off, the excitement wouldn't. This was something Eden wanted, and she'd be great at it. And it would honor her mother. If he'd had a fleeting thought — or more — of asking her to come to Baltimore, this squashed the idea.

You could stay here.

He tried to shake off the thought as he got ready for bed. She rolled into him when he got under the covers, and he put his arm around her, bringing her close, breathing in the floral scent of her shampoo. He couldn't imagine being more comfortable with someone, not that he'd had much experience one way or another.

Stay here.

It was tempting, the thought of being with her day in and day out. Opening and running a New England branch for Prometheus. Spending time with Adam, Millie and Martin, even hanging out with the other firefighters. As frustrating as the case had been, and as worried as he was about how many more fires would be set before he caught this guy, he couldn't deny that his time, when he wasn't working, had been more fun than he expected.

Some things never change.

Alice Bruce's voice rang in his head. He couldn't forget the people like her. Not to mention Eden's father. What if Patrick found a way to threaten Eden's happiness again? There weren't a lot of buildings she'd be able to buy or rent for her new studio and many of the ones available probably belonged to Patrick in one way or another. If she had to avoid those properties, it could cost her money or the location she wanted. And what about Adam? If Theo got involved with Eden, would Patrick cause problems when it came time for Adam to purchase his building? Patrick had his fingers in too many pies in Fable Notch and neighboring towns. Theo didn't doubt for a minute he'd make trouble wherever possible for Theo and anyone connected to him.

He wouldn't give Patrick the chance. He'd go back to Baltimore as if nothing had changed. He was up for visiting the Sinclairs in the future, and he hoped to stay in touch with Adam, but he wouldn't do anything that might hurt the people he cared about. Staying here was not an option.

Chapter Thirty

♥

Eden woke slowly the next morning. Her head was a little fuzzy, and it surprised her when the clock told her it was almost ten. The Seven Brothers. Too much beer.

Oops.

She remembered last night, Dani bringing her home. She kissed Theo and then... he tucked her into bed. Turning her head slowly, she saw the glass of water on the nightstand. *Drink me first*, said a note. It was nice to be taken care of.

Eden did as the note suggested then followed the smell of coffee into the kitchen where she found Theo reading something on his tablet, Harlow sitting at his feet as though waiting for something to do. "Good morning, sleepy," he said. "There's a mug by the pot for you."

As she added cream and sweetener to her drink, she asked, "Isn't Sleepy what you used to call Jeremy?"

"Good memory," he said, taking a drink from his own cup. Laurel's brother, Jeremys, who'd been a friend of Nick's, hated mornings even more than Eden did. "For a woman who had a lot to drink and no coffee yet, you're pretty clear-headed."

"Sleeping in helps," she said.

"No ill effects from last night?"

"Thanks to the water you gave me then and this morning, I think I'm good."

"One of the few good things to come from growing up with my mom. I know how to avoid a hangover — and before you say anything again, no, you're not reminding me of my mother."

"I don't have anything to apologize for, do I?"

He came around the island and gave her a soft kiss. "Not a thing. Dani said your car is at the Seven Brothers, so whenever you're ready, I'll take you over."

"Am I keeping you from anything this morning?"

"No, I'm going to meet with a few of the volunteers at the station and then we're going to talk with the stations who helped us on Thursday. And I'm supposed to go over to see Martin and give him an update. Do you have a busy day?"

She shook her head. "Two classes, one patient. I don't have many appointments on the weekends, but occasionally there's someone who can't make it during the week."

"What would you think of taking Harlow with you? She won't have anything to do if she's with me."

"Not a problem. I enjoy having her for company. Millie is in my yoga class this afternoon. Maybe she can take Harlow after so the Duncan twins can play with her."

"Oh, she will love that. Good idea. I'll call her and make sure they'll be around."

The coffee worked its way through her morning fog, and she asked, "We can have dinner later if you're free."

She thought he hesitated before saying, "Sure, I can do that. Is there someplace you'd like to go?"

"I can't think of anything off the top of my head — coffee hasn't worked that well yet — but if I think of something, I'll let you know."

"I'll be on the lookout for your text. Nothing fancy — I've got nothing to wear."

Eden laughed. "I'm having dinner with my dad tomorrow, and I have to dress for that, so causal is fine with me."

A little while later, he'd dropped her at the brewery and kissed her goodbye. It was a simple, boring way to start the day, and Eden thought it was perfect. As she and Harlow headed to Maximum Results, she couldn't deny the truth. It had taken less than a week, but she was in love with Theo.

She didn't think it could come to anything, but Eden was determined to enjoy whatever she could before he left. She'd lived through loss before — including losing Theo — she would find a way to handle it again.

The afternoon passed easily, even with being occasionally distracted by thoughts of Theo. She waited in her studio for Millie to come back after changing and take Harlow when an unexpected—and unwelcome—visitor came into the dance studio.

She had no idea what to say to her ex-husband's current girlfriend. If there was proper etiquette for this, Eden wasn't familiar with it. "Hello, Monica. What brings you here?"

"I heard you know about me and Keith. I wanted to talk to you, to explain."

Harlow, who had been standing by Eden, walked around and sniffed at Monica. She returned to Eden's side when she was done and gave two loud barks, which echoed in the studio and made Monica jump. Eden liked the idea Harlow didn't care for Monica either and scratched the dog between her ears. "There's nothing to explain. Keith's free to see who he wants. You two being together doesn't bother me. He and I are through, and it's been legal for over two weeks."

"Your divorce is final?"

"You look surprised. There seems to be a lot of miscommunication going on. You didn't mention you were seeing Keith, and he didn't tell you we're no longer married. Anything else that's gone unsaid?"

Monica crossed her arms across her chest and stood taller. "Maybe I shouldn't tell you this, but Keith and I have been seeing each other for over two years."

Longer than Eden thought. And despite the other woman's words, Eden got the impression Monica was more than happy to give her this news. "I'm not surprised."

"I'm sorry, Eden."

"No, I don't think you are, but it doesn't matter. You are welcome to him. Clearly you get something from him I never did. Hell, I wish he'd left me for you years ago. It would have been better for us all."

Monica's expression changed instantly, from feigned kindness to complete frostiness. "He's not a castoff, Ms. High and Mighty Barrett. He's a good man," Monica said, taking a step forward.

Eden stepped back. She didn't feel comfortable near the anger in the other woman's eyes, and she trusted her instincts. "That's not what I meant."

"You think you're entitled to whatever you want because your father is rich and controls so much of this town."

"I've never thought that."

"Oh, please, I can tell. The way you walk around, so proud and haughty, and the way people always rush to do things for you. You'd be a skinny little nobody without your father's name and money. Keith wouldn't have looked twice at you if it weren't for Patrick. Everyone knows he wanted me until he found out you were available."

Eden didn't know what to say. She never expected this kind of venom, nor was she aware Monica had disliked her for so long. Eden was saved from having to respond when Millie came in. "I'm ready to take Harlow. Grace's kids are looking forward to seeing her." Millie must have seen something in Eden's expression, because she looked at the two women and asked, "Is everything all right?"

"It's fine, Millie," Eden answered, not taking her eyes off Monica. "We were clearing the air. I think we've said all we need to, Monica, don't you?"

"There's a lot more I'd like to say," Monica said, "but I don't suppose it would change anything." Eden thought it was more likely Monica didn't want to say anything in front of an audience. "Goodbye, Eden."

Eden said nothing as the woman turned and left.

"I get the impression I interrupted something," Millie said when they were alone.

"Only Monica letting me know she and Keith have been having an affair for several years."

"Holy shit," Millie said, her hand flying up to cover her mouth. A beat later, both women burst out laughing.

"Thank you, Millie. That was exactly what I needed," Eden said as her giggles subsided.

"I knew you were well rid of Keith, but I never would have guessed he had something going on the side. Are you okay?"

"I'm fine. Part of me wishes I knew sooner. I wasted a lot of time with him."

Millie shrugged. "You can't control these things. It was time when it was time."

"Thanks," she said, giving Millie a hug. Harlow chose that moment to bark. Eden squatted down and gave the dog a hug, too. "And to you, girl, my sweet protector. You didn't like her, did you?"

"Didn't you say Keith is still pursuing you?"

Eden nodded. "He came over yesterday to tell me it wasn't too late for us. He didn't know I had seen them together or that my father knows about our divorce, but there's a lot of that going on. Keith hadn't told Monica the divorce was final. I got to give her the news."

"Lord, no wonder she isn't happy. I'm glad your future is much brighter."

Eden smiled, thinking about the truth of Millie's statement. No matter what — if anything — happened with Theo, things were going to keep getting better for her.

Hours after he left the house, Theo was sitting in the Sinclair's living room with Martin, reviewing where he was on the case and watching the Red Sox. Meeting with the other station's volunteers hadn't let to any new ideas. At least he had dinner with Eden to look forward to. They'd leave from the house at 5:30, then decide where to go. The twins had agreed to "babysit" Harlow while he went out.

As he and Martin talked and passed pictures back and forth, Theo's phone pinged with a text from the lab. The results on the accelerant came in. Kerosene. Great, all he needed to do was question everyone on the list who also had a backyard grill. He might as well have Harlow sniff the whole town. He hated not having anything concrete, which is what he told Martin.

"We knew this wasn't going to be easy," Martin said.

"I'm sorry I'm letting you down." It hurt to say the words.

"Because it's not solved yet?"

"Yes."

"Have you ever solved a case in a week?"

"No, but —"

"But you thought a small-town firebug would be easy to find."

Theo shrugged. "I thought I'd see something everyone missed. After all, I'm supposed to be the professional. At this point, I haven't helped any more than the state fire inspectors could have."

"I disagree. Your being here has meant a lot to me and the volunteers."

Theo was too frustrated to be placated. "Hardly."

"I saw how you managed at the fire the other day. Things were smoother with three departments than they would have been with two because you knew how to make the teams work together."

Theo could see the truth of Martin's words and had to take the compliment. There had been chaos at first, but things fell into place quickly. It hadn't occurred to Theo that this might be because of his presence and training. "I wish I had more to go on."

"I know, son. Keep going the way you are. It will come."

"You sound confident."

"I am. Always have been with my boys."

"Even when we screwed up?"

"Especially then," Martin said. "Because when you did, all of you worked to make it right. That told me what I needed to know."

They fell into watching the game again until the doorbell rang. Theo went on alert, but Martin said, "It can't be a fire. We'd have gotten a call."

Theo relaxed as Millie answered the door and Valerie Stewart walked in with a pile of boxes she was having trouble carrying. Theo got up automatically to help. "It's for the Duncans," she said, when he could finally see her face after taking the top two off her stack and walked with her to the corner of the living room. Other boxes and bags waited in a large pile to be moved when Grace found a new home.

"I was hoping to get a chance to see you," Mrs. Stewart said, as they tried to find a place among the growing mounds. "I heard from Adam you two got together."

"It's been good to see him."

"He's missed you. We've missed you."

"Thanks, Mrs. Stewart." She had a warm heart and an open door for everyone, a lot like the Sinclairs.

"You could call me Valerie."

"Nah, too weird."

She laughed. "I understand. Come with me to my car. I've got more in the trunk." They walked out to her SUV, the back door still opened. As she handed him a stuffed contractor's bag she said, "I'm glad I didn't get rid of all this bedding when we updated three of the cabins a few months ago."

"The Duncans are getting a lot of help."

"Of course. It's what neighbors do."

Theo couldn't stop the snort but said nothing as they went inside. Once the car was emptied, Valerie joined Millie in the kitchen for 'tea and talking', as Martin called it, and Theo dropped into the recliner Millie used when she and Martin sat in the room together. After a few minutes of watching the Red Sox make a valiant effort against the Yankees, Theo said, "I guess it's different when something happens, and people don't think it's your fault."

Martin looked at him and said, "What do you mean?"

Theo gestured to the boxes. "When my dad left, we needed help almost as much as the Duncans, but no one was there for us. Guess because dad was a shit and mom made the choice to stay with him, we were on our own."

"That's not true."

"The hell it isn't." Theo didn't bother keeping the bitterness out of his voice.

"You don't know what was going on." Theo was surprised by Martin's angry tone. "When Russell left, your mother turned down every offer of support. People reached out. Me and Millie included."

Theo let that sink in before responding. "Why would mom do that?"

"I can't pretend to know what was in Susan's head, but by the time your dad walked out, she was broken. I didn't know your mom, but I knew your grandparents a bit. They doted on their only child, so proud of her. They never approved of Russell because he was several years older than her and a bad influence. But the more they told her to stay away, the more she rebelled. I think they would have cut her off when she eloped if she hadn't been pregnant with Cole. They tried to have a relationship with her after that for their grandson's sake, but it was never good. How much of it was Susan and how much was Russell I couldn't say. They died in a car accident when she was pregnant with you."

"Yes, I'm named after her father, Theodore. My dad hated that. I assume it's why he called me 'Kid' most of the time."

"Russell was a hard man. He kept her separated and made her suspicious of everyone. By the time he left, I think she was either too proud or too embarrassed to accept help."

"But people offered?" This was the first Theo had heard of it.

"They tried. Several times. I remember Millie and Valerie went over to bring food and clothes for you boys. It was two or three months after Russell left. When Millie came home, she still had the meatloaf, and she'd been crying."

"I never knew Mom turned people away. I assumed people judged her for choosing an asshole and were...."

"Punishing her? And you kids? No, Theo. No one would do that."

Theo wasn't sure how to take this information. What he'd thought were looks of pity could have been people feeling sorry his mom cut them off. The abandonment came from his mother, not the people in this town. Which meant the reasons behind him hating this place were wrong. "Why didn't you tell me this sooner?"

"When? And what could I say? 'I know you hate this town, but it's your mother's fault for cutting you all off'? How could I tell you things might have been better if it weren't for her pride and, quite frankly, stupidity? You already had so many mixed feelings about her, mixed memories. I couldn't add to that. Besides, fate had a way of letting Millie and me help you boys out anyway."

"I have said thank you for that, right?"

Martin smiled. "Many times. And not only said it — shown it. Including being here now."

Martin turned back to watch the game, leaving Theo with a jumble of thoughts he didn't know what to do with. Things he would have sworn to be true... weren't. He didn't think anything could confuse him more than his reawakened emotions for Eden, but this was beyond anything he imagined.

Chapter Thirty-One

♥

By the time Eden and Theo were ready to go out, most of the local places were busy with Saturday night crowds. It took longer than usual to find parking in the downtown area and by then there were lines and wait times. Theo was getting more and more aggravated, and Eden sensed this was about more than their inability to find a place to eat.

"I'm sorry," Theo said after the third place, told them it was an hour wait. "Guess I'm out of practice when it comes to taking a woman out on a Saturday night."

She didn't hate knowing that he didn't date much. As she ran through alternatives in her head, she came up with a possibility. "I have an idea." She sent a quick text to Laurel telling her about their situation and asking if there was a way to pick up dinner to go. Laurel did boxed lunches for hikers to take with them, but Eden wasn't certain if take out at dinner was an option. It wasn't long before Eden got a message back: *No problem. Come to the front desk in thirty minutes.*

"Laurel's going to let us pick up dinner from the brewery. We could go to Silver Lake to eat."

At first, Theo didn't say anything, and Eden worried he didn't like her suggestion. Then he answered with a kiss that warmed her everywhere. They spent the time waiting for dinner to be ready walking around the main street of Fable Notch. Eden could tell Theo was grateful for not running into people they knew, although they did stop in The Bright Spot to chat with Adam until he got busy. "Hey, I'm short-staffed tonight. If you're bored later, feel free to come by and help me scoop."

As they left, Theo said, "I suppose there are worse jobs than serving ice cream."

"You could work for my dad," Eden suggested.

"That sounds truly horrible. I'd rather clean cabins at the Stewart's Lodge."

"You had to do that once, didn't you?"

"Yup, me and Adam, along with Nick, and Adam's brother, Drew."

"I can't remember if you ever told me why."

He probably hadn't. It was embarrassing. "We were taking their truck out for a drive. None of us had a license yet. Adam's dad caught us as we were leaving. He offered the cleaning punishment versus telling Mrs. Stewart and Millie and letting them decide our fate."

"Cleaning was the better choice?"

"Absolutely. Disappointing Millie and Mrs. Stewart would have been worse. But it was a horrible weekend, I assure you."

When the time came, they drove to the Seven Brothers, which wasn't within walking distance, to pick up their dinner. A bag of food and two bottles of beer were waiting for them. From there, it was a short drive to the lake. Fortunately, it was late in the day, and most of the people had left, making it easy to find a bench in a quiet location and spread out their dinner.

"This is what Laurel serves at a brewery?"

The food looked amazing. There were two containers with Caesar salad, entrees of steak tips and chicken and waffles, along with fries and steamed vegetables. "Laurel knows how to cook."

"I don't know which one to choose," Theo said.

"Then we'll put it between us so we can have it all."

"I like the sound of that."

So did Eden. As they ate, they talked about, then Eden told Theo about her encounter with Monica. "I almost feel sorry for Keith. When he finds out she knows about the divorce, it's going to get ugly."

Theo looked into the distance before quietly saying, "Who knows, maybe facing the truth will do him good."

There was more behind Theo's words. A few days ago, she might have hesitated before asking what was on his mind, but after what they'd shared, that wasn't necessary. "You've been distracted since you got back from the Sinclair's. Did something happen when you visited the other stations? Or with Martin.?"

Theo filled his mouth with food. Interesting delay tactic. Eden waited. When she was sure he wasn't going to answer, he took a deep breath and said, "It turns out I was wrong about people in Fable Notch not wanting to help my family when my dad left. It was my mother's doing."

Not what Eden expected. "What did she do?"

Theo explained how Susan turned away offers of support. Eden was shocked, and her heart ached for Theo and his brothers. They'd been through so much, and although Martin and Millie had helped, Theo hated what he saw as the town's snubbing his family.

"I can't imagine what knowing this means."

"I can't either. Truthfully, it hasn't sunk in yet. I'm sorry if I'm not good company. I thought dinner out would be fun. Instead, I couldn't find a place, and I'm so wrapped up in my own thoughts I might as well be on another planet."

Eden took his hand and gave it a squeeze. "First of all, I think this is a wonderful place for dinner and somewhere I couldn't imagine being with anyone other than you. And second, this news about your mom is a bombshell. If you were fine with it, I'd say you were in denial."

"Ah, the benefits of therapy," he said with a smile and matching humorous tone. She was glad he could tease.

Theo moved the food and slid over to sit by her side. She leaned against him, wrapping her arms around his waist. They sat in silence, and she was more comfortable being quiet with him than she could ever remember being with Keith.

"I'm sorry," Eden said finally. "About what Susan did."

"Thanks. It's going to take some processing."

She wanted to say more, something to make him feel better or even okay with what he'd learned, but this was something he'd have to deal with on his own. If he wanted to talk, she'd listen. And if he didn't, she'd simply be there for him.

Chapter Thirty-Two

♥

Eden didn't entirely dread her monthly Sunday dinners with Patrick, but since this would be the first time they'd spoken since he found out about her divorce, she expected it to be more difficult than usual. And when he suggested The Dining Room at the Castle on the Hill, she knew he was going to try to convince her again to go back to her marriage and lead the life he thought best for her.

The restaurant, easily one of the fanciest places in the area, was one of her favorites. She and her parents went there for her sixteenth birthday and her graduation dinner. Her parents had spent nearly every anniversary there, and it was where Patrick had taken her and Keith to celebrate their engagement. It had been years since she'd been back. If Patrick was hoping to remind her of happier times, he didn't understand she had no interest in returning to her past. She had too much to look forward to.

Theo offered to kidnap her and bring her to dinner with him at the Sinclair's, but as tempting as the suggestion was, Eden needed to face her father. She was dressed and ready when he came to pick her up at five o'clock — no one left Patrick waiting. She managed to get through opening pleasantries, but once they hit the main road, she asked, "Do you want to talk about it now or over dinner?"

"Talk about what?"

Eden kept the exasperated sigh to herself. "Fine, we'll talk about it at dinner." She turned on the radio and let a Mozart Piano Concerto fill the silence for the rest of the drive.

At the restaurant, they were immediately shown to a table by the window with a beautiful view of the sunset she wasn't able to appreciate. Sunday nights at the restaurant weren't busy, and she was glad they wouldn't have an audience for what was certain to become a heated conversation. Her father ordered a Maker's Mark on the rocks as they were handed their menus. Eden considered a glass of white wine, then decided she didn't want anything impairing her thoughts. She didn't need liquid courage to speak with her father. When the waiter came back with her father's drink, they ordered dinner and said nothing. Eden almost regretted not ordering the wine. She decided the best way to do this was by jumping into the deep end. Wading in wouldn't work.

"Theo told you my divorce from Keith is final."

Patrick sipped his drink before answering. "He did. Which begs the question, why didn't you? Why did I hear it from him?"

She heard the disdain in the way her father said "him." Some things never changed. "It happened a week after my apartment burned down, and it wasn't as important as getting the rest of my life in order. Knowing your reaction, I wasn't in any rush to give you the news."

"Are you certain that's the only reason?"

"What other reason could there be?"

"Maybe you're having regrets."

Eden was proud of herself for not laughing out loud. "You think I didn't tell you because I changed my mind, and the divorce went through before I could stop it?" Her voice escalated, and she looked around the room to see if anyone had noticed. Bringing her tone down, she continued. "Let me be perfectly clear. I have never had one moment of doubt about ending my marriage. If I could have made the process go faster, I would have."

"You can be a very stubborn woman, Eden."

"And here I was hoping you might see me as determined and clear."

"Oh, you're determined, but that doesn't mean you're right. You're walking away from a good thing. Your marriage to Keith gave you stability, security."

"I don't need a marriage for that. My job covers my living expenses." She wasn't going to tell him her plans for the new studio. He'd have a litany of questions and concerns, and she wasn't going to give him the opportunity to voice his doubts. She had no more room in her life for people who didn't support her. "Trust me when I say Keith was not as good to me or *for* me as you might have been led to believe."

Patrick scowled. "Did he hit you? If he laid one hand on you —"

"No, Dad. If he had, things would have ended a lot sooner, I assure you. But there are other ways to hurt a person." He gave her a look she didn't understand, but she needed to get this out. "Both of you like to make decisions for me and think you know what's best. In your case, it came from love and worry. With Keith, it was about control and him wanting me to be a certain way. And I admit, there was a long period where I was happy to turn off my needs and go through the motions, pretending everything was fine. But it's not what I need or want. I can take care of myself whether or not you choose to believe it."

"I wanted you to be safe and looked after."

"I understand, Dad, and I know why you thought Keith might be the right choice, but there's more to marriage than security and there's more to feeling safe than having a husband with a job. My work and my friends — the life I've been able to have since leaving Keith — have given me all of that and more, because it's more of what I want."

"Parents can't turn off worry."

She heard the concern in his voice. She reached across the table to give his hand a quick squeeze, then pulled back. It was as much affection as Patrick would accept in public. "You can't protect me from everything. I'm an adult."

"I couldn't even protect you when you were a child." Patrick looked as though he said something he didn't intend. That alone was surprising.

And his words didn't make sense. He might not have been as present as her mother, always putting in long hours at the office and bringing work home with him, but he'd always been there in his own way. Hadn't he? "What are you talking about?"

Before he could answer, the waiter came with their appetizers. Her father finished his drink and asked for another. He tasted his soup, and she was going to ask her question again when he said, "Do you remember why you started dancing?"

"Yes, I broke my ankle and after the cast came off, the doctor thought it would be a good way for me to gain strength back."

"Do you remember how you broke your ankle?"

"I tripped and fell down the stairs."

"Not exactly," he said.

Eden didn't remember much detail about the day, always assuming the trauma had affected her memories. It was mostly flashes and images from the first days trying to manage with the cast on. Her mom had set up a bedroom for her in the living room, so she didn't have to go upstairs. Eden loved how fun and different it had been. "Mom said I was running down the hall, tripped, and fell."

"I'm sure that's what she said, but it's not the whole truth. Your accident was my fault."

Eden, about to take a bite of her salad, put down her fork and leaned back in her chair. Her heart skipped a beat. "How could it have been your fault?"

"You never knew him, but I grew up with a father who had a terrible temper, who lashed out and hit. I swore I wouldn't do that to my family, and I never once hit you or your mother. But the yelling?" He shook his head. "I couldn't stop that. Your mom tried to keep it from you, making sure doors were closed, but it didn't always work. During one of our fights, you came into our bedroom. I raised my voice. Your mother yelled back. You got scared and started crying. I got mad and yelled at you. You ran out of the room and your foot slid at the top of the stairs. You lost your balance. I've never forgotten the sound of your scream or the look of your ankle as it swelled. You wouldn't let me near you, not even to carry you to the car. It took a long time before you trusted me again, and you never stopped getting upset when I yelled."

Eden blinked back the tears welling in her eyes. She didn't recall the fight, but hearing the story she remembered when he came to her after her fall, and she curled into her mother. It was one of her earliest memories. Did that instance begin the distance she felt between her and her father? His guilt and her fear? It explained her discomfort when people raised their voices or even when she thought they might. Because his yelling had caused her accident.

"I promised myself I would never let it happen again." He pounded the table with his fist. Eden was amazed she didn't jump. "If I could keep you from getting hurt, I would. It's why I had you choose between dance and Theo Hanson. And why I've wanted you to stay with Keith. I thought one would hurt you, and the other was safe."

"You got the men mixed up," Eden said. "And there are better ways to show someone you care for them than by controlling their life."

"It was all I could think to do," he said, rubbing his hand across his jaw. "It may have been wrong, but it doesn't mean I don't love you. I hope you know that."

"Excuse me. Is everything all right?" The waiter's comment made Eden realize neither of them had touched their first course.

"It's fine," Patrick said, his eyes still locked with Eden's.

"I could have your soup reheated or bring you another?"

Patrick brushed his hand in the air. "No, need." Gesturing with his chin to Eden he said, "What do you want to do about your salad?"

She couldn't care less about the salad. "Take it away," she said. As the waiter left, she fidgeted with her napkin and didn't know where to look. She needed to process the last few minutes. This was the most emotion her father had shown since her mother had died and the most honest they'd ever been with each other.

As if this week needed more emotional swings.

Accepting she loved Theo was wonderful, if overwhelming. Her father's honesty was a different revelation, and she wasn't sure how to respond. Part of her wanted to yell at him for the choices he thrust on her, and the way he treated her. Part of her wanted to cry for the wasted years of distance between them, while another part was relieved to understand the underlying issues a little better.

Patrick broke the silence. "Are you angry with me?"

Eden didn't know how long she'd been quiet, but the salmon she'd ordered was magically in front of her. "I wouldn't say angry. I've got a lot swirling in my head, but mostly I think I'm sad."

"Sad?"

"Yes, because instead of us trusting each other, we acted out of fear. Your fear was my getting hurt. My fear was angering you. Not a great basis for a father-daughter relationship."

"I'm good at business, not relationships. That was your mother's area."

"And once she was gone, we didn't know what to do."

Patrick gave a self-deprecating laugh. "And you know how much I like not being able to control a situation."

"About as much as I like being controlled."

They let the silence return and picked at their meal until Patrick asked, "So, what do we do?"

"I don't want us to always be fighting. You need to accept that I'm an adult and trust me to live my life, even if it means I make mistakes."

"Are you willing to accept this isn't going to be easy for me, and I'm likely to overstep again?"

Honesty and understanding from her father. Would wonders never cease? "I'd be surprised if you didn't, but I'm going to push back. You're going to see how strong I can be."

He paused, and Eden waited for him to question her. "I will be proud to see that," he said.

Eden's heart ballooned with hope and love.

Chapter Thirty-Three

♥

Theo and Harlow arrived for dinner at the Sinclair's at four thirty. When he walked in the door, his mouth instantly watered at the smell of pot roast. Oh yes, he was definitely seeing the value of things that didn't change.

"Oh, good, you're here," Millie said, coming into the living room as soon as the door closed behind Theo. "Martin said he got in touch with you, but he never said if you were coming."

"I told you he would," Martin said, not getting up from the brown leather recliner where he was watching another Red Sox game.

"Do you need any help, Ma?"

"No, Grace and I have things under control, and Rosie and Helen should be here any minute. Sit and watch the game with Martin, but remember, I'm not holding dinner for baseball," Millie said, nodding toward the television. "Plan to turn it off when the food's ready or you're eating it cold."

As she went back into the kitchen, Theo sat in the matching recliner, putting the book Millie left there on the table in between. "Has she ever held dinner because of a game?"

"Not that I recall. Although for the fourth game of the World Series in 2007, we had a bunch of people over, and we ate dinner in the living room in front of the television. Only time I can remember it happening. Thank God we won."

"Millie loves her Red Sox."

"She sure does. And they've disappointed her more than I have."

Theo looked at Martin. "I understand about the Red Sox, but not about you."

"Oh hell, Theo, I've been married to the woman for over forty years. You don't think I've made some serious bone-headed moves during that time? Spent my share of nights on the couch or had to go over to Rosie's begging Millie to forgive me and come home?"

"You always seem happy and in love to me."

"We're always in love, but that has nothing to do with being happy. Mostly happy, sure. Always? Anyone who says they are is lying."

"I thought that was the point of being with someone. To make them happy."

"And you don't think you can, do you?"

"Of course, I...." Theo stopped. He almost said "can't." The word, the thought, was automatic, but as he was about to say it out loud, he also heard — and felt — it wasn't true. "I'm not sure. If you'd asked me a week ago, I would have told you I don't know anything about happiness or what another person needs, but these last few days have been more than I expected. And that's not only about Eden. It's you and Millie, seeing Adam again. Even being able to talk to Dylan and hang out with the volunteers."

"You've grown up."

"I suppose I have." Thirty-one wasn't too late, right?

"And you're in love with Eden again."

Theo took a second before saying, "I am." There was no need to deny it. Martin wouldn't believe him anyway. "Although it may not be 'again'. I don't think I ever stopped."

"I think that's more likely. What are you going to do?"

"I'm not entirely sure. First, I have to find a way to tell her, and hope she feels the same way."

"I think you know she does. Then what?"

"And then I'm going to figure out a way to open a New England branch of Prometheus Consulting so I can stay here and be with her." The words came out without him thinking. He didn't know when he'd made the decision, but as soon as he said it, he knew it was true.

"Not going to ask her to move to Baltimore?"

Theo shook his head and told Martin about Eden's idea for her own studio. "I won't take her away from that or the friends she has. We both have family here." Martin's eyes filled with tears. "Don't say anything to Millie, okay? I'm not sure how any of this is going to work or what it's going to take. For all I know, Prometheus won't be ready to expand, and I'll be scooping ice cream for Adam."

"If that's your choice over going back to Baltimore alone, then I think you're going to be just fine."

Theo hoped so. There was still the hurdle of Patrick and making certain he didn't meddle with him and Eden, or any of the other people Theo cared about — not to mention how they were going to deal with his PTSD. But he knew what he wanted and was determined to make it happen.

Dinner was noisy, fun, and filling. He couldn't wait for the Sunday when Eden would join him. Looking at the clock, Theo saw it was almost 7:00. He expected Eden would be back from her dinner in less than an hour. He could get to the house before her, set the scene, and tell her he loved her and wanted to have a life with her. He was fairly certain she felt the same for him, but he couldn't stop a moment of insecurity. What if she thought they were rushing? Or it was too soon after her divorce.

He'd wait.

This time, he would not leave and cut himself out of her life. If she needed time, he'd give her time. If she needed space, he'd give her that, too. Hell, they could keep dating if she wanted. As long as they were together, it didn't matter.

Eden was getting in Patrick's car when she got a text from Courtney. *At the studio. Gym about to close. Can't find lights. Need help.*

Saturday night and Courtney was practicing. Eden smiled at the girl's commitment. "Dad, could we stop at the gym? I need to help a student who's there to use the studio."

"You won't be long?"

"No, in and out."

She texted Courtney she'd be there in twenty minutes, then again when they were closer. Eden made her way through the darkened halls, her nose wrinkling at an odd smell. One of the dryers must be on the fritz. She'd let Leslie know tomorrow.

"Courtney?" No answer. Eden called again when she got to the studio. Having done this in the dark before, she found the lights, but when she turned them on, no one was there. She sent *Where are you,* then waited. When she didn't receive a reply, she texted again. This time, three dots told her Courtney was typing.

The message arrived. *Sorry. Forgot about school as-signment. Went home.*

Teens, Eden thought. She sent a *NP* to Courtney and turned the lights off. The light in the room changed from fluorescent to an unfamiliar yellow glow. When Eden stepped out of the studio, she faced a hall filled with smoke, the exit barred by a wall of flame.

Chapter Thirty-Four

♥

Theo and Harlow were halfway home when the call came in. Maximum Results was on fire. From the information, he knew this was the next arson. Only three days since the last one. Not a good sign.

Theo responded, saying he was going directly to the site. All available volunteers should meet him there. Even without seeing the state of the fire, he called the two closest stations and requested their help. He'd rather have too many people than too few. Running through a list of what else needed to be done, he thought of reaching out to Eden, but decided to wait. He didn't need her worrying or coming to watch the fire. He looked over at Harlow. "I can't take you home, girl. Plan to stay in the car." He banked a U-turn and headed to the gym.

By the time he was at the site and getting out of his truck, he heard sirens getting closer which was good, because from what he could see it looked likely he would be calling for additional help. Fable Notch's first four alarm fire. Through the front doors, flames were visible, already consuming the main workout room. Fortunately, this was the one night the place closed early. On any other day of the week, the gym would be bustling with members. And unless Theo missed his guess, the sprinklers weren't working. The fire wouldn't be this out of control if they were.

The volunteers arrived, got their assignments, and got to work. Martin showed up soon after, followed by the other two departments. Before long, the teams were working in sync. This time there was no danger of other buildings being affected since the gym sat alone on its property. As far as Theo knew, nothing in the building was explosive. One less thing to worry about.

Theo was pulling up his fire pants when he heard a deep voice yell his name. Looking over, he saw Patrick Barrett running toward him. He didn't think the man ever ran. Did this mean he set the fires and something had gone wrong? Before Theo could ask, Patrick grabbed him by both arms and yelled, "She's in there!"

There was only one 'she'. Theo was certain he heard wrong. "Why..."

"We were leaving dinner, and she got a text from a student to meet at the studio, so I drove her over. I was reading something on my phone. When I looked at the building, I saw the fire, but no Eden."

Theo didn't think his heart could beat so fast without coming out of his chest. The studio was at the back of the gym. If she hadn't come out, there was a reason. What if the arsonist had knocked her unconscious so she couldn't leave? The last time Theo had been in a fire he'd lost a friend. If he lost Eden, his life would be over. He had to go in and get her. He yelled out to anyone who could hear, "I need full gear. There's someone in there."

Dylan was closest and responded immediately, "I'm on it."

Within seconds, Theo was putting on boots, a jacket, and an oxygen tank and grabbing an ax. He ran into the building as quickly as the heavy equipment would allow. As he opened the door, he saw Dylan next to him. "What are you doing?" he yelled through the visor.

"Got your back, Chief."

It hadn't occurred to him not to go in alone. Damn, he was already making mistakes and he couldn't afford to do that. Theo nodded and hoped he conveyed his gratitude, and they stepped inside.

Their helmet lights did little more than show them the smoke-filled space. He knew he was looking at the lobby of the gym, but what he saw was every building he had gone into in Afghanistan. His thoughts dragged him back in time to when he and his team didn't know from one day to the next what they could be walking into, how bad it would be, and who might get injured—or worse. He could hear his ragged breathing inside his mask, feel the sweat dripping down the back of his neck, and he prayed it wouldn't get so bad that it got into his eyes. The oxygen from the tank meant he couldn't smell the fire, but he knew exactly how acrid and overheated the surrounding air was. For a split second that lasted forever, his legs didn't want to work, and he wondered if he could do this. Then in the next moment, he thought of Eden.

He had to get to her. Now.

Snapping back to the present, he turned to Dylan, pointed to the direction they needed to go, and headed further in. They stayed against the wall that led down the corridor to the back, glad it wasn't one of the things burning. He knew they were moving quickly, but he felt as though he was trying to run in a lap pool. The corridor seemed infinite. Time was speeding by, and he didn't know if he'd reach Eden in time. When the wall finally ended, he turned left down the hall and saw a nightmare come to life.

This was the reason Eden hadn't gotten out. The back exit, only a few feet from where she should be, was in flames.

When they got to the studio entrance and the doors didn't open immediately, Theo panicked, thinking Eden might be collapsed against them. Fearing what he would find when he pushed inside, he breathed a sigh of relief when he saw the towels on the floor. She must have put them there to stop the smoke. Smart woman. He stepped in, lifted his mask enough to yell her name and listen for a response.

He waited, stomach churning, until he heard a muffled, "I'm here." She came running to him, a towel over her nose and mouth.

He'd never been so happy to see her. He gave her a quick hug before putting his face close to hers to yell, "Is there anyone with you?"

"No, it's just me," Eden said, then coughed. Not a good sign.

He undid the straps of his oxygen mask and put it over Eden's face to let her breathe clean air. Immediately, the smoke in the room had his eyes stinging. He wanted to take off all his protective gear and put it on her, his own safety be damned, but he knew better. She took a few breaths without coughing, then handed it back to him, and he did the same. He hoped she was ready for what was next. "We need to go."

"What do I do?"

"Stay next to me. Dylan will be right behind us." He looked to Dylan who gave an awkward thumbs up. "I'm going to give you my mask every few steps. Try to take deep, slow breaths. Keep the towel over your mouth when I have the oxygen. It's not far. Can you do that?"

"I can. I will."

If ever she trusted him, now was the time he needed her to show it. "Keep hold of my hand and close your eyes. Are you both ready?"

Eden gave a hurried nod. Dylan said, "Let's do this."

With his hand gripping hers as tightly as the gloves would allow, they left the studio and went into the hall. The fire had gotten worse since they came in, and he could see both flames and smoke. He took a step, but Eden stumbled as the air changed. He understood her fear. Even with her eyes closed she'd feel the heat and hear the noise. Being terrified was to be expected, but forward was the way out. He shouted to her over the thunder of the fire, "We're getting out of here together."

He hoped he sounded confident enough to help her get moving.

As they walked in a tight group, Theo could feel Eden shaking next to him. He ached to comfort her, but that couldn't be his priority. There would be time for that later.

There had to be time.

He traded the oxygen mask back and forth with her and did his best to keep his focus on his next step, watching as best he could for anything that might cause them to trip. His awareness of her hand in his was the only thing keeping him sane. When they turned the corner, it was his turn to stop. The interior walls were burning. He hoped Eden was keeping her eyes shut. He didn't need her having nightmares, too.

Eden asked, "What's wrong? Where are we?" He hated the fear he heard in her voice.

"Home stretch," he said. "Eyes closed." He turned back to Dylan and tilted his head to the side to let his teammate know they needed to walk in the center. As they stepped into the tunnel of flames, Theo could sense the heat through his clothes, which meant it was worse for Eden. As if to confirm his thoughts, she leaned closer into him, pressing herself completely against him as she tightened her grip on his hand. He quickened his pace and hoped Dylan would keep up. It wasn't much further.

Eden had the oxygen mask, which was why, when they neared the lobby, Theo was the one who heard a familiar sound. He looked up but couldn't see anything. It didn't matter. If it was loud enough to hear over the fire, they had only seconds. The exit was ahead. They would make it. He screamed, "Run!"

They were at the door when the ceiling gave out behind them. Through his jacket he felt the searing heat as he pushed Eden in front of him and outside. Dylan was behind them by a step. They were out. He turned to see the fire consuming where they stood moments before.

As they stepped into the fresh air, water showered down on them. Firefighters came rushing to help them. As he took off his helmet, he could hear cheering from the gathered crowd.

Theo watched as a paramedic brought Eden to a waiting ambulance. They helped him and Dylan out of the heaviest of their equipment. They both brushed off the need for medical attention, and Theo went to get an update on the status of the fire. It was consuming the structure from multiple hot spots. The ceiling collapse created a hole in the roof, and when he looked back, he saw flames shooting through the top of the building. It would be a total loss.

Once he knew the men had things as under control as possible, he found Dylan and thanked him, then headed to the ambulances to assure himself Eden was alright. He found her sitting at the back of an open vehicle with a blanket wrapped around her, her hair wet from the dowsing they got as they left the building. He noticed the oxygen mask over her nose and mouth, the monitor on her index finger, and watched as someone checked her heart. The fact that they didn't have her on a stretcher was a good sign. Patrick hovered over his daughter, uncharacteristically silent. Theo never thought he'd see fear on the man's face, but he understood it.

Theo stared at her soot-streaked face and bloodshot eyes, thinking of how close he'd come to losing her. It would take days for his heart rate to return to normal. When the paramedic stepped away, she looked up and found him. He walked closer and took her hand. "How are you?"

She removed the mask from her face. "Better than I would have been if you hadn't come to get me. They tell me my blood pressure is high and my oxygen a little low but acceptable. No surprise, right?"

"Good, then I need to do this." Not caring who might see, Theo pulled her into his arms and kissed her. He needed to convince himself she was safe and unhurt.

She tasted of smoke and Eden, and he was unendingly glad she was safe. When he was finally willing to let her go, he set them down on the back of the ambulance. Keeping an arm around her shoulder, he put the mask back over her face. "Your father said you were here because you got a text from a student."

She nodded. "Courtney. I went in to help her find the lights, but no one was there. When I went to leave, the fire and smoke trapped me." She stopped remembering something. "The place smelled weird when I went in."

"Probably kerosene, like the other fires. He lured you, Eden. Someone tried to kill you tonight."

Eden's face, already pale, lost its remaining color. "But I'm okay," she said, as if to convince herself.

"And I'm forever grateful for that."

"So am I," said Patrick. Theo had forgotten he was there. "It's because of your quick thinking and skill that she's alive."

Theo stared at the man, not sure he heard him right. Did Patrick Barrett give him a compliment? "Just doing my job, sir."

"I think we both know it was more than that. Thank you for going in after her, Theo. For saving her. I don't know what I'd do if I lost her."

Theo knew the feeling all too well. "I'd do anything for Eden. It's why I walked out of her life all those years ago. It wasn't for you. It was for her. Because I thought she'd be better off without me. But I think you should know I'm not going to do that again. Ever. If she'll have me, I am going to spend the rest of my life with her."

Theo couldn't believe he'd said what he did. It wasn't planned, but it was true. He braced himself for her father's explosion, sure the moment of peace was about to be destroyed. But it didn't matter how the man reacted. He was going to be with Eden no matter what her father said or did.

When Patrick responded, he surprised Theo for a second time. "Then you better make her happy."

Chapter Thirty-Five

♥

I t wasn't smoke inhalation making her heart race. Theo was staying. They would be together. And he was shaking hands with her father, something she never thought she would see. She couldn't stop the tears and didn't want to.

Patrick gave Theo a quick pat on the back and said, "Will you see to it she gets home?"

"As soon as I can."

Patrick moved to Eden and kissed the top of her head. "I'll call you tomorrow to make sure you're okay."

Eden nodded, not trusting herself to speak. When Patrick was gone, she took off the oxygen mask and put her arms around Theo. She never had to let him go. Shifting from wondering if she was going to die to having so much to live for in only a few short minutes was dizzying, but she'd manage.

He pulled back to look at her. "I almost lost you again. God, Eden, I don't know if I could bear that a second time."

She couldn't stop smiling. "You want to spend your life with me?"

"I always have. Before, I wasn't convinced I could be the man you needed."

"You've always been the man I needed." He pulled her into an embrace which nearly squeezed the breath out of her. They were still holding each other when Harlow joined in the reunion, first walking around them, then bumping into their legs, and almost knocking them off balance.

"What's she doing here?"

"She was with me when I got the call. She was supposed to stay in the truck, but apparently, she jumped out the window."

"It's okay, Harlow, I'm fine," said Eden. "See?" She opened up her arms, but instead of moving closer, Harlow took a step away and gave a sharp bark. Eden moved closer and Harlow repeated the action. "What's wrong with her?"

"Holy shit. Absolutely nothing. Harlow, go, I'll follow." He took Eden's hand, and she went with him, not understanding why he looked as eager as his canine partner.

"What is it? What's she doing?"

"I told you I don't typically fight fires, and if there's another blaze while we're on a case, it's my job to watch the crowd."

"I remember."

"That's one thing I haven't been able to do since being here. Take crowd shots to look for anyone who shouldn't be there or looks suspicious. This fire started after you went into the building. Chances are he's here watching, and if he is, he's going to have traces of accelerant on him."

Harlow took a few steps, then turned to make sure they were behind her. Then she broke into a run until she stopped in front of Monica. She walked around the woman sniffing and bumping, and when Eden and Theo got close, she barked and sat. Monica took a step away. Harlow followed and sat again.

Monica was clearly annoyed by Harlow's attention. "Get this crazy dog off of me." Then she caught Eden's eye and her expression changed from irritated to shocked.

Eden might not like the woman, but she didn't want her to be unnecessarily concerned. "Monica, it's okay.

Courtney's not here. She left before I arrived." Monica said nothing. "Wait, how did you know Courtney had come over here to practice?"

"She didn't," Theo said. "Monica is the one who texted you."

"What?" Eden looked at Theo, then back at Monica, and made the connection Harlow and Theo already had. "It's you? You did all this?"

Monica turned to run, but in the space of a blink, Theo grabbed the woman's upper arm. "I didn't see it, but I should have," he said. "She has something against you. You're standing between her and Keith. And sticking it to your father by setting fire to his buildings was a little extra fun. Maybe she even thought it would help Keith."

"Let go of me, you bastard," Monica said.

"My parents were a lot of things, lady, and many of them were not good, but I assure you they were married when my brothers and I were born. You will never hurt anyone again."

"You can't prove anything."

"Oh, there you are very wrong," Theo said. "You're coming with me."

As they walked toward the emergency vehicles, Eden couldn't stop staring at Monica, still not believing what the other woman did. "How could you?"

Monica struggled to pull out of Theo's grip, growling in frustration. Finally, he stopped walking and called over one of the police officers who was helping with crowd management. Monica whirled to face to Eden and said, "It's your fault, Miss Perfect. You messed up my life."

Eden was genuinely confused. "How could I have done that?"

"Keith was mine until you came back when your mom got sick. Then all he could talk about was how good it could be for his career if he was with the boss's daughter. You were supposed to leave in the fall, but you stayed. If you'd gone then he and I would have gotten back together, and I wouldn't have ended up with a loser like Rob Russo. Even after you separated, Keith wouldn't give you up. I was not meant to be anyone's second choice."

"So you set all these fires? And you intended for this last fire to...?" Eden couldn't bring herself to say the words. She never imaged she could be the focus of so much hate. "Why?"

"I'm the head cheerleader," Monica said, as though that explained everything. "The girl everyone wants. I'm supposed to marry the quarterback, have the family and life everyone envies. But is that what happened? No! Turns out I can't have kids, but my sister can get knocked up without trying and without a husband. Then she goes on non-stop about how great you've been for Courtney. And Keith can't get over you, no matter what I do for him."

"He doesn't care about me. You said it yourself. He only wanted the boss's daughter."

"What's the difference?" Monica's voice continued to rise. Once she started talking, it was as though she couldn't stop, and people were watching them instead of the fire. "He should have been mine. I had to put you and your high-and-mighty father in your place."

If Monica's actions weren't so serious, Eden would laugh. In trying to hurt her, Monica brought back the man she'd never stopped loving. She'd made Eden's life better, not worse. "You burned buildings, Monica. You temporarily hurt the people whose livelihoods depended on those properties. They will recover. My father will rebuild. I'll find a new place to live. You are the one who's going to lose everything."

"No, Keith is mine. You don't get to win." As she screamed, two policemen who'd been listening to the confession handcuffed Monica and led her away.

"What a crazy bitch," Theo said when they were alone again. "Arsonists are rarely women. I've never come across one before, so she wasn't on the suspect list."

"Guess you won't make that mistake again."

"There are a lot of mistakes I won't be making again."

"Like leaving me?"

He put his hand under her chin and lifted her face up for a kiss. It was the only answer she needed.

Eventually the noise and chaos around them broke through her bubble of joy. Theo must have noticed, too, because he pulled back and said, "I need to finish here. Let me get you my keys. After you get cleared by the EMTs, take my car and Harlow, and go home. Maybe you should call someone so you're not alone."

Eden didn't want to leave Theo but sitting around waiting for him to be done didn't seem like a good idea. "I'll call Janelle." Then she remembered, "My phone is in the gym. I had it with me when I discovered I was trapped."

"As losses go, that's no big deal." Eden had to agree. "Just drive carefully and I'll be with you as soon as I can." He walked her back to the ambulance, kissed her, and went back to his team. When her oxygen levels were acceptable, she and Harlow got into Theo's truck and drove home. Once she was there, she called Janelle, gave her the basics, and asked her to come over. Then she warmed up some leftover chicken and gave it to Harlow. "You deserve steak for what you did tonight, sweet girl, but that will have to wait for another time."

She got out of her smoky clothes, dropping them directly into the washing machine. Theo was right — the smell was awful. She looked in the mirror and saw tear tracks and the outline of the oxygen mask on her soot covered face. It was off-putting. She jumped in the shower to rinse off. As the dirty water swirled down the drain, she found herself shaking with residual fear. She put a hand on the wet shower wall to brace herself as she let the emotions run through her. She'd talk with Theo about this later. He'd understand and help. By the time she came back to the kitchen, Janelle was waiting with a mug of tea and a hug.

Eden burst into tears when she saw her friend. Until that moment, she didn't realize how much she'd been holding back. Being trapped by the fire, then having to get through the burning building with Theo by her side, only to discover that someone she knew tried to kill her. It was a lot. She didn't even notice Janelle had walked them to the couch until she was sitting, curled up against Janelle on one side with Harlow resting on her other. When crying subsided and she could talk, she told Janelle everything that happened, from her father's revelations at dinner to Monica getting arrested. It took a while since she kept having to stop and sob occasionally. It had been a crazy night.

"Holy shit," Janelle said when Eden finished. "I'm not sure what's most shocking."

"Seeing my father shake hands with Theo," Eden said. It was also the best part of the night and an image she was using as an anchor to keep her from falling apart further.

"And he's going to stay."

"That's what he said."

Janelle gave Eden a hug. "Best news ever."

Eden agreed. They talked for a while, then put on *Notting Hill* and snuggled under a giant blanket. Hours later, Harlow's bark told her Theo was home even before she heard his truck. The three of them greeted him at the door. And before Eden could say anything, Janelle said hello to Theo and goodbye to them both, promising to call tomorrow.

Once they were alone, Eden asked, "Is it out?"

"Finally. At the end, all we could do was watch for flare-ups and let the fire run out of things to burn. I'm exhausted, but relieved beyond words. You're safe, the arsonist is caught, and your father doesn't hate me anymore."

"Quite a night."

"What matters most is that you're safe." He kissed her, and she fell against him. The smell of smoke on him made her heart race again. It was going to be awhile before she didn't react strongly to anything having to do with fire, but she wouldn't be alone. Neither would he. He toed off his shoes and said, "I've got to get the smoke and soot off of me."

"I did that already. You're right — you can't stay in clothes after a fire. But I don't mind getting wet again. Would you like company?"

He considered it, and she knew he was wondering if it was a good idea given the night they'd had and what showering might lead to next. She smiled when he said, "I'd love it," and took her hand to lead her to the master bath. Once there, he turned on the water and untied her robe as she helped him out of his clothes. It was more about staying close to him than anything romantic at this point. Now that he was home, she didn't want to be apart.

The room filled up with steam and Theo opened the door to the giant shower stall, clearly big enough for two. She hadn't been in the master bath. Like every other part of the house, Nick had done an amazing job with the renovation. Looking up she said, "I've never been under one that big."

"From the direction of your gaze, I know you're not talking about me."

"Nope, the shower head."

"I'm jealous. Here I am, naked, and all you can do is stare at a spray of water."

She dropped her eyes. "Nice hose."

"Firefighter jokes?"

If he needed her to be serious, she would, but something told her humor might go a long way in comforting them both. "Don't you think we could use a little laughter after the night we've had?"

"Laughter, kisses, anything that will keep you by my side and help me remember I didn't lose you tonight sounds wonderful. I never want to go through an experience like that again. It took only minutes to get you out, but those were the longest minutes of my life." He gave her a deep kiss, hotter than the water could ever be. She pressed against him, enjoying the strength of his body. She needed him, too.

Looking along the wall, Eden found a bar of soap, grabbed it, and ran it down his back, slowly kneading his muscles as she went, working to soothe and reassure him. He closed his eyes, and she hoped he was relaxing. "This may not have been the biggest fire I've ever battled, but it was definitely the worst," he said.

Good. He was talking. The articles said that helped. She continued what she was doing. "From what little I saw, it looked as though everyone worked well together."

"I never thought a group of volunteers could do such a good job." As she watched, she saw understanding soften his features. "Turns out love of a place can be a benefit. They weren't simply fighting a fire. They were fighting for something together. It made a difference."

This was a big change in perspective for him, as big as anything that happened between them. "How are you feeling now?"

He opened his eyes and looked at her. "Better because it's over. Better because you're in my arms."

"It's my favorite place," she said and went up on her toes to kiss him. His quick response excited her, and she let her hands roam down his back. He moaned against her lips when she grabbed his ass. She rocked her hips, feeling his erection press against her stomach. She didn't know when the shower had gone from comforting to arousing, but she wouldn't complain. This was a much better focus than where her thoughts would go otherwise.

When they were sure he was soot free, he took the soap from her and returned the favor. Before long, they were covered in suds, their bodies sliding together, touching in tantalizing ways but not getting the full satisfaction they craved. Her hands skimmed along his hard length while his covered her breasts then moved between her legs.

"You make me hungry," he said.

"There is nothing stopping you from taking what you want." She stepped under the water and rinsed off, but before he could grab her again, she opened the shower door, jumped out, and wrapped herself in a towel.

She handed him one as he joined her. "You missed a spot," he said, and leaned down to lick water droplets off her shoulder.

"How am I supposed to get dry when you keep making me wet?" she said.

"Is that what I'm doing?"

"Yes."

He continued to lick, first behind her ear, then her neck. When he reached the tops of her breasts, she let the towel drop. She shivered, but it had nothing to do with the cold. "I cannot get over how incredible you make me feel."

"Good, because I want you to feel amazing," he said. "You deserve that and more."

She took his hands and pulled him to the bed, where they slipped under the covers. Within moments, they were wrapped around each other. His body heat was better than any shower or warmed towel. Something to savor and enjoy. She kissed him deeply, tasting his passion and giving him hers in return.

He slid his hands between their bodies and found her center, swollen and sensitive. He slid first one, then two fingers deep inside of her, making her wetter. "You're right. The towel didn't dry you in the least."

"You do that to me." After so many loveless years, he'd awakened a passion she never wanted to live without. And never would.

"Do you want more?" His voice was husky with need, and the sound gave her a shiver.

"Yes, please," she said. He caressed her with his thumb as his fingers continued to move inside of her. Aching to touch him as well, she reached for him and found him hard and a touch wet. She teased the head of his erection, lubricating the tip with his pre-cum, then stroked the length of his shaft, sending the only fire he wanted to be around through his body.

"Do you know what I want now?" he asked.

"Tell me."

"I want you to come for me."

Before she could say anything, he moved between her legs and took her into his mouth. She was so aroused it didn't take long for her climax to build. She couldn't slow her responses, and she didn't want to. In no time, her back arched in pleasure. She couldn't hold back her scream. He sucked her core hard, sending an additional jolt of desire crashing through her.

"God, Theo, yes," was all she could say.

Keeping his fingers inside of her, he turned and opened the nightstand drawer. He unwrapped the condom package with his teeth, then quickly covered himself. She was still shivering from her orgasm when he plunged into her. The sensation of being filled while her body was contracting set off another flood of desire. She wrapped her legs around him and lifted her hips to take him more deeply.

"Eden, my God, you are perfect."

She had no words to express the emotions running through her, so she took his face in her hands and kissed him, hoping it would tell him everything she was experiencing. It was enough because he increased his pace and thrust harder. Her nails raked down his back, making him gasp, and they moved together until they both came in a cry of release and delight.

He fell against her, breathing rapidly. She could hear her heartbeat in her ears — and feel it between her legs. The intensity of their lovemaking thrilled her, and she basked in the weight of him on top of her.

"Nothing is as wonderful as being with you," he said, echoing her thoughts.

She let his words into her heart. They were going to stay together this time. So much had happened in the years they'd been apart. She could hardly believe they'd found each other again. She'd never stop being grateful.

When he rolled off of her, she curled next to him and let herself be lulled by the sound of his beating heart, still a little fast from their lovemaking.

"As much as I love holding you, I think you should consider sleeping in your own bed tonight." She sat up to look at him. What she was thinking must have been clear in her expression because he said, "I understand that you probably don't want to be alone, believe me, but having to find you in a burning building was a nightmare come to life. I doubt I'll make it through the night without one. I hate knowing I could hurt you."

She appreciated his concern, but knew this was important for them going forward. "There are a lot of ways to get hurt. We can't avoid them all. You don't have to save me." He raised an eyebrow. "Okay, tonight you did, but you don't have the only say in what's best for me. If we're going to make this relationship work, we need to figure out a way to do things together. Other couples manage with one of them suffering from PTSD, and if it means separate beds occasionally or couples counseling, we can do it."

"Together," he said.

"Can you think of a better way?"

"No," but he didn't look convinced.

"Let me stay with you tonight."

She watched as he considered her request and hoped for the answer she wanted. Finally, he said, "I'm willing to give it a chance." He opened his arms, and she curled against him, exactly where she wanted to be.

Theo woke with a yell. Moments before, the fire was everywhere. He couldn't see. He couldn't find Eden. He could barely breathe. Then he heard her voice. "You're awake, Theo. It was a dream, and it's over. I'm here."

He looked and found her sitting at the foot of the bed. "Eden?"

"I'm here," she repeated.

"What are you doing there?" He sat up abruptly as it occurred to him what he must have done for her to put distance between them. "Did I hurt you? Oh God, I knew it. I...."

"I'm fine," she said, joining him on the bed. "I was giving you — and your dream — some space."

"You got out of bed when I woke you?" She made it sound so simple.

"I did a little research on what to do when someone had a PTSD nightmare. It suggested first waiting to see if it passed. If it got worse, I was to stroke your arm and say your name to help calm you. When that didn't work and you got louder, I moved away and let the dream run its course. I told you I can take care of myself."

He reached out to her, and she took his hand, then moved to sit next to him. He was so relieved to find he hadn't hurt her. "You've always been strong and capable."

"I let myself forget for a long time. It's good to remember." He loved seeing her confidence bloom. He'd never get tired of seeing her succeed as well as knowing she'd be with him for whatever challenges lay ahead for him.

"I can understand. I forgot what it means to have someone believe in me. Not in the way Millie and Martin cared for me, which is wonderful but parental. You...

You know me, the good and the bad along with the frustrating and painful and still you believe in me. You..."

"I love you."

"And I love you. I never stopped, and I know I never will." He kissed her and allowed himself to revel in the knowledge that he'd be doing this for years to come.

Epilogue

♥

Nick Hanson

Nick couldn't believe what his brother, Theo, was telling him.

Not about catching the arsonist. He'd known Theo would be successful at that as soon as he heard Martin had reached out for help. And the part about Theo discovering he was still in love with Eden wasn't a shock either. Nick knew what it was like to never get over the first woman you loved.

No, the surprise was that Theo was moving back to Fable Notch. Permanently.

Nick was pretty much the only one of the three Hanson brothers who ever went home. Theo couldn't get out of there fast enough, and his oldest brother, Cole, was based in Colorado when he wasn't touring with his rock band. Nick didn't have as many hard memories of the town as his family. When he'd started to make enough money, he visited the Sinclairs once or twice a year and, depending on the season, take time to ski in the White Mountains.

With the first big bonus he'd received years ago, he'd gutted and renovated the house he and his brothers grew up in. And he'd been doing so well recently, that last fall he'd started building his dream home on land in the area. According to the most update Nick received a few weeks ago from his contracto, Ed Franks, the place would be done by July. Nick was looking forward to spending time there this coming winter. Assuming he could get away. His bank account was in great shape, but his free time was minimal. He hadn't been to New Hampshire in over two years. Theo being there gave him a little more incentive.

And a recent loss gave him an additional reason to get away. Maybe he'd have time in the fall.

Stepping from his office desk, Nick walked over to the wall of floor to ceiling windows and looked over the New York skyline, six hours and a world away from where Theo was. "Let me see if I have this straight. You found the arsonist, got the girl, and won over her father. That's a lot to accomplish in only a few weeks."

Theo's laugh came through the phone, and Nick thought his brother sounded more relaxed than he'd heard in years. Theo had wanted out of Fable Notch since they were kids, but he'd always hoped Eden would be with him when he left. When he lost her, a sadness crept into his voice that remained, until now. "Tell me about it. Not sure which of those is the most surprising."

Thinking about what Theo shared, Nick said, "Between Patrick shaking your hand and you deciding to move home? Yeah, that's a toss-up. Never thought I'd hear about either of them."

"You and me both, but it really happened, and I'm really staying." Theo went on to tell Nick about what he'd learned about their mother and how she'd refused all offers of help when they were little. Believing that the people in town turned their back on the Hansons was one of the things Theo held against Fable Notch. It was good to learn it wasn't true.

"Do you need the house for a little longer?" Nick asked. If it hadn't worked out so well, Nick would feel bad about the mix up that landed Theo in a situation where he and Eden had to live together. Best miscommunication ever. Nick wished that could be true in more situations.

"Yeah, for a few more weeks if that's possible. We're looking for a place to rent, but it could take a while. Especially since I need somewhere that accepts dogs." Harlow, Theo's arson dog, had been one of the reasons Theo agreed to stay in the old house in the first place. "We can pay you."

"You can, but you won't. It's not a problem." Okay, it was a small problem. There was a rental coming up in two weeks that Nick would need to cancel, and he'd been counting on that income to help him out of some of the hole he'd dug himself into, but he wasn't going to share that.

"My brother, the big financial success. At least that's something we predicted."

"What can I say," Nick said with a laugh and hoped Theo didn't hear how forced it sounded. "Some of us were clear about what we wanted."

Nick had planned to have a career on Wall Street since he was in his early teens with a goal of making his first million before he was thirty. He'd graduated from college in three years to make it happen sooner and hit the goal a few months after his twenty-ninth birthday last year. There had been some costs along the way, but a lot of rewards.

"You've done an amazing job," Theo said. "I'm proud of you, baby brother."

"Thanks," Nick said. He looked to the closed door of his office feeling panic rise in him at his brother's words. There wasn't much to be proud of recently, but Nick was determined to come up with a plan to change that. "Listen, someone is standing at my door waiting for me, so I need to get going. The house is yours as long as you need it. Let me know when you're ready to move out."

"Thanks. I – we – appreciate it." He was glad he could do something right for someone. "When will you be coming up for a visit? Millie tells me you haven't been here in ages. There are some changes you really need to see."

There was something cryptic in Theo's words, but Nick didn't have the time to ask about it. There was too much work to do. "Maybe for the holidays at the end of the year. Things slow down then."

"Great. I'll look forward to racing you down the slopes," Theo said. For all the challenges he was having, Nick would never get tired of hearing his brother sound happy. If anyone deserved it, it was Theo.

They got off the phone, and Nick continued to stare at the city. He'd come here with his best friend to conquer the Big Apple and to take as big a chunk of it for himself as he could. Everything had been going according to plan, but for the last few months, Nick had been struggling.

In the eight years since he'd been working for Jeffries and Waters, he'd done good work and every year his bank account and portfolio grew substantially. No, he didn't have a perfect track record, but no one did. And he'd never had a setback like the one that happened in the last week.

There had been too much going on in his life outside of work. What he needed was time to think, get a better perspective on what was happening, then turn it around.

He stepped out of his office and his assistant looked up from her desk. "Ordering dinner in again," she said with a knowing smile. It wasn't a question. He hadn't gone home before eight o'clock for the last two weeks.

With a nod he said, "Greek tonight, I think." *Add some vegetables to that,* said a voice in his head. It must be because he'd been talking to Theo that he thought of Millie. "And a salad on the side."

"You got it. Do you need me to stay?"

She'd put in plenty of late nights in the last few weeks as well, but tonight he planned to focus. "No, head home whenever you're done with what you're working on.

Leave whatever you order for me on your desk, and I'll see you in the morning."

She must have heard something in his voice because she asked, "You okay, boss?"

He'd gotten a thrill out of her calling him that initially. Tonight, he heard the pressure of the word. He had responsibilities. Clients and team members who were counting on him to continue to be as successful as he always was. He plastered on a smile. "I'm great. Planning to make us all very rich. How does that sound?"

"Wonderful," she said. Assistants got bonuses based on how well the people they reported to did. She was as invested in his success as he was. "I'm hoping to go on a cruise at the end of the year."

"Then start looking for bathing suits." Did he sound confident? He hoped so, because he sure as hell didn't feel it.

Nick went back into his office, leaving the door partially open in the hope that someone would walk in with an idea of how to salvage the project he was working on. When he'd taken on this merger, he'd been so sure it would be hugely successful. Yes, there were a few red flags, but he'd worked his way around those before. It was like navigating a black diamond ski run, the most difficult. You couldn't anticipate every turn, but he had skills he could rely on.

Had he overreached this time?

No, he thought shaking his head hoping to clear his concerns. He'd be fine. This was nothing more than a stumble. He had plans for his future and even with the latest losses, he was going to make them come true. He looked out the window again as the sun set and lights came up around the city. He was going to make a new plan and find a way through. This was where he belonged.

Find out what happens when things don't turn out as
Nick plans in
Meant To Be His
at https://books2read.com/mtbh

Acknowledgements

♥

You read these?

Me too!

As you may know, writers work in solitary and in solidarity. While I wrote much of this book sitting in my home office (a converted garage), it would not have happened with the support of many people, both in person and virtually.

First, I have to thank the writers in my life.

- Sara and Lisa, thank you for your friendship, encouragement, knowledge, and patience as I navigated the world of self-publishing for the first time. I am grateful for every milestone you cheered me through and every ledge you talked me off of. Here's to many wonderful adventures in writing!

- And to June and Trish, the other members of our Monday night cohort. It's amazing the magic that happens when you bringing writers together. Thank you for your support and encouragement.

- The Saturday Shenanigans: Paula, Misty, Win and Delia. When we started meeting, I never imaged how much our time together would come

to mean to me—or how much I'd get done because of you. Thank you for your joy, humor,
talent and unwavering compassion.

- The Better-Faster Academy morning Office
  writers. Your Zoom faces help me get my butt in
  the chair every morning. I appreciate your sharing your struggles and your smiles and allowing
  me to share mine with you.

- And the various Facebook communities I've
  been lucky enough to find, especially 20Book-
  sto50k, Wide for the Win, and Sarra Cannon and
  Publish and Thrive. I am grateful for all I've been
  able to learn.

To my editor, Kelly at DogStar Creative, thank you
for being willing to tell me the hard truths that not only
made for a stronger book, but made me a better writer.

And then there are the non-writers folks who gave me
much needed support. To Adrienne and Margaret, who
are always willing to listen and never let me give up on
my dreams. And to my husband and sons—thank you for
accepting and loving the crazy woman you live with. You
make all of this worth it. I love you more than I have
words for – which from a writer, says a lot.

About the Author

♥

Elena Markem writes emotionally rich contemporary romances about dreams, love, and taking a chance on both. Her stories reflect her belief that life is about the passions we pursue, the people who support us along the way, and never giving up on what we want.

She can't start work without coffee, fall asleep without reading, or listen to Broadway musicals without singing along (badly). She loves time spent with her husband and sons as well as weekends with girlfriends, rom-com and old movies, and anything that sparkles.

Feel free to join her on her ongoing quest for the perfect planner, the best diner breakfasts, and the gooiest chocolate chip cookie. In the meantime, she hopes you'll enjoy spending time in her sexy books where you'll find strong heroines, heroes who find them irresistible, and at least one scene involving comfort food.

Stay in touch by signing up for her newsletter at www.elenamarkem.com to get updates, sneak peaks, and free stories and don't forget to follow her on Facebook, Instagram, and Tiktok!

Books By Elena Markem

Fable Notch

Once More With You – Theo & Eden
Meant To Be His – Nick & Dani
This Time For Us – Cole & Mia
Can't Let You Go – Janelle & Ash
Bring Back Her Heart – Laurel & Hunter
What You Wish For – Casey & Derek
Just Right For Him – Ryan & Sheridan